ADVANCE PRAISE FOR *RIVER MUMMA*

"*River Mumma* is a mad-dash hero's journey of mythical proportions carried out in the span of a single day. It is both a love letter to Toronto and a meditation on ancestor gratitude. A masterclass in fusing cultural stories with current struggles, both internal and global, *River Mumma* will have you conflicted on whether to speed ahead or slow down to savour the deft writing and unforgettable imagery. Zalika Reid-Benta has created a story that will make you want to live fully, with eyes wide open to take in all the magic around us. There is so much to learn from this book, and so many loveable characters and locales to relish (and a badass spirit you wish you could be more like). Wholly original, remarkably crafted, and unmatched in voice, atmosphere, and action, *River Mumma* should be on every must-read list this season. I loved this book!"
—Cherie Dimaline, bestselling author of *VenCo* and *Empire of Wild*

"Prepare to be seduced by this book the way Alicia Gale succumbs to the pull of her ancestors' messages. An emotional quest painted with magic realism and folklore and set against the vibrant backdrop of Toronto's York region, *River Mumma* is more of the Zalika Reid-Benta magic I've been waiting for."
—Catherine Hernandez, award-winning author of *Scarborough* the novel and screenwriter of *Scarborough* the film

"*River Mumma* has everything you want in a great read—magic, adventure, and mystery—all with incredible characters you're rooting for from the very first page."
—Jael Richardson, author of *Gutter Child*

"Zalika Reid-Benta's latest novel moves with the urgency and inevitability of a river. Her shimmering prose and evocative characterizations make it a joy to follow Alicia and her friends on this tense, but powerful journey—not only across Toronto, but into Alicia's own family history. *River Mumma* is the type of vivid, rich novel I love best. It left me turning pages and pondering possibilities well into the night."

—Alicia Elliott, author of *A Mind Spread Out on the Ground*

"*River Mumma* is a love letter to culture, home, and coming of age—and will spark important, relevant book club conversations, too. What a ride! I loved every moment."

—Marissa Stapley, *New York Times* bestselling author of *Lucky*

"A fast-paced and absorbing adventure steeped in Caribbean folklore and mythology, *River Mumma* is a treat for the senses. Zalika Reid-Benta does magical realism right—with delicious storytelling and characters both relatable and compelling, plus the best parts of Toronto on display. . . . this novel has it all. I enjoyed every page!"

—Uzma Jalaluddin, bestselling author of *Much Ado About Nada* and *Hana Khan Carries On*

"*River Mumma* is a profoundly moving celebration of kinship, following the journey of a dynamic trio that turn into a family and find ancestry that is at once defining and liberating. It's funny and colourful, and it paints a nostalgic image of a Toronto where communities create homes, all while specifically honouring Caribbean wit and magic and joy. Zalika Reid-Benta's writing is riveting; it is meant to entertain and inspire and leave you one step closer to your truth."

— Téa Mutonji, award-winning author of *Shut Up You're Pretty*

ALSO BY ZALIKA REID-BENTA

Frying Plantain

RIVER MUMMA

A NOVEL

ZALIKA REID-BENTA

PENGUIN

an imprint of Penguin Canada, a division of Penguin Random House Canada Limited

Canada • USA • UK • Ireland • Australia • New Zealand • India • South Africa • China

First published 2023

www.penguinrandomhouse.ca

"The River Mumma Wants Out" from *Controlling the Silver*. Copyright 2005 Lorna Goodison. Used with permission of the University of Illinois Press.

Publisher's note: This book is a work of fiction. Names, characters, places and incidents either are the product of the author's imagination or are used fictitiously, and any resemblance to actual persons living or dead, events, or locales is entirely coincidental.

LIBRARY AND ARCHIVES CANADA CATALOGUING IN PUBLICATION

Title: River Mumma / Zalika Reid-Benta.
Names: Reid-Benta, Zalika, author.
Identifiers: Canadiana (print) 20220426023 | Canadiana (ebook) 2022042604X |
ISBN 9780735244764
(softcover) | ISBN 9780735244771 (EPUB)
Subjects: LCGFT: Novels.
Classification: LCC PS8635.E4355 R58 2023 | DDC C813/.6—dc23

Book design and maps drawn by Emma Dolan
Cover design by Emma Dolan
Cover image: (Wave) © Pannawish Jarusilawong / iStock / Getty Images Plus

Printed in Canada

10 9 8 7 6 5 4 3 2 1

To the Afro-Caribbean girls,
the Toronto Black girls.
To the children of the diaspora,
and to those who came before us.

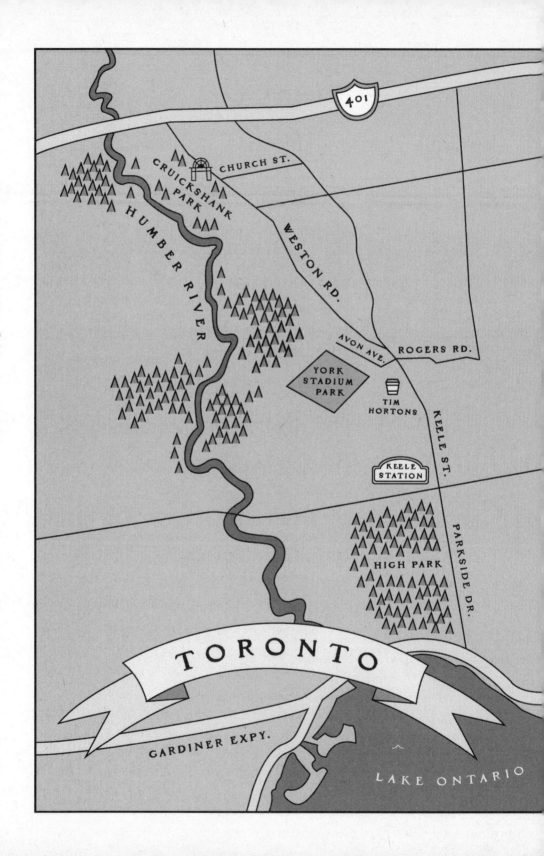

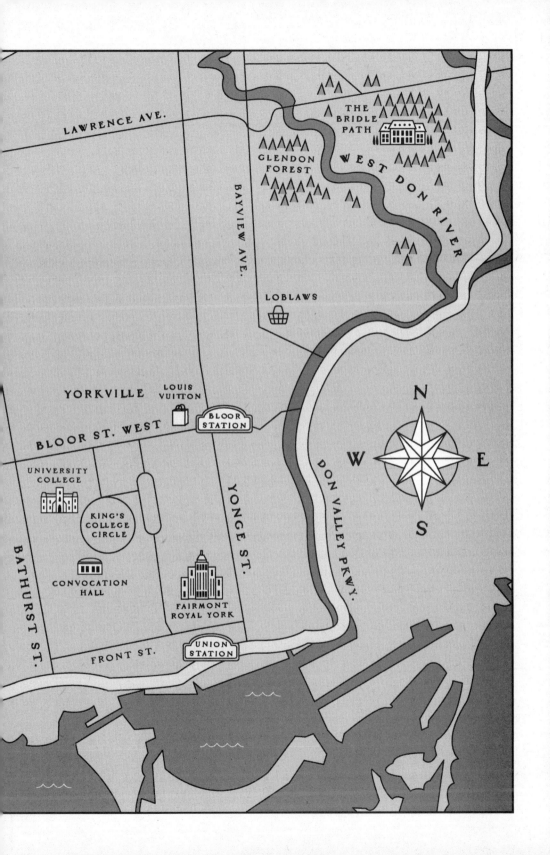

THE RIVER MUMMA WANTS OUT

You can't hear? Everything here is changing.
The bullrushes on the river banks now want
to be palms in the King's garden. (What king?)

The river is ostriching into the sand.
Is that not obvious? the nurse souls ask.
You can't take a hint? You can't read a sign?

Mumma no longer wants to be guardian
of our waters. She want to be Big Mumma,
dancehall queen of the greater Caribbean.

She no longer wants to dispense clean water
to baptize and cleanse (at least not gratis).
She does not give a damn about polluted

Kingston Harbour. She must expose her fish
torso, rock the dance fans, go on tour overseas,
go clubbing with P. Diddy, experience snow,

shop in those underground multiplex malls,
spending her strong dollars. Go away, she will
not be seeing you, for you have no insurance.

—Lorna Goodison

RIVER MUMMA

I

Alicia sat on a couch, watching people laugh and drink and talk in the living room, and wondered if she'd always hated parties. The fireplace boasted a real fire, thawing the winter frost that seeped in through the bay window, and the ska coming from the phone on the mantelpiece wasn't too loud, keeping the mood mellow but festive. The space was homey, with patterned wallpaper and woollen rugs. Everyone was clustered into groups of three or four, many of them drinking mulled cider, absorbed in their own conversations, saving Alicia from any forced socializing. She wouldn't know what to say anyway.

The house belonged to Heaven, or well, her parents, but they were in Niagara-on-the-Lake for a few days. Alicia hardly even knew Heaven; they were friendly co-workers but not exactly friends. Shifts at their store were just more tolerable if they worked together. If Heaven was around, a manager wouldn't have to remind Alicia to, at bare minimum, *appear* as if she liked working the cash register or the fitting room or the "floor." She and Heaven were bonded together by the horrors of retail and not much else. Alicia showed up tonight only because her apartment building was ten minutes away, and her mother wouldn't stop asking if she'd been invited to at least one holiday party by at least one friend.

She took a sip from the bottle of Corona she didn't want, remembering last year, when a date told her she should be embarrassed for ordering it off the menu with all the other brews available. That same night, she'd deleted Hinge and hadn't been on since. Over the music, she made out snippets about natal charts and exam schedules and upcoming holiday plans and—

"He's a sellout!"

"Bredren, he's a *celebrity*. There's a difference."

Two men next to her were having a heated conversation.

"OK, but who needs walls that high, though?" said the first man, quickly clapping his hands between each word. "Like honestly, fans love him off that bad? Nah."

"Do you work for the city? Are you getting paid? 'Cause, legit, I would only hate this hard if someone was paying me *bare* bones."

Alicia tuned out their conversation, partly annoyed and partly envious that they felt so strongly about a celebrity's walls, something so plainly trivial, when she couldn't even care enough to dress up for the party. She had showed up in the grey sweats she'd been wearing all day, with small, December-induced dry patches dotting her hickory-brown face. The only accessory she wore was the one she never took off: a bracelet Grandma Mabel had given her as a child, when the two of them went to Westmoreland to visit family.

"Yuh have nightmares, nuh true? This here is protection from duppy, from the bad spirit that try fi catch yuh in yuh dreams," she'd said.

They had gone to see an elderly lady who lived down the road from Grandma Mabel's childhood home. "Even from when I was small, she was old, but she's trustworthy."

The bracelet was made of strips of black leather and had a gold clasp with the Roman numeral X engraved on it. The very night Alicia put it on, the nightmares stopped, never to return in fifteen years. Now the bracelet helped to elevate her drab grey appearance.

In the time Alicia referred to as Before, things weren't like this. *She* wasn't like this. Four years of undergrad completed in three, another eighteen months in New York, earning an MA and founding a graduate lit mag, and internships at two boutique literary agencies. She was on her way to becoming the next Toni Morrison of publishing, only to graduate and discover a wasteland in place of the opportunities she'd been promised. She'd returned to Toronto when her money ran out, applied everywhere, and got no interviews. Now everything seemed pointless, including and especially this party.

Alicia resolved that she would leave in thirty minutes. All she'd done was idly check her phone and complete Facebook polls that asked questions like "Do you say plant-IN or plant-AYNE?" (plant-IN, obviously), or online quizzes that guessed her age based on what kind of fries she preferred (McDonald's and seventeen) or her Blackness by which answers she chose (she barely passed those—the references were American and largely irrelevant to her: for instance, where they put "sweet potato pie," she'd have put "black cake").

A couple walked into the living room from the dining room. The man wore a sweater that had a small outline of an owl in the corner, and the woman wore one with "WE THE NORTH" splayed across the chest. They walked up to a cluster of people sitting in front of the fireplace, and a floppy-haired man held out his fist for a bump.

"Wahgwan!"

"Wahgwan, Dennis?"

Alicia rolled her eyes at the exaggerated accents. Thirty minutes was starting to feel like too long a wait. She put her empty bottle on the coffee table and was readying herself to get up and go when there was a shift in the room. A shift that only she seemed to notice. Her focus was pulled to a leggy woman with a burgundy afro and a hooped nose ring. Alicia hadn't seen her come in.

The woman was draped in a long blazer bright with African prints, and she was wearing denim shorts over ripped black tights like it wasn't minus sixteen outside, yet she had a chunky scarf around her neck like it was in fact below freezing. She'd joined one of the larger circles in the living room, the one that seemed to talk only about astrology, and Beychella, even though it'd been a while since the performance. Everyone in the group tried to get her attention, but she was too busy looking at Alicia, her eyes bright with recognition like they were old friends.

The woman smiled and pointed to her own tight curls and then to Alicia, mouthing, "Love it!"

Alicia touched her hair, slightly dazed. She'd gone to the salon earlier that day, the one just up the street, on the corner of Church and Weston Road. Weeks of neglect had knotted her hair, and she'd forced herself to shell out the money for a professional to wash and detangle it. She'd decided to get single braids done so she wouldn't have to think about her hair for another eight weeks. At the salon, she'd responded to Heaven's "what time you think you'll be coming thru?" texts with "I don't know" because she was getting braids in and didn't know when she'd be finished. Heaven had pressed for details, complained that black was a boring colour to get, and talked her into getting ombré so that her braids would blend from indigo to blue to light purple.

"That's Oni."

Alicia turned her head to see Heaven in front of the couch, looking exponentially more stylish than she did. She was wearing an off-the-shoulder sweater dress with leg warmers over her bare copper-brown legs, and her Havana twists were pulled into a high bun. She held a thin black vape pen like she was a flapper girl gripping a cigarette holder. Heaven could make even the most mundane things look glamorous, as if she was practising for a future life of luxury.

"The girl with the Afropunk vibes," she continued, nodding her head approvingly at the braids. "Her name is Oni. She's from Saint Catherine."

"Ontario?" said Alicia.

"No, Jamaica. Catherine, not Ca-tha-*rines*. She's in my breadth class, postcolonial lit? I helped her with an essay on the imperial context of the omniscient narrator." Heaven paused. "Like, the 'voice of God,' looking down on everything from above—"

"I know what an omniscient narrator is, Heaven."

"True, you were an English major."

Alicia snorted. "I don't think that's actually a requirement for knowing that piece of information, just FYI."

"Touché." Heaven sucked on her vape pen and exhaled. "Anyway, Oni's cool," she said, the vapour billowing out of her mouth with every word. "Does birth charts, readings, some tarot. She inspired me to start learning about that too."

"So she's done a reading for you?"

"Me? No. I mean, I like the *idea* of a reading, but I don't think I actually want to know what the cards say? I feel like that could fuck me up, and I'm all about the positive vibes, enuh."

Heaven was really into the idea of things—the idea of starting her own podcast, the idea of a cross-country road trip. She'd detail all the research she'd done on a particular subject and then laugh off any questions about actually following through on it. "Maybe in ten years, when I'm rich and have the time," she'd say. To which

Alicia always asked, "Aren't you planning on doing a master's in library sciences or something? Do you know any rich librarians?"

Heaven's eyes flickered down to Alicia's bracelet; it was what had got the two of them acquainted in the first place. Heaven was the best employee on staff, and the managers had paired them on Alicia's first day as a way for her to acclimate to the store. Heaven had asked about her bracelet when they were tidying up shirt-strewn tables during closing.

"A talisman, right?" she'd asked.

Alicia hadn't answered right away, too surprised that Heaven had noticed something people usually acknowledged only absently.

"I don't know if I'd call it that. I used to get nightmares. This helps."

Heaven raised her eyebrows.

"I'd dream about these people, right?" Alicia explained. "They didn't walk, they'd kind of glide above the ground. They were dead. Had no eyes, feet pointed backward. Sometimes they weren't even people, just balls of red."

"Girl, a duppy dat," said Heaven, easing into an accent.

Alicia smiled slightly, feeling the kind of affinity that came with cultural recognition.

"Yuh sound like mi grandma fi true," said Alicia. "Talking about ghosts and ting."

"It's my thing. It started because of a paper I did for my early Caribbean history class, but when something interests me, I kind of want to know everything I can about it, and this, especially, is something I want to know more about. So you could say me and your grandma have the same interests."

"Had, anyway. Car crash. Years ago." Alicia didn't pause so Heaven could offer her condolences. "She gave this to me when I was ten. It helped," she said, quickly folding a polo shirt. "Well, it did the trick. I know that there's nothing to it—it's just a security blanket."

Heaven glanced up at Oni now while she pointed to the gold clasp. "You know, Oni might like that. You should go talk to her."

"And say what? I wear this out of habit more than anything else. I don't really know what it's supposed to do or how it's supposed to work."

"Then you should listen to one of the podcasts I keep telling you about. Reclamation of spirituality and traditional religions in the diaspora—"

"OK, I don't want *you* getting into academic podcast mode. I'm just saying, I'd like to get in touch with a yearly salary before anything else. You'll get it when you graduate."

"I swear, one of these days you won't end a sentence that way. Still, you should talk to Oni. It's my party. You have to mingle."

Heaven was the most social person in the store, always suggesting late lunches at the nearby pho restaurant before it turned into a gastropub, or after a closing shift, a few rounds at the gastropub before it was bulldozed for a condo. Sometimes Alicia wondered if anyone wanted to go. Admittedly, part of her did want to walk up to Oni and get a better understanding of what she was feeling, but the other part just wanted the feeling to go away.

"I cyaah friend she up just because she liked my hair and might also like my bracelet."

"And I can't help you if you're determined not to have a good time."

"I'm having a good time."

"Lies. Since you got here, you've had that look on your face," said Heaven, taking another hit of her pen. "Don't bullshit me, you know the look I'm talking about, the one you have when they make you hand out the 40 percent off coupons at the store's entrance."

Alicia laughed at that. "But really, though, I don't even know why they make me do all that greetin' and ting."

"It's just Pradeep trying to shake things up as the new assistant manager, blah blah blah."

"Well, whatever strategy that is, it's chupid, because I suck at being a greeter."

"You suck at anything involving people. Yuh nuh skin dem teeth, Leish." A young man in a cream cable-knit sweater and jeans slunk between Alicia and Heaven like he'd always been a part of the conversation.

"Mars," said Alicia. "For a second, I thought you were Heaven's friend Dennis over there." She pushed her mouth toward to the floppy-haired man, ignoring Heaven's correction of "guest, not friend." "That's how bruk up your accent is."

"Wow, 'low me, eh?" He paused to listen to Dennis excitedly yell "Brap! Brap!" and chuckled. "He just appreciates the culture; 'low him too."

"That's the wrong A-word," said Alicia. "But 'appropriate' and 'appreciate' sound similar, so I understand the confusion."

"Is it really that deep? When it's so ingrained in the city?"

"It's ingrained when he puts the accent on, but when it's my mother's natural voice, all she gets is racism? Cool story, Marcus."

"Why it gotta be all that?" he asked, shaking his head. "Why are you so extreme?"

Before Alicia could respond, Heaven interjected. "Why is Alicia the only one who can call you by your actual name? I've known you longer and I can't. That one time your brother came to the store, even he didn't call you Marcus."

He grinned. "Jealous?"

Heaven put up her hand. "Relax yourself. You are a mistake I will not be making, Mars."

Alicia shrugged. "If it makes you feel any better, he's the only one who calls me Leish."

Mars—who'd once revealed to her that he was named for Marcus Garvey—was the closest thing Alicia had to a friend at work, other than Heaven. When they'd first met, she stared at him a second too long and he'd grinned and said, "Nah, you're not seeing Trevante Rhodes. My name is Marcus. Mars," and she was determined to hate him. But he was also twenty-six and understood her ennui in a way no one else did, though it didn't seem to eat away at him the way it did Alicia.

"I think this is the first time either of you have come to one of my things," said Heaven.

"My brother said I've been working too hard," said Mars. "And that dude is *focused*, on that valedictorian track, so if he tells me to take a break, I'm going to oblige."

Heaven snorted. "Work hard? I stay catching you napping in the break room when you should be on the floor."

Mars said nothing, though Alicia was sure his expression darkened slightly. He wasn't a serious person, but whenever he spoke about his younger brother, even in passing, he became one for a few seconds. He smiled and put his arms around Heaven and Alicia, but when Heaven saw a spliff in his hand, she shrugged him off.

"Is that lit?"

"Not yet." He plopped down on the sofa with bravado, took a lighter out of his pocket, and sparked the spliff, taking a puff before extending it to Alicia. She waved it away.

"I have work first thing. Seven a.m. Pradeep put me on cleaning duty."

"We're working the same shift."

Alicia shook her head and Mars laughed, scratching the black stubble on his chin.

"Wouldn't want to actually have a good time, eh?"

"What do you mean? I'm practising my right to just say no, Mars."

"Shit's been legal for a minute, now."

"Barely. So you're fast-forwarding time?" said Alicia.

He started to laugh again as he exhaled. "Just saying. I bet since you've been here, you've just been in the corner doing polls or some shit on your phone."

Alicia kissed her teeth and leaned forward, taking the spliff out of Mars's hand and ignoring his mutterings about bad smoke etiquette, then took two short puffs before giving it back.

"Seriously, wah mi ah seh? If you're gwine fi smoke di ganja, do it—" Heaven didn't finish her sentence; a guy in a bucket hat walked past her, and she touched his arm before he could leave the living room. He turned around to face her.

"I don't know how you got in," she said, before he could speak, "but you can leave." She pointed toward the front door.

He threw his head back. "Tiana isn't even here."

"She doesn't stop being my friend just because she isn't physically here. Out."

"Are you seri—"

"*Out.*"

He kissed his teeth and headed to the door. Heaven turned to Alicia and explained.

"He was dating my friend and was having this side ting with

some girl from Sauga and shit got ugly. I don't know how he thought I would let him into my party."

Mars raised his eyebrows. "Damn, you take your friendships seriously."

Alicia didn't know when she'd stopped paying attention to the conversation, but she found herself looking at Oni across the room.

"Why does it feel like everyone knows this person but me?" she asked.

"Who do you really know besides me, her"—Mars pointed to himself, then to Heaven—"and the person who creates all those BuzzFeed quizzes you do?"

Alicia gave him the finger. And then giggled. Which made her giggle more. Get a grip.

"Wait, did I say that out loud?"

"Yes." Heaven eyed the two of them passing the spliff back and forth. "Fam, I'm officially kicking you out. If the walls start to stink, my parents are gonna give me licks, twenty-two years old or not. Go out on the deck by the kitchen."

Mars waved his hand but got up. Alicia motioned that she was staying inside and not joining him.

Heaven watched him leave, then turned to Alicia. "So what's up with that?"

"Nothing. You?"

Heaven shook her head. "He's gotta be playing the long game, still. Why else would he hang out with us?"

"For the scintillating conversation, obviously."

"The same dude who has different girls come into the store every other shift asking for him?" Heaven looked at Alicia like she should know better. "I thought he wasn't trying anything with me because you two had a thing and he had some basic semblance of boundaries."

Alicia looked at her. "Why, do you want him to try something?"

"Ew, no." Heaven clarified. "Not 'ew' in terms of appearance— I'm not saying he isn't cute—but he's waste. He'd bring too much drama, and I don't need that in my life." She took another hit of her pen. "You sure there isn't something between you two, with your only-we-call-each-other-by-these-nicknames bit and the not-really-but-kind-of *Living Single* Maxine-and-Kyle bickering?"

"It just feels like we've known each other forever, that's all."

The laughter from the other side of the room turned to cheers.

"Let me just go get my deck," said Oni.

It was the first time Alicia had heard her speak, and she found her raspy, accented voice relaxing, or maybe that was just the smoke.

"She did a reading for me last month, and it was so accurate, like uncanny, you're gonna love it, I swear," said one guest to the other people in the group.

Heaven narrowed her eyes, looking at the intrigued expression on Alicia's face, and then took her by the wrist. "Come on."

"I don't—"

But Heaven ignored her and led Alicia over to the crowd. She was starting to get drowsy and didn't have it in her to argue. They waited with the others, Heaven talking to her friends. Alicia stayed quiet beside her.

When Oni returned to the living room, the gold chain of her Ankara handbag looped over her shoulder, Alicia blinked. She wasn't sure if she was hallucinating, but she could see a light arcing over Oni's head, a radiant white halo that turned her into a living medieval painting. The glow shifted with her body, intensifying with each little movement.

"Holy shit," Alicia whispered.

Oni caught her staring, but Alicia no longer had the inhibition to look away, like she would've if she were sober. The recognition that had brightened Oni's eyes before shone even more vividly now, and she started walking toward Alicia.

"I'll get to whoever wants a reading," she addressed everyone else in the group. "But first . . ."

She stood so close to Alicia that she could count the freckles on Oni's pecan-brown skin and see the tiny Adinkra symbol for knowledge tattooed in white ink just below her collarbone.

"I just feel a connection to you," said Oni. "Like an energy?"

An energy. She was *exactly* right. Alicia traced the aura around Oni's body. Her fingertips touched nothing but air, and yet she could feel something faint on her skin—a frequency. Oni's eyes followed the movement of Alicia's fingers and she smiled, a breathy chuckle at the back of her throat, and that made Alicia smile.

"Are you human?"

Heaven muttered, "Raas, Alicia, you didn't even smoke that much."

She knew it was a strange question, but she didn't feel strange asking it.

Oni cleared her throat. "Will you pick a card from the deck?"

Not a question but an invitation, one that Alicia could, maybe should, decline. There was no logical explanation, but she heard caution in those eight words, a warning of potential change should she accept what Oni offered. Or perhaps Alicia was simply high. She nodded her head.

"Of course," she said.

II

O ni opened her purse and took out a bottle-green suede envelope case. Unwinding the leather strap, she turned the case on its side so the cards could fall into her hand. Tarot had never been something Alicia was interested in even mildly, and if Grandma Mabel could see her, she'd balk at her participating in a public reading. Things like this were done rarely and privately in her family. When her mother helped her move into her apartment for grad school, her first (and so far only, she thought bitterly) place on her own, in a city that wasn't her home, she'd cleansed the studio and its bathroom with sage. Alicia had never seen her do that before, and she'd understood that they weren't to talk of the cleansing while it happened or after it finished.

"I want you to reflect before choosing a card." Oni's eyes searched Alicia's.

"What, like a Magic 8 Ball?" Alicia's voice sounded far away even to her own ears.

Oni smiled and Alicia somehow felt her amusement, as if they could share the same emotions.

"Not exactly, but you can ask a question."

Alicia swallowed hard. "Do I have to tell you what it is?"

"Not if you don't want to."

She leaned in so only Oni could hear. "Why don't I have a job?"

Oni didn't say anything right away and continued to look at her, but Alicia could sense that a look was never just a look with her.

"Come now, is that really the question you want fi ask?" Oni said finally. "Did you reflect?" She narrowed her eyes a bit. "I think it troubles you to reflect."

She said it like a musing or an observation, but it felt more like an indictment. Rather than bristle, Alicia felt desperate for Oni to see her as someone who did reflect.

"A job I'm good at, I mean." Her high made it difficult to be articulate. "A career. That's the word."

That had to be the right question when she was always being confronted with her own failure. Last week, Elliot from grad school (who'd once told Alicia she was just following popular opinion for saying she didn't like *Infinite Jest*) updated his "works at" description to "*The New Yorker.*" A few months ago, Kennedy from undergrad shared housewarming photos of her new condo right by High Park. Rachel, also from undergrad, posted the articles she'd written for *Vice* and *Maclean's*. Meanwhile, Alicia spent her shifts half worried she'd be fired— she didn't fold jeans to standard, she didn't clean fitting rooms fast enough, she didn't convince unsure customers to buy polos. She wasn't striving at anything.

"You're not putting your mind to it," Pradeep had said. "Look at Heaven. She made a five-hundred-dollar sale."

Alicia had adopted an autopilot stance to keep from feeling anger or resentment or embarrassment with any true rigour, and the blank expression that came from her detachment only compelled the other assistant manager on shift to give her another talk about appearing friendly to customers.

"That's the question," she insisted now.

Her mother had told her a degree would give her the power to go wherever she decided, and yet having two did nothing to push her forward.

Oni blinked, and there was a shrewdness in her expression. "The answer might be more complicated. It might address the question behind the question. Don't discount it." She fanned out the cards and held them out to Alicia. "Like I said, nuh rush. You have all the time in the world."

Alicia somehow knew that if she took hours before choosing a card, Oni wouldn't say a single word. But an instinct told her exactly where to put her hand. She pulled a card from the middle of the deck, and another one at the end fell to the floor.

"Does that one count too?"

"Yah, man," said Oni, bending down to pick it up. "What does the one in your hand say?"

Alicia flipped the card over. There was a golden outline of a tall spire perched on a mountaintop. At first glance the drawing looked pretty, but Alicia took in the golden lightning bolts surrounding the tower and the flame that almost looked like a crown bursting from the parapet, and she felt an unease that made her heart thud the way it did the first and only time she'd eaten an edible.

"The tower," said Oni, which was met with a few mutterings from the people behind her. "Which means that—"

"You're going through significant internal change," said Heaven, cutting Oni off. "And you're probably resisting the inevitable, to delay the change."

Oni didn't take her eyes off Alicia but smiled. "You didn't lie about studying up, eh?"

Heaven shrugged her shoulders but looked pleased.

"Still," said Oni, "there are layers to a reading. It all depends on if the card is reversed or not." She gestured to Alicia to confirm the direction of the card.

"It's not upside down," she said.

Oni stared at the card she'd picked up before turning it around to show Alicia.

"The wheel of fortune, also not upside down," said Alicia. "So what do they mean?"

Oni didn't answer for a while. Alicia wondered if the long stretch of silence was real.

"They do mean that a change soon come," Oni said finally. "A big one. On the one hand, it will take you by surprise; you didn't ask for it, it'll seem abrupt and destructive. But all chaos isn't bad chaos, all destruction isn't bad destruction, weh eye nuh see, heart nuh leap, yuh understand? That's the tower. But the wheel of fortune, that card tells you the change been put in motion from time, destiny like."

Oni's eyes met Alicia's. "It's important," she said quietly. "Be careful."

Alicia took a step back. She felt another shift. The vibe in the room was changing, and she knew it was time for her to go. Heaven followed her to the foyer.

"You're not going to wait and say bye to Mars?"

"I'll see him in the morning."

"And Oni?"

"I don't need to say anything, she understands." Alicia bent down to put on her Sorels, lacing them up with hurried fingers. "I need to go home."

Alicia couldn't appease Heaven when she herself didn't understand what had happened—or if anything, in fact, had happened.

"How far up on Weston are you?" said Heaven. "Should you get an Uber or something?"

Alicia opened the foyer closet for her coat and took a knitted white hat out of the left sleeve. "I'm a fast walker. It should only take me ten minutes, fifteen tops," she said. "I'm just across the street from the Cash Max."

"Oh, bless," said Heaven.

Alicia walked to the door, making sure she had her phone and house keys in her pockets before putting on the winter gloves she'd just bought at the Dollarama on Lawrence Avenue earlier that day. She glanced back at Heaven.

"Thanks for inviting me. I know more about you now, like you come from mad money."

"Why, because of the house? Please. My parents can barely keep up with the payments. They're only gone for the weekend because my dad won the holiday raffle at work." Heaven paused. "Damn. Every time I'm around Oni, mi get labba-labba. She has a way of making things come out. Anyway, text me when you reach home, eh?"

Alicia nodded and stepped out onto the walkway. Getting distance from Oni was an odd relief. It was one of those December nights absent wind but sharp with a chill that sank deep into the skin so you felt the cold inside and out. She'd resent the cold after a few minutes, but for now she was grateful for the way it cut through her buzz and anchored her to reality.

Snow crunched beneath her boots as she headed up the street, shoving her gloved hands into her pockets, balling them into fists for more warmth. There were many ice-frosted trees around her, their leafless branches casting spiked shadows in the light of the streetlamps. A dog barked in the distance, its whining the only noise Alicia could hear next to her own footsteps.

Ding! Her phone sounded with a notification and she felt it vibrate against her hand, but she didn't check it right away. Only one person really texted her these days. The friends (if you could call them that) from her grad program all still lived in New York, and like the ones from undergrad, they had become friends on social media only. After a second ding interrupted Alicia's thoughts, which were drifting back to Oni, she stopped and took out her phone. The texts from that morning and afternoon were still visible:

MOM: A BC park ranger got attacked by a bear outside his home yesterday.

. . . OK? What do you want me to do with this information, mom?

A few hours later, her mother had sent her a picture of the bottle cap from the Grace Island Soda she'd drunk with lunch. The photo was for the Jamaican proverb stamped into the underside of the cap—each Island Soda came with one. After Grandma Mabel died, Alicia had got into the habit of collecting the caps instead of throwing them away after she'd finished drinking. She did it at first because she recognized a proverb as one Grandma Mabel had said frequently, and then she started keeping ones she thought Grandma Mabel would have enjoyed reading. Her mother started contributing to her collection, and they kept the bottle caps in a jar in the living room, beneath a photo of Grandma Mabel. They never spoke about their tradition. The new message from her mother, Miss Gale, was a link and an image of an article.

MOM: Did you see this? AUTHENTICITY "EXTREMELY IMPORTANT" FOR LOCAL JAMAICAN RESTAURANT.

Beneath a picture of Bob Marley was the opening sentence: "Caribbean cuisine is all the rage, with chefs and restaurateurs of all backgrounds getting in on . . ."

Alicia knew this was her mother's way of checking to see when she was coming home, but the link she had sent as an excuse to text her was surprising. Normally, she picked the most gruesome news stories to send, as if knowing about all the terrors in the world would somehow help Alicia protect herself from them. This article didn't fit into her mother's usual repertoire. Alicia made a mental note to read it later, but for now she texted back "be home soon," put the phone in her pocket, and kept walking, picking up her pace a little.

Church Street could be lonely after dark; a street of bungalows and red-brick houses and a few mid-rise apartment buildings, its busiest hours were before and after school, and yet she felt like she had company tonight—a presence that stalked her, like hot breath against the back of her neck. It made her hunch her shoulders, readied, her apartment keys nestled between her fingers like a makeshift claw. Every few seconds, Alicia glanced behind her. She told herself it was to see if she could spot the two blue lights of the Maple Leaf bus and not to check if she was being followed, though she was prepared for that.

"Keys are good," said Heaven once, when they discussed their DIY protections for walking home alone at night, "but I prefer an umbrella. You can mash up a face with the handle."

Even with distance, Alicia's thoughts circled back to Oni's reading. The shift she'd felt in the living room was still affecting her, even as she tried to shake off its strangeness. She passed Rosemount Avenue, putting a five-minute distance between herself and Heaven's house, but the barking dog, still unseen, seemed to follow her, alternating between growls and high-pitched yelps, like a warning. It put Alicia on edge. A gust of wind blew, and just ahead, the yellow diamond-shaped sign at the railway track wobbled. The streetlamps started to flicker. Alicia tried not to think much of it.

She approached the Canadian Pacific Railway track that passed through Weston Village. Usually she heeded the red-and-white X-shaped sign that cautioned cars to slow down, even though she was a pedestrian and even when there was no chance of a train barrelling down the tracks. Tonight she cut across without thinking twice.

The breeze turned into a violent bluster, sweeping snow up from the ground in the middle of the road—a twister that looked so much larger with each turn that Alicia could imagine the cyclone picking her up with the snow and planting her in an entirely new world.

If she hadn't felt so nervous, she would have stopped to record; she'd never seen anything like it, and she was sure no one else on her timeline had either. Everyone had homes, careers, wedding engagements even, but none of them had ever witnessed a terrifying phenomenon like the one before her now. This was something she could boast, she could update about her life, maybe she could even say it was a near-death experience. But the hot breath against the nape of her neck intensified, as did the sense that she was being watched.

One by one, the streetlights stopped flickering and the bulbs blew out entirely, exploding with sudden and individual pops, white and yellow sparks flittering like gently falling snow. Alicia picked up her pace.

She no longer heard barking. The dog quieted with a final squeal, and in its place, Alicia heard a distant clanging, metal scraping against the ground, scratching like nails against a chalkboard. She looked behind her to see if she was hearing the wheels of a train screeching on the steel tracks, but she saw nothing. Alicia thought of Oni's caution and how it mirrored Grandma Mabel's old warning. Instinctively, she fingered her bracelet.

"Duppy know who fi frighten."

She muttered the old adage before ripping off her bracelet and throwing it to the ground. The golden X glinted in the night. Quickly, Alicia broke into a run.

III

CRUICKSHANK PARK. GATEWAY TO THE HUMBER RIVER. Alicia read the sign fused to the wrought-iron archway mounted atop two stone plaques. She didn't remember reaching Weston Road. She only remembered running. And fear. She remembered that too. It didn't make sense to her, but she somehow knew she was out of immediate danger. Weston wasn't busy but it was well lit, and a couple of restaurants in the plaza across the street from her were still open. She heard music coming from Bonita, the Italian restaurant she often passed by but never dined in, and someone had just walked out of China China, the takeaway she always ordered from. It had comforted her upon returning to the neighbourhood that the plaza was still there without a single development sign in place, that nothing about that plaza had changed, not the barbershop, the mobile store, the dentist. Seeing it now, she didn't feel so alone.

Her apartment building was only two minutes away, the mint-green balconies within sight, but she couldn't go home. Not until she did this first. She couldn't explain it, but she knew she was wanted in the park. It was connected somehow to Oni, to the reading. The change was starting. Right now. Someone was wait-ing, someone was—

Alicia was standing on the other side of the archway. No memory of walking beneath it. Just—*blink!*—and she'd moved from one spot to the other. Right below her feet were six flights of stairs that led into the park. They were steep and ice-slicked. Alicia put her hand on the snow-covered railing for balance, wetting her cheap gloves.

One flight finished.

Shuffling on the landing. Alicia's shuffle turned into a skid. She slipped. Sliding down the next flight of stairs. *Wutless!* Sorels were supposed to prevent this from happening. They had "traction" and "grip" and something else the sales associate mentioned that had made her feel like a proper adult for spending over a hundred dollars on winter boots and not the forty she'd normally spend at Urban Planet (now, *there* was a woman who was good at customer service). When she stood up on the next landing, dusting the snow off her coat and sweatpants, she felt bruised but not in pain. Alicia wasn't as cold as when she'd left Heaven's either. It was like she was feel-ing everything second-hand—shadows of sensations.

Finally, there were no more stairs to descend. She was in the park. Even at night, Alicia could see the trails and steps and benches sprawled out in front of her. In warmer months, the oaks and willows and maple trees stood like gentle giants, but there was a certain majesty in their current nakedness. Alicia probably shouldn't be there. Her mother told her she'd seen a coyote lurking in the bushes one night, but that was in the summer, and now that Alicia thought about it, her mother probably saw an unleashed dog anyway. A noise. Alicia hesitated. A rabbit or a hare scurried across her path and she relaxed—those things were harmless. She had nothing to worry about. To her left, she saw the yellow-and-blue playground with the red slide that twirled in on itself and the metal A-frame swing set with the bucket swings that looked like dangling diapers. To her right was the Pan Am Path, which led to another set of stairs that climbed up to St. Phillips Road.

Alicia walked straight.

There was no trail ahead of her, only leafless trees, so the snow was untouched. She felt as if she were gliding. Everything was strange. It was stranger that as spooked as she was, she had to keep going. Alicia passed between the trees. Now she was on the riverbank. Across from her, in the distance, high-rise apartment buildings towered behind the park.

In daylight the Humber River looked muddied, but tonight it glistened a deep blue. Large patches of snow floated downstream. This was where she was wanted. She stayed where she was and watched herself breathe out white puffs of air, imagining them as small misty clouds. She waited.

Psst! Psst!

Alicia looked to see if there was anyone around. No one.

Psst! Look 'pon di water!

It was a strange request. It didn't matter. This was what was drawing her, pulling her forward despite the nervousness that knotted her stomach. Alicia inched closer to the bank's edge. Once she was close enough to fall in, the blue of the water shimmered to a lizard green. A boulder emerged in the middle of the river where there hadn't been one before. A figure sat atop the rock. It looked to be a beautiful woman, but that was too ordinary a description. A shapely woman with blue-black skin and gorgeous loc'd hair. Coiled black strands that fell below her bare shoulders, covering her naked breasts. She wore nothing but beaded necklaces of varying lengths and colours. Some red. Some blue. Alicia spotted some orange. Both of her wrists glinted with golden bangles that nearly reached her elbows. Her face was a mystery. Neither young nor old, or maybe she was both at once, Alicia couldn't be sure. She couldn't be sure of anything because the most striking detail about this woman was that in place of her legs was a scaled green fishtail. Not quite a human.

Alicia reached into her coat pocket and took out her phone, then swiped up with a gloved finger. "Siri, am I still high?"

Ah yes, mi a vision fi true, but yuh eye nuh deceive yuh.

The woman—mermaid—hadn't opened her mouth, and yet an ethereal voice penetrated Alicia's head, its dreaminess making the words unfurl in her mind and take root like some kind of enchantment. It felt terribly pleasant, and that made Alicia nervous.

"I swear, this is, like, the weirdest night," she said, putting her phone back in her pocket.

The mermaid wasn't listening. *Why mi haffi be so foofool fi want fi experience snow?* She seemed to be talking to herself, though Alicia still heard the voice in her head. *Mi live so long and mi never once feel so raasclaat cold!*

Alicia laughed, surprising herself. The short burst of sound didn't even feel like it came from her own body. There was just something so normal, so *human* about swearing that it seemed at odds with the mermaid's mystique, that both entranced and unsettled her.

"How long have you been alive?" she asked, slightly emboldened.

The mermaid raised her chin, her eyes narrowing imperiously. She examined Alicia. Then her expression changed, almost becoming maternal.

Oh, mi roam dis earth since Wappy kill Phillip.

Alicia hadn't heard that saying in over a decade. Grandma Mabel used to say it all the time, and one day, when Alicia was around twelve, she'd finally asked who Wappy was and why he'd killed Phillip. But instead of answering, Grandma Mabel simply cackled and continued braiding Alicia's hair. That was the last conversation they'd ever had.

"So you've been around a long time, then," said Alicia.

Yuh cyaah even begin fi understand time.

Somewhere beneath the voice's possession of Alicia's mind, recognition clicked into place. She had a fuzzy memory from years ago of an older cousin, Winston, visiting from Jamaica around this time for the holidays. He told stories to all the younger cousins—fables and legends and jokes from back home. There was Anansi the Spider, and Big Bwoy for the older kids, and when they were feeling brave, Winston whispered about Annie Palmer, the White Witch of Rose Hall. But then there was also—

Alicia took a quick step back from the edge of the bank. Her unease had morphed into an educated fear. The mermaid smiled, at once a threat and a comfort.

Yuh place me now, eh?

This was no ordinary mermaid. Alicia moved back a little more. She stumbled and threw out her hand, planting it firmly on the snowy ground to keep from falling completely. She scrambled back even farther. It didn't matter how much distance Alicia put between herself and the river, the woman was still clearly visible, as if she were only a few feet away.

Pickney, if mi want fi take yuh, mi just haffi sweet yuh wid mi song. She moaned in imagined relish. *Mmm, yuh wudda never die so nice.*

She wasn't wrong, Alicia realized. That was what the stories said. Death came to whoever looked upon her. It was certain and immediate. In an instant, Alicia could disappear beneath the Humber, her body never to be found. If any of this was even real. It definitely *felt* real. But Alicia wondered if her nightmares had returned—if this mirage was different from the ones she'd dreamed as a child.

"How are you here?" she asked, deciding to use logic to test reality.

How water walk go ah pumpkin belly?

All the answers were in proverbs and sayings that threw Alicia's questions back in her face, but she couldn't betray her utter bewilderment. Not when she knew who she was dealing with. As the warning entered her mind, Alicia heard a mischievous laugh. She tried again.

"What I mean is, you aren't, this isn't real, but if it was, the legend is Jamaican."

So?

Alicia didn't understand the question. "Well, this isn't Jamaica."

A misstep. The woman drew herself up, straightening her back, volatility unleashed. Her locs whipped around with a fury, her voice resonated with an anger that made Alicia jerk even farther back in alarm. She collided with some brambles.

Pickney! She stayed seated on the boulder, but the water around her harshened, its current quickened to a turbulent flow. *Ah wah mi name?*

"Well—"

Water sloshed onto the bank, soaking Alicia's boots and socks.

Speak 'pon mi name!

The river around her continued to crash against itself, threatening to flood the park.

"River Mumma!" said Alicia, a wobble in her throat, a plea that she'd survive.

River Mumma! The voice was surround sound in Alicia's head, the airiness replaced with a terrible wail.

Mi nuh just some ordinary mermaid splash splash inna di water, mi guard all di river, all di pond, all di fountain inna Jamaica!

River Mumma poised herself on the rock, regal and ancient.

Mi used fi get heap ah heap ah offering!

"I—"

Kibba yuh mouth! The voice grew louder. *Mi and yuh ah nuh size! Mi a deity! And yuh nuh think mi have di power fi go ah farrin'? Fi go wherever di water dem flow?*

Alicia doubled over in a half-bow, partly because the cold finally seemed to be getting to her, but mostly because she didn't know what to do with herself, how to act in such a presence.

"I really didn't mean it that way. I just—"

River Mumma put up her hand, and Alicia stopped speaking at once. She wondered if she'd do anything River Mumma told her to.

Yuh read, pickney? Yuh read about di chupid gods who did give dem wives bun, having intercourse with mortals as stag and swan? What if one of dem gods did show himself, eh? You wudda ask him why he inna Canada?

Nothing by way of a response or justification came to Alicia's mind. She didn't expect to feel guilt or shame, but River Mumma's accusation saddled her with both. The situation made no sense either way, she understood that. Still, she wondered how different her reaction would be if she were standing before one of the Greek gods she'd studied in her elementary school ancient civilization class. If she'd be skeptical of seeing Poseidon, not only because of its impossibility but also because of geography.

"I'm sorry." Alicia let her apology hang between them.

When the river calmed to its original near-still current, she took that as the sign she needed.

"Sorry," she said again. "But can I ask why you're here?" She kept her tone respectful.

River Mumma didn't answer right away—as if considering whether Alicia was worthy of speaking to—but eventually, she relaxed into a more informal posture, placing her chin on her right hand and her right elbow on the top half of her tail.

Ah wah di stories dem say?

The details came to Alicia in sluggish bouts of memories from different years of her childhood.

"There's a golden table you guard," she said slowly. "Stories say it's Spanish treasure from when they invaded the island, or, well, from when they colonized it. You drown the people trying to get it, right?" Alicia looked up briefly at River Mumma, aware that one story warned against looking into her eyes for fear of being irrevocably spellbound. "But I'm guessing the table isn't here with you."

River Mumma shrugged, giving nothing away.

Alicia tried to concentrate. It was difficult. When the water soaked her boots, it was like physical reality had returned to her. Her body throbbed from when she'd fallen, and her feet and lips were numb.

"A comb," she said. "You have a golden comb."

Yes. Mi want it back.

Alicia massaged her wrist as she waited for an elaboration, but River Mumma simply stared.

"Oh, I don't have it," said Alicia.

No, but mi know it's here inna dis country, dis city. Tourist dem tief it.

"So, what, you think I know them?"

River Mumma trailed her fingers in the river. *Mi nuh think so.*

"OK, real talk: I don't get what's going on." It was too cold for Alicia to continue focusing on her tone; she wondered if the bottoms of her feet had turned white.

"Like—with all due respect and everything—why can't you get it? Stories say you can get gully when you need to, like you torment people until they bring back the shit they stole from you. Or you offer them treasure, or you . . . I don't know, but you do something. So *do* something."

Ay, look here! Di woman who tief from mi have nerve fi steal, but she nuh believe inna mi power. Mi punish she, but it nuh change nuthin! Mi still need mi comb and mi trust yuh fi get it.

"I don't know what you expect me to do." Alicia felt silly explaining something that seemed obvious. "I don't even know them."

River Mumma waved a hand, unbothered. *Sharp spur mek meagre horse cut caper.*

Alicia paused. It took her a moment to work out the meaning. "You're just telling me that I'll have to deal with the circumstances," she said. "That doesn't help me."

River Mumma's expression flickered between a kindly smile and a severity that narrowed her eyes and set her jaw.

Look here, yuh washbelly baby! Mi nuh here fi help yuh, yuh here fi help me! Yuh owe it to me fi give something back to yuh roots!

"But I actually didn't do anything, though—"

And yuh have til sundown tomorrow fi get it.

"One *day*? What happens at sundown?" Alicia reminded herself that she hadn't agreed to anything and wasn't going to, but the short time frame compelled her to ask questions.

Mi g'way.

River Mumma's tone shifted again, and she extended herself on the boulder, a luxurious stretch, as if her possible disappearance was a trifle.

"That's it? You're just going to go away?"

There had to be something substantial.

Dis here di problem. Yuh nah know what mi disappearance gwine fi mean. Unuh forget about unuh environment, about di spirit, and yuh nuh know about yuh past. Nuh matter. No use fi chat 'bout hypothetical. Mi just warn yuh fi be careful. Mi nuh put yuh 'pon an easy path, yuh know? Yuh work fi spirit, spirit gwine follow yuh, and duppy know who fi frighten, so yuh haffi be on alert.

Alicia had whispered that exact saying only moments before. It wasn't a proverb she said often. She didn't say proverbs often at all—the weight, the importance, the memory of those sayings was saved for collection, for the jar in her living room. Perhaps the words weren't her own. Perhaps River Mumma had repeated the saying because she was a figment of Alicia's imagination.

A flicker of irritation passed over River Mumma's face. *I am real. Mi talk this way because mi know proverbs mean something to yuh.*

Alicia could see the Mason jar full of bottle caps in her mind's eye and bit the inside of her lip, not knowing if she found it manipulative or oddly touching that River Mumma had tried to appeal to her by tapping into something so personal.

"I never said I'd do this for you," she said.

Too late. Yuh already been chosen, and duppy already know how fi find yuh.

The metal clanking. The barking. The lights. Alicia shook her head. "That's not really an incentive to help you. What makes you think I will?"

Yuh feel lost. Nuh true?

Alicia flinched. Lethargy was a state of being she'd resigned herself to, but "lost"? That word, that concept, it felt too serious, too chaotic for her to acknowledge as a possibility.

"That's not an answer," she said quietly.

River Mumma reached out her hand, and even though she hadn't moved from her boulder, Alicia could feel a gentle caress beneath her chin.

It is.

And then River Mumma dove into the Humber. At once, the boulder vanished and the river picked up again. The rushing of the water turned to whispers, hisses, sounding one word over and over: *Alicia, Alicia, Alicia.* It became a song. Alicia could hear River Mumma's voice in the current. Intoxicating and haunting. Waves splashed onto the bank, breaking upon Alicia's feet, encircling her ankles like hands gripping her joints. She felt an ever-so-delicate pull toward the river, and she complied. She should resist, but she couldn't. She had to listen to what the voice said.

Alicia couldn't remember climbing into the river. But now she was battling the waves. She spluttered. She choked. Panic pushed her heart to beat faster. She had never felt so cold. Everything inside of her was screaming. The words came back to her, the voice soft and hungry: *If mi want fi take yuh, mi just haffi sweet yuh with mi song. Yuh wudda never die so nice.* Was she dying? Did it matter? It didn't feel very nice. She was leaving. Being pulled somewhere. That knowledge loosened something within her, eased her into a sudden surrender. Then the waves overtook her.

IV

The water spat Alicia out as quickly as it'd swallowed her, her head breaking the surface of a river. The emergence split her consciousness in two. She saw out of her own two eyes, listened out of her own two ears. Yet she could also view herself from outside of her body. Within and without at the same time.

Had to be a dream now.

Everything was different. The cold of the water was different. Clear and deep, rushing past sleek rocks. Harsh and rejuvenating. Buoyed in the river, Alicia watched herself look up at her surroundings: Snowy banks—gone. Bare trees—gone. Lush foliage, so deeply, vividly, Dorothy-crashing-into-Technicolor green, enclosed her instead. Ferns and shrubs were rooted to brown boulders that towered over the river with a magnificence born of their prehistoric existence. Plummeting from their apex, a waterfall fed into the river she treaded in.

History lived here. History Alicia knew in her bones rather than her memory. A Queen had fortified herself in these waters, in that fall. A Queen of resistance. Independence.

Women appeared where there had been none before, as if

conjured by air. They stood in white dresses, knee-deep in the river. They stood in front of the crashing waterfall, gathered in a half-circle, one side longer than the other. Arms linked by the crooks of their elbows, their palms open in front of them, the backs of their hands touching the water's surface. Alicia had never seen any of these women, but none of them were strangers. They felt more than familiar. Echoes. As if Alicia had been split into ten separate bodies external from her own. But they weren't *her*. They were family. Family unremembered. Family unforgotten.

Three women at the shorter side of the curve caught her attention. They were each crowned with different hairstyles: Bantu knots. A braided updo. Tightly coiled curls.

They had something for her.

Come. They said, *Come. Come. Come.*

Alicia didn't have a choice—they drew her to them. There was no saying no. She waded through the water, and once she'd reached them, standing in front of their half-circle, she looked at what the women were holding. A white veil. Draped over each of their palms. Cradled. Cherished. Held by all the women in the arch. Alicia didn't understand the feeling it inspired in her. It was only a veil. Unease shivered through her, and yet she couldn't resist the allure of the veil, the emotion it invoked, the affinity she felt for it. The veil drew her to it the way the women drew her to them.

Still, something wasn't right. The veil was long—too long. It trailed into the river.

That's when Alicia understood. She looked at the women. All the women. At their arms. At how they looped together. They were a chain. But one that was broken. The woman at the end of the shorter side stood with her left elbow crooked, but there was no arm to loop with hers. No palms to catch the tail end of the veil. Grandma Mabel. She was missing. Alicia swallowed her disappointment.

To the right, Alicia turned her head. The same thrall she'd felt at Cruickshank Park compelled her to. She saw a tableau in the distance, a snapshot of yet another time. River Mumma rested on a boulder—she had thick tresses of black hair and umber skin, the same ageless, extraordinary face, her tail blue instead of green. And she had the comb.

The women spoke again.

The comb is to River Mumma what River Mumma is to the waters. No comb, no River Mumma. No River Mumma, no rivers.

Alicia could suddenly see it, as if the women had put the picture in her mind: dried rivers and barren streams in the dozens, in the hundreds. The skeletons of cattle. A total wasteland.

Do your duty.

Somehow, those words turned Alicia's attention to the rest of the tableau. Several feet away from River Mumma was a scene that looked peculiar outdoors—a man at a dining table set for five with mutton and fish and vegetables rotting away on fancy dishes. Alicia was possessed by a hatred so intense it scared her; she was surprised by how personal it was, how she felt it so deeply in her being. The man had white skin and blue lips. He stood up, gesturing to his throat. Abruptly, he coughed up fish bones and fish guts, he coughed up blood, splattering red on his white shirt and breeches. In between the coughing man and River Mumma stood a barefoot woman—a woman who looked exactly like Alicia but was dressed in a white blouse and striped skirt, a headwrap around her hair, a red beaded necklace draping her neck. She looked up at Alicia, and Alicia gasped.

In an instant, River Mumma was in front of her, her hands on either side of Alicia's face as if she were pulling something down, and suddenly, her vision was obscured. Her face was cloaked. Netting over her eyes. Alicia looked over to the women, to their hands. The veil was gone. It was draped around her head.

She reached up to touch it—

She sank.

The river called her back with its song. The melody pulling her into its depths. *Alicia, Alicia, Alicia.* Too many voices at once. River Mumma. The women by the falls. The river itself. All singing just for her. All mingling together, growing louder and louder.

Bright colours clouded her vision. Like the tie-dye she used to do in daycare. And the song of her name would be the last thing she'd hear: *Alicia, Alicia, Alicia . . .*

"Alicia!"

A hard bang on something solid. A violent mechanical click. Alicia opened her eyes to a flurry of noises she couldn't distinguish or put together. A dull pain throbbed in her left temple. Her throat hurt. She spluttered for air.

". . . the 89 will come and gone."

"What?" Alicia blinked rapidly, trying to bring her surroundings into focus.

"Get up so you don't miss your bus! I don't want you taking Uber. You know I saw on the news that a man from Mississauga— an Uber driver—got arrested last month for sexually assaulting passengers? It was a year-long investigation!"

Alicia realized that she was at home, lying in bed. Her mother had opened her bedroom door without knocking but stood in the hallway to technically honour the conversation they'd had a few days earlier about boundaries. Alicia rolled onto her side, coughing; she expected to regurgitate some water, but her airway was clear. She could hear her mother's voice tinted with worry.

"Are you sick? See the Vicks in the bathroom there, and gargle your mouth with salt. Let me make you a shot. Crushed ginger and lime, a bit of rum—not too much because you're going to work."

"No, I'm fine, Mom. I'm just . . ." Alicia didn't know what she was, except alive. Alive and not at the bottom of a river. She pressed two fingers against her temple in a vain attempt to squeeze her headache out, then sat up a little to look at her mother.

Strangely, it was like looking at her for the first time. In her face she saw the faces of the women who had stood before the waterfall, and Alicia wondered if she'd see the same eyes, those noses, those lips when she looked in the mirror, and what that would mean if she did. She risked the pain and shook her head slightly in an attempt to knock herself into reality.

She saw that her mother was looking at her with pursed lips.

"What is it?" Alicia asked.

Ms. Gale folded her arms over her white satin robe. "You just got your hair done and you didn't even tie up your head before you went to sleep?"

Alicia sighed, grateful for her mother's mundane observation. The maternal sixth sense she sometimes had didn't alert her to Alicia's not being quite right this morning. She looked up at the pink silk bonnet on her mother's head, the one she never failed to put on before sleeping so that her curls were perfect for the next day. She gestured to Alicia's braids.

"The scalp is already frizzing. This is why your braids never last as long as they should."

"I was too tired." It hurt to speak. Alicia's mouth was dry, and her eyes were like sandpaper.

"Ah your money dat. Let me mind mi cahna." She started to close the door.

"Mom, wait." There was still that morning fog clouding her consciousness, but she really was alive. "What time did I get home last night?"

Ms. Gale smiled with what looked like triumph. "I thought you were grown and it wasn't my place to check on you," she said. "You have all the answers at twenty-six, remember?"

"OK, OK." Alicia rubbed her eyes. "It's too early for this."

"Not early enough. Get up, Miss Twenty-Six. You're going to be late for work. If you did have a licence—"

Alicia grumbled. "No one who grew up and still lives in the city has a licence."

Ms. Gale kissed her teeth before closing the door, and Alicia lay back down, staring up at the stucco ceiling. It had been a dream, then, or a nightmare. She repeated this revelation silently. Of course it hadn't been real. River deities and waterfalls and cryptic messages—she didn't know what she'd expected. It was only that this was the first time a dream had left residue in her mind, in her body, like muscle memory.

Without looking, Alicia reached for her phone on the nightstand. Her hand brushed against the empty mugs and glasses she hadn't yet put in the sink. Her fingers ruffled the stack of CVs her mother had made her print, but she knew she'd never have to use them because no employer took hard copies anymore. These were the ones she'd made when she applied to be a grant writer or a program assistant, office manager, executive assistant. She felt the tops of pop bottles and the rim of her penholder, but no phone.

Alicia looked around at the mismatch of plastic bins and card-
board boxes, suitcases and duffel bags that crowded her room; even
the steelpan she used to play in elementary school hung from its
stand in the corner. Her mother had moved apartments while
Alicia was in graduate school and used the second bedroom as
storage, to save the monthly two hundred dollars she'd otherwise
have to spend on a commercial unit. When Alicia came back home
earlier than anticipated, the room had been cleared just enough for
her expendable duffel bags to join the collection of luggage, and for
a twin bed to be pushed against a wall. During the second month
of Alicia's homecoming, her mother had offered to give in and find
storage space so Alicia could be more comfortable. Alicia told her
not to, that the discomfort would serve as motivation.

She spotted her coat and her sweats on a beige bin nestled atop
two others, and braced herself to get up and walk the few steps
across the room. Her head twinged painfully with the movement
of standing up, and her left leg was so stiff she had to hobble the
short distance. She started to look through her clothes but drew
back her hand in surprise: everything was wet. Her coat was
drenched. There was even a small pool of water at the base of the
stack of bins, and the sight of it was like a cold stone weighing
down Alicia's gut.

"No," she said, verbally challenging her own thoughts. "No
fucking way, that would be ridiculous." But then she asked herself
why she was in so much pain.

Quickly, she pulled down the pyjama pants she didn't remember
putting on, exposing a large red splotch on her left thigh. The logical
explanation was that perhaps she did go to Cruickshank Park after
Heaven's and perhaps she did fall down the stairs, but that was it,
that would *have* to be it to stay within the realm of possibility. Yet

the bruise felt like incriminating evidence. She had the same pit in her stomach that she'd get on the mornings of exams.

Alicia reached into her coat pocket and pulled out her phone. No shattered screen. She had to click the power button a few times for the phone to boot up, and once it did, vertical bars flickered onscreen and it turned off after a few seconds. Alicia mimed bashing her head against the phone before trying again. Most, if not all, of her next cheque would have to go to fixing the *blasted* ting. On the second start, she managed to open a search engine.

It took her a minute to decide what to type, to weigh which of last night's experiences was more bizarre than the others. Finally, she searched the words "River Mumma, Jamaica."

She clicked on the first link and read: "River Mumma is both sacred and feared in Jamaican folklore. Legend has it that the fish in her waters are her children and should not be caught, as suffering will be a consequence for such an action, and to catch her will cause all of the rivers to dry up."

It said nothing about what would happen if she left. Neither did any of the other sites Alicia skimmed. Not one article or blog said anything about whether River Mumma could even leave, and whether taking off would mean taking the rivers with her. Before Alicia could type the question, her phone shut down again.

"RHATID!" she yelled.

"ARE YOU TELLING ME YOU'RE STILL IN BED?" her mother's voice sounded from the living room, along with the whistling of a kettle.

V

The grogginess persisted even after Alicia washed her face with cold water. Getting dressed in a fog felt like a mild case of sleepwalking. She pulled on a blue-and-white colour-block hoodie that nearly reached her knees and a pair of fleece-lined jeggings that she'd got for fifteen dollars at Ardene. This would have to make up for the autumn jacket she now had to wear.

"I made you the ginger. It's in the shot glass by the microwave. Also, when you get home from your shift, make sure to stop at Greenland down the street to get some curry seasoning and browning. Alicia? Alicia, what are you looking at?"

Alicia had meandered from her bedroom, down the hallway, through the darkened living room to the kitchen, which was brightened by the light over the stove, her eyes never straying from her phone. She was trying to see, in the moments that the phone charge held, if there was any news about any kind of water shortage in Jamaica. She put Google Alerts on certain words and phrases: "Jamaica." "Jamaica, rivers." "Jamaica, drought." "Jamaica, water."

"Just looking at the *Gleaner*. The *Observer* too," said Alicia, picking up the shot glass and throwing back the concoction her mother had made. The ginger and rum scorched her throat, and the burn of the lime juice made her eyes water a little, but she was grateful for the boost and smiled her thanks to her mother.

"You're talking Jamaica's *Gleaner* and *Observer*?"

Alicia wiped the tears away as she returned her attention to her phone. "Yes."

"Really? I didn't know you read those."

She looked through the archway to Ms. Gale, who was sitting at the round glass table in the connected dining area, steeping a tea bag in a Mason jar.

"Why wouldn't I read it? We have family in Jamaica. Should I not care about what's going on there? You read them both all the time."

Ms. Gale let go of her tea-bag string to put her hands together on the table, interlacing her fingers, and looked at Alicia with an authoritative coolness.

"One, dial it down, Miss Twenty-Six. Me and you nuh size, understand?"

Alicia flinched, hearing River Mumma's voice in those words. "Sorry, Mom."

"Two, I just didn't know. It was a question. Three, are you finished cosplaying as a white teenager?"

Alicia regretted teaching her mother about Comic-Con but nodded her head all the same. When Ms. Gale declared the conversation over with an "OK, then," Alicia put her phone in the pouch pocket of her hoodie and opened the fridge.

"You don't have enough time for a proper breakfast." Her tone indicated that their tiff was indeed behind them.

"I know," said Alicia with the same kind of airiness. She scanned the shelves, grinning at the scent of the curry chicken that had been left to season overnight. "Any more bammy?"

Her mother snorted. "You ate them all. I only got one."

"More like three," said Alicia, closing the fridge. "Cookies, then? Ovaltine?"

"Check the cupboard."

She rolled her sleeves up to her elbows and took out the step-stool that was stored in the space between the fridge and the stove. At nearly five-nine, her mother was significantly taller and put the more valued snacks on the highest shelf she could. Alicia could see the bright orange package of biscuits she was looking for and had to stand on her tiptoes to grab it, even on the stool.

"Your hair looks nice even with the frizz," said Ms. Gale.

Alicia continued reaching for the top shelf but turned her head to the side, raising an eyebrow. "Mmhmm."

"Nuh lie, the colours do suit you," she said, stirring her tea.

"Thank you." Alicia finally gripped the package and brought it down with her as she stepped off the stool.

Ms. Gale took a sip of her tea. "Will your work let you wear your hair like that?"

Alicia raised a finger, as if to say, "There it is."

"What do you mean 'let me'? I already did it." She took the clear plastic tray out of the box, revealing two sealed packs of biscuits.

"So they're not going to find some dress-code excuse to penal-ize you like what happened to that girl who wore her hair natural at Jack Astor's?"

"I don't know," said Alicia, putting a biscuit between her teeth. "I don't think so."

"You didn't think about this before getting it done?"

Alicia heard her mother's voice start to turn. She bit the cookie between her teeth and started to chew.

"What's the worst thing that can happen? I get fired?"

Ms. Gale put the Mason jar down on the table with a thud. "Ah wah she sey?" she asked to no one in particular. "Yes, getting fired is the worst thing that can happen! It took you three months just to get this part-time job."

"OK, well, I am sorry I decided to pursue a degree in English and not—I don't know—engineering."

"Engineering? With your math skills?"

"Funny."

"I looked it up. If publishing is what you want to do, there are programs that—"

"Excellent, more school. Look, everyone else I know got their dream job with just their degree and had no issues. I don't know why, for me, suddenly that's not enough."

"Twice as hard—"

"Not the speech, Mom. I know the speech by heart."

"But did you know, if yuh want good, yuh nose haffi run."

Alicia rubbed her head. "How would I even pay for this program on minimum wage? Take out another loan? Add to my already ridiculous debt just to really make sure I won't pay it off in my lifetime?"

"Watch your tone."

"Sorry," said Alicia again. "I just . . ."

"Mm-mm." Ms. Gale threw up her hands. "I'm not going to give you the argument you're so clearly looking for this morning. What is with your mood, anyway? Are you still tired? Because mi nuh gwine fi lie, yuh nuh look so good."

Alicia put another cookie in her mouth and turned around to lean against the counter. "What if I told you I feel even worse than I look?"

"Mi nuh feel sorry for yuh. I don't know why you'd get drunk the night before you have to go to work."

"I didn't get drunk," said Alicia. It was technically true. "I just had a weird night, that's all."

"Does it have anything to do with why you're not wearing your bracelet?" She nodded her head toward her daughter's hand.

Alicia rubbed a finger over her naked wrist as if to confirm that the bracelet really was gone.

"I've never seen you take it off," she continued. "Even when I keep telling you wearing it all the time will make it tarnish."

Alicia remembered now. She had taken it off purposely because of a feeling. She didn't know what to say; her mother was cagey about this kind of stuff, always had been.

"I'm actually surprised you let Grandma Mabel give me the bracelet."

Ms. Gale got up from her chair and walked over to the kitchen. She ran her fingers through Alicia's braids before taking a section of them in her hand. She didn't speak for a while.

"Back home, your great-grandmother used to draw an X—and by that, I mean a ten—outside of her house to ward off any evil duppy, because they can only count to nine," she said, twisting the section of braids into a medium-sized bun on the top right side of Alicia's head. "Don't ask me why that's the number, it just is. Grandma Mabel brought some of that here with her, and it would've felt wrong to keep her from passing down a bit of what Granny Joycelyn believed in to you."

Alicia flinched at hearing "Joycelyn." Those faces came to her again, and one in particular stood out: the last woman in the chain, a mixture of soft and fierce in her expression. Granny Joycelyn.

"So she was really into that stuff? Like she practised it even more than Grandma Mabel?"

"She had her ways," said Ms. Gale vaguely. "It was the time.

Mummy held on to some superstitions here and there, but she didn't practise anything much. She didn't encourage her gifts."

"But she gave me the bracelet. Why didn't she get you one?"

Ms. Gale touched up the bun to make it perfectly round. "Well, like I said, she held on to *some* superstitions, and you were . . . She called you sensitive."

Alicia cocked her head. "How am I sensitive?"

"Not like that—stop being so sensitive." She moved to Alicia's left to make another bun. "I mean like how she was before it finally went away. She thought you were—I see you cringing, there are enough loose braids, I know how to do the style, it's Sailor Moon–like, cha—she thought you were prone to 'seeing things.'"

"Because of my nightmares?"

Ms. Gale shifted her weight and cleared her throat. Alicia could tell this conversation was going on longer than she would've liked, and she felt a combination of exasperation at her mother's hang-ups and appreciation that she was temporarily getting over them to have this talk.

"She didn't think they were nightmares; she thought it was some kind of sight, because you were born with a veil—or if you want to be scientific about it, a caul."

"A veil," Alicia repeated.

"Mm. The bracelet was supposed to help guard you from it as much as from duppy."

She didn't know if this information made her feel better or worse, if it added weight to what she thought had possibly happened the night before or if it was just nonsense and she shouldn't even entertain the idea of veracity. She had never questioned her dreams as a child because she was told they were just that—figments of an overactive imagination.

"This seems kind of important, Mom." Alicia tried to tamp down the accusation in her tone. "Why didn't you tell me any of this before?"

"Because I have my limits, and I think this sight business leads to obeah, myal, all that bush, and it's—"

"You're not going to tell me you think it's 'evil' and 'devil work,' are you?" said Alicia. "This isn't some internalized 'heart of darkness'—"

"That was in reference to the Congo, Miss Twenty-Six. Or the African continent as a whole," said Ms. Gale, making sure both buns were sturdy and tight so they wouldn't unravel.

"You know what I mean! It's all related. Colonial-mentality shit. You realize the British made obeah illegal as a way to suppress rebellions, right? Heaven, this girl I work with, she did a whole paper on it worth, like, 45 percent of her grade."

Ms. Gale nodded her head. "I suppose I wasn't the first one to tell you that Queen Nanny was a priestess or was said to use obeah against the British during the Maroon Wars, then? Raas, don't try to out-woke your original educator."

"That's not what I was—"

"I just thought—and think—that it's all ruled by fear and suspicion, and I wasn't going to encourage that."

"So which one is it to you? Negative or positive? Do you even consider it real?"

Alicia was desperate to find some kind of indication of what to believe, if only so she could move on and return to her life, stagnant but predictable in its stasis. Her mother opened her mouth but said nothing, and Alicia could see years of conflict and contradiction battle across her face. Finally, she shook her head, walked back to the table, and sat down again.

"It's not any of your business what I think. And why is this suddenly so important to you?"

Alicia didn't answer right away. She walked into the dining area and looked at her reflection in the mirror hanging on the wall next to the table. Her lips, eyes, nose—they all did seem different now. She was awakened to the fact that these features didn't begin and end with her. Joycelyn was staring back at her, so was Grandma Mabel, and yet Alicia didn't see Grandma Mabel at the waterfall. The chain broke with her.

"You mentioned Granny Joycelyn and I know I never met her, but"—Alicia paused—"it feels like I met her last night, or dreamed her," she added, quickly correcting herself. "Her and other women from before I was born. Before *you* were born. It felt like some kind of induction."

Ms. Gale looked at her wryly. "Induction into a family you're already a part of?"

Alicia could see the veil clearly in her mind's eye. They had given it to her. Put it on her. Regifted her something that Grandma Mabel had tried to repress, had turned away from herself, at least partially. Maybe that was why she wasn't with Alicia's other foremothers.

"That's all you have to say about my dream?" she said. "I'm surprised."

"Well, dreams are real. Spirits can hang around. That's why we did have set-up for Mummy so her spirit could go where it needed to."

That had been a point of contention during the funeral preparations; part of the family had wanted to do the celebrations properly, with a wake held every night for nine nights, with drums and live bands and dancing, and the other part had wanted to do away with it altogether. In the end, the wake was one night, the ninth night after Grandma Mabel had died and the night before the funeral. There'd been a lot of cooking and a lot of rum, a lot of singing of hymns, a lot of games of dominoes, a lot of swapping of stories. And each time Grandma Mabel was mentioned by name, they spoke of her as if she were still alive.

A candle had burned all night long on a table of white and red flowers, and next to it was a glass of rum and a plate of plantains, rice and peas, and curry goat—no one touched the food until the next morning. After midnight, the candle had burned out and Alicia gasped, unaware of why exactly, but her mother had heard her sharp intake of breath and looked at her, a sad joy in her eye.

"She left," she'd said.

Alicia remembered walking in on her mother and other family members covering the mirrors and moving the furniture around in Grandma Mabel's apartment the day before the wake, and when she'd asked why, all they'd said was, "It's what you do." Winston had been the one to tell her what it all meant, because he always told her things the other adults wouldn't.

"You move the furniture around fi help the spirit of the dead. You don't want fi tempt it to stay, you want it fi get back to the homeland, fi get back to Africa, so you move the furniture around to confuse it. We put the food there so Grandma Mabel can eat and listen to all the stories about her before she leave, and when the candle blow out, her spirit g'way."

Alicia looked at her mother now. "And you believe that? The furniture, the candle, the table, the whole tradition?"

"It's what you do," she said. "People have been doing that—"

"Since Wappy killed Phillip," Alicia finished.

"Mm."

"Well, the dream about Granny Joycelyn happened after . . ." Alicia didn't even know what to call it. She tried again. "When I was walking home, I felt like I needed that bracelet, and it came through for me. There was this *presence*, and *that* was after the tarot reading and—"

Ms. Gale raised her hands. "I don't want to hear any more," she said. "Just don't go around telling people you've been dabbling in all this business, you hear?"

Alicia laughed, exasperated and amused about where her mother's lines were when it came to this conversation. "OK, first of all, who would I tell? I have no friends. But even if I did, it's different now. People my age, we're curious about this stuff; no one is going to shun me."

"Ah, so yuh say."

"And besides, my mind is on more important things, like, you know, starting my career. Really, I was just having a conversation." She turned to her mother, narrowing her eyes affectionately. "You don't believe me, do you."

"What I *believe* is that you have five minutes to catch your bus." She pointed to the clock on the wall.

Alicia jolted. "Oh, shit."

She walked quickly around the table to give her mother a quick peck on the cheek.

"Wait! Before you go . . ."

She picked up the bottle cap she'd taken a picture of the night before and handed it to Alicia, who turned it over to read the proverb again: *Gi mi sponge fi go dry up sea*. It was common to find this saying—it was probably the most popular one—but Alicia laughed at receiving, today of all days, a proverb about tackling an impossible task.

"OK, see you, Mom," she said. "Love you."

"Mmhm, love you too," said Ms. Gale. "And remember, bring

back some browning and curry seasoning from Greenland! You have no reason to forget!"

Alicia rushed into the living room, stopping briefly in front of the shelving unit pushed against the wall. Grandma Mabel had a shelf to herself; candles flanked her photo, and the frame that housed the picture of her mid-dance in her traditional white blouse and checkered red-and-white bandana skirt rested on a lace doily in front of which was the glass jar full of bottle caps. Alicia tossed the newest one into the jar, taking a moment to look at Grandma Mabel's smiling, joyful face before heading into the foyer.

VI

The 89 was ten minutes late. By the time it reached the stop at the intersection of Weston and Church, it was six in the morning. When she rushed out of the apartment building, Alicia could see a small crowd forming down the street and knew she wouldn't have to run to catch the bus, which was a blessing. Her Sorels were as wet as her coat, so she was wearing the red boots she'd scored in a trade on Bunz last year; they had no grip, but they were the less expensive option and Manhattan winters were different than Toronto ones anyway—slush was the danger down there.

The bus was already packed when Alicia stepped inside. It smelled like wet socks, and the front was congested with bodies; a few people had knapsacks and computer bags slung over their shoulders instead of between their feet. A man sitting up front was playing dancehall—Vybz Kartel—on his phone without earphones, aggravating her headache. The other tired-faced passengers glared at him, muttering beneath their breath, but two teenage girls shimmied their shoulders and snapped their fingers.

"Ayyee!" they exclaimed before singing along to "Fever."

Alicia squeezed past the passengers, making her way to the back, but she stopped in front of the two steps that led to the higher level of the bus. Nothing seemed out of place and yet she had the strangest sensation that her world was about to be disrupted. The music from the phone blared in her ears and turned into humming in her head, humming that produced an image in her mind: a group of women to whom the humming belonged. They were outdoors in white aprons atop blue dresses, crowded around one woman in a coarse white shirt—a woman Alicia had seen at the waterfall the night before. Then, her braided updo had been a natural tiara, but now, she was heavily pregnant.

The image expanded. A lush riverbank replaced the interior of the bus, and Alicia now saw the women place lit beeswax candles on the grass alongside the river, together with a few baskets of apples, a single jar of honey, and a couple of bottles of rum. There was a small pile of silver coins and even some scraps of white lace taken from the buckra mistress's dress. The pregnant woman, whom they called Adelaide, had one hand on her swollen belly and the other clasped on to an older woman in a turquoise headwrap— a midwife holding a calabash.

The midwife freed Adelaide of her shirt and dipped her fingers into the calabash, rubbing a kind of lotion onto Adelaide's skin. The two women then waded into the river until they were a little more than waist-deep, and the midwife began to bathe her, smoothing her knowledgeable hands along Adelaide's body, massaging her face, her arms, placing her hands on her stomach. She cupped water in her palms and then poured it over the mother-to-be's hair, tiny rivulets streaming down the curve of her nose, dripping down her chin, back into the river, while the humming grew louder and louder on the shore.

Though Alicia had no insight into the thoughts of those around her, she understood what was happening, as if she were one of the women humming: they were participating in a custom. The river was to protect Adelaide and her soon-to-be-born child, to keep sickness out of her spirit, to keep her body from harm, and once the child was born, the women would return to this spot to cleanse Adelaide and ease her pain. It was a tradition. This river had eased many pains in the past, soothing brutal and unjust wounds on the backs of others. Alicia also knew that Adelaide would come back with the child. That was what the fruit and the rum and the pretty, pretty lace were for—offerings to the River Maid, who presided over their waters; the River Maid some called Ribba Missus or River Mumma. Adelaide sought her protection and gave her gifts in return. As if in acknowledgment, the river foamed and frothed around her, the water pushing against her body without sweeping her away in its current. It flowed toward her like encouragement. Adelaide cried out. It was time. The baby was pushing to get out—

"Leish?"

The bus came back into view like a jump cut, but Alicia wasn't entirely reoriented. Whatever had just happened to her was sensory. Tactile. Her consciousness had been transported to another place, another time, while her body remained in the present, except that wasn't possible. Alicia covertly looked around to make sure she was in fact inside a bus.

"Ay, Leish!"

She finally looked up. An exhausted Mars sat at the back of the bus in a black North Face jacket. Slumped against the window next to him was Heaven, who seemed to be in a state between sleep and consciousness yet still looked chic, with makeup and a beige faux-fur coat. Alicia shouldn't have been surprised. She once saw Heaven simultaneously fix her unravelling headwrap and take down a customer's email at cash.

"So you're alive," Heaven mumbled. "You never texted me that you got home OK last night."

"Yeah, sorry, I was . . ." Alicia didn't have a ready-made excuse and so decided to change the subject. "What are you doing here?" She walked up the steps toward them. "Didn't you say you live by Vaughan and Oakwood or something, Mars?"

"I got way too faded to go home, so I crashed on Heaven's couch. We got breakfast at the McDonald's up the road."

Alicia raised her eyebrows at Heaven, who gave her a look that confirmed his story. Mars held up a small brown paper bag, oblivious to their unspoken conversation. "The one by the—" He paused. "What highway is that?"

"The 401," said Heaven.

"True," he said, looking warily at the breakfast burrito he took out of the bag.

Heaven raised an eyebrow. "You're looking at that like it shot your dog or something."

"Nah, just if I made it home, I could've warmed up leftovers. My brother cooked last night and his cooking game is unparalleled. But it's fine."

Alicia looked at Heaven. "Why are you still here, though? You missed your stop, you know. We just left Church."

It looked like Heaven was gearing up for a diatribe. Alicia knew she'd only half listen to it, even though she was the one who'd asked the question. Her mind was still on Adelaide, who was presumably her ancestor, and her connection to River Mumma. The mermaid's words came back to her: *yuh nuh know about yuh past . . .*

Heaven was saying, "And Jalyssa kept asking, you know, like it wasn't even six o'clock yet, the *moon's* still out, she really needed the shift covered. I felt bad, so I said I would do it."

That focused Alicia. "You broke the number-one rule, fam. Never pick up the phone if anyone from work calls. Listen to the message or read the text, and then answer if you want."

"None of that matters anyway. Pradeep said he'd stop accepting shift changes that aren't done in writing, you have to sign the schedule in the managers' office, it's a whole fucking process now," said Mars.

Heaven shrugged her shoulders dismissively. "What are they going to do, turn me away when I show up? And I actually do need the money too. Band launch for Caribana is, like, four months away, and I have to start saving for my costume from now. I *will* be frontline this time, and that means a bigger deposit."

The static of the intercom sounded. "Move to the back of the bus to let on more passengers. All the way to the back of the bus."

Nobody moved.

"You better sit down before we reach Lawrence," said Heaven. "Bus will full up."

"Yuh nuh lie," said Alicia, sitting down next to Mars. "My mom was like, 'Get a car so you don't have to deal with this bus life.'"

"What city kid has a licence?" said Heaven.

Alicia made a gesture of agreement when Mars made a noise. "What are you even talking about? I've got my G1."

"What are you, sixteen? That's a baby licence," said Alicia. "That doesn't count."

"OK, chill. Look—"

The bus halted, the wheels hissing with the effort, and Mars stopped talking to brace himself against the abrupt stop. Alicia could hear an echo in the sibilance—the clanging of what had to be a metal chain dragging on the ground. It set her teeth on edge. She felt the same sensation she had last night, like she was being watched.

"Do you hear that?"

"What?"

"You have to be more specific," said Heaven. "A lot of noises happening."

There was an exodus of passengers, but their exit was a slow, shuffling march as people from different sections tried to leave.

"Let us off first before you try to get on!" A man shoved his way through people trying to step onto the bus.

The driver spoke into the intercom once more: "There is no boarding at the back of the bus. I repeat, no boarding through the back doors."

"Never mind," said Alicia, stopping herself from covering her ears. "You'd know what I mean."

The rattling was dull and loud at the same time, a chilling pest. Alicia looked around for someone who looked as if they heard what she heard or felt the same simmering trepidation she felt. All she saw was a young woman around their age making coy glances at Mars, who pretended not to notice, though there was a small grin on his face, and all she heard from other passengers were irritated whispers because the headphone-less man had turned up the volume of his music. The teenage girls danced their way off the bus, singing along to the song, belting about finessing on Weston Road.

As an influx of passengers entered, scrambling for the few remaining seats, the bus lurched forward. Everyone in the aisle stumbled. The clanging sharpened to a painfully high pitch that made Alicia grab Mars's coat, inhaling sharply.

"You good?"

"I'm fine," she said. The woman who had been checking Mars

out looked away, annoyed. "I need a phone. I don't care whose. I just need to look something up."

"What's wrong with your phone?" said Mars.

"It got wet. So can I just—"

"Dropped it in the sink?" asked Heaven.

"No—"

"Oh, damn," said Mars. "The toilet?"

"I fell in the river behind my building last night, OK? Or I didn't, I don't know." Alicia motioned frantically with her hand. "I was kinda blem still."

"Bro, what?"

"Is that why your hair is already starting to frizz? It hasn't even been a full twenty-four hours, Alicia."

"What, you and my mom have a WhatsApp group or something? Just lend me a phone, yah."

"Not me, my data plan sucks," said Mars. "Maybe you can hop on real quick when we get in the radius of a Tim's or something."

Heaven rolled her eyes and reached across Mars, handing Alicia her cell. She stared at the screen, assuring herself that the rabbit hole she was going down was no different from the YouTube videos she sometimes wound up cycling through at two in the morning. It was all just curiosity; her grip on reality was firm and intact. *Firm and intact*, she repeated to herself.

Alicia closed her eyes against the noise she decided she wasn't actually hearing and started to type. Mars peered over and exclaimed at the photo of a baby, its head en caul.

"That's sick. What is that?"

"Something I was born with," said Alicia, skimming the Wikipedia page. She changed her search and added "Jamaica" after "caul," then decided on the third result that appeared.

A very rare occurrence wherein a baby is born with a thin layer of skin covering its face. Once upon a time in Jamaica, it was believed that cauls, sometimes colloquially referred to as "veils," gifted the bearers with supernatural abilities, including the ability to commune with spirits or the ability to see duppies.

She clicked on the link for "duppies" and found herself on another page.

Duppies are believed to be the spirit of a person who was "wicked" or "cruel" in life and wasn't afforded the proper burial rituals, and so has stayed on earth to haunt the living.

Alicia started searching for another site—this one couldn't be trusted. She didn't know much, but she did know that the description was only partially correct. Sure, whenever she heard "duppy" used, it was to refer to an evil spirit, but duppies weren't *necessarily* malevolent; sometimes they were friendly relatives. Once, Winston swore up and down that his dead father dreamed him the winning numbers for the Supreme Ventures Lotto, but because he couldn't get to the store in time, he didn't reap the rewards of the jackpot.

She read from the next site:

Legend states that some animals, particularly dogs, can sense duppies and will howl when they are near. Sometimes duppies assume demon-like forms, like the Rolling Calf, the most feared duppy of all.

Heaven leaned forward. "Rolling Calf? Let me see that." She took the phone from Alicia.

"I was reading that!"

Heaven ignored her and continued scanning the site. She shook her head and then put the phone away.

"I can tell you everything you need to know. It's a shape-shifter—it can look like a three-legged white goat with black spots, and one of those legs is a human leg. But I've read other descriptions that said it's a black bull with eyes made of fire and has a large metal chain."

Alicia looked at her. "Chain?" She tried to brush off as a coincidence the metal jangle that kept disorienting her but was unsuccessful in stymieing her panic.

"My Auntie Em from down inna country says it's the most frightful noise she ever heard. She swears she escaped it by carving a cross in the ground and lighting some rum on fire." Heaven paused for a second, contemplating the story she'd been told. "I guess she poured the rum on the ground too? That's what she'd have to have done, nuh true? Anyway. Why she had rum, I don't know, but trust, I will be well prepared if I ever meet a duppy."

The sounds of the bus became garbled, and Alicia could hear only snippets of the commotion clearly. Even A$AP Ferg's "Plain Jane" blasting from the phone at the front sounded like white noise. She rocked back and forth in her seat—she needed to get off this bus.

The static from the intercom crinkled, adding to the noise. "Ladies and gentlemen, this bus will be short-turning at—"

A collective roar of outrage erupted, and all the passengers started yelling at once. Alicia bent over and put her head between her knees.

"Are you *kidding* me?"

"This bus was ten minutes late, and now it's not even going to the *subway*?"

"I need to get to work!"

"It is 6:20 in the morning. How could you possibly already need to short-turn?"

In the chaos of noise, Alicia pressed herself against the seat, as if she were trying to escape through a nonexistent back door. A roar sounded with the invisible chain, and she dug her fingers into her ears so violently and so deep, she scratched skin and made herself bleed.

"Nope, I need to get off this bus." Alicia stood up and said it again like an announcement. "I need to get off the bus!"

"Did you not hear? We *all* need to get off the bus."

There was a panicked voice. "Wait, we all have to get off *now*?"

"No, the last stop is St. Clair. That guy doesn't know what he's talking about."

Alicia pushed her way to the back doors, social civilities and codes forgotten. Even though the STOP REQUESTED sign brightened red after a commuter rang the bell, Alicia demanded that other passengers keep pulling the yellow cord and pressing the red buttons on select poles to indicate she wanted to get off. She could hear Heaven and Mars asking her to wait, to slow down, to explain, but she had to keep moving.

The driver stopped in front of the Rogers Road bus shelter, and Alicia pressed her hands against the yellow bars fused to the doors like handles, pushing against them so she could finally leave. But the doors remained firmly shut.

"You have to push the yellow bars," said a man leaning against one of the dividers.

"I am," said Alicia.

"You also can't *keep* pushing," said another man, leaning against the other divider. "You gotta wait for a sec."

Heaven spoke the way she did when she was asked to help new employees on cash at the store. "Wait for the green light or else pushing won't do anything."

Alicia kept pressing against the yellow bars, willing the doors to open, and started hyperventilating when other passengers attempted to help her, only to be met with the same resistance. Finally, the doors folded open, seemingly at their own behest, and Alicia cried out in triumph, stumbling out of the bus.

VII

Alicia didn't know where she was. On Weston, she'd passed a blue-and-white automotive centre and just ahead there'd been a Tim Hortons and a Petro-Canada gas station, but now she was running on a residential crescent, turning down a second side street, and she'd lost her bearings.

The cold shredded her lungs, but she was sweating through her hoodie. Heat seemed to chase her, like a sentient predator working its way into her body. It made her nauseous.

On her left, a rusted chain-link fence spanned the length of the sidewalk. Alicia saw an opening and ran into what a Toronto Parks Department sign called York Stadium Park. There was nothing inside of the fence but snow-covered grass—it was probably used as a soccer field in warmer months—and clusters of leafless trees along the perimeter. Behind it in the distance were brown-brick apartments and a modern-looking grey building.

It wasn't until Alicia stopped running, putting her hands on her knees to catch her breath and looking up to the steadily brightening sky, that she heard her name being called.

"Are you related to Shelly-Ann Fraser-Pryce or some shit?"

Heaven and Mars weren't too far away. Mars held out Alicia's scarf as he approached. She wrapped it back around her neck in a sloppy twirl.

"What the hell is going on?"

"I saw something last night," said Alicia, her words rapid-fire. "Something that didn't make sense, but I'm starting to think it was real, and what I saw, it made me go into the river and I was drowning, and then I was in this *next* river and there was a veil, and I was about to die again, then two-twos, I'm in my room and it's this morning."

"None of that makes sense," said Heaven. "Slow down, start again."

Alicia shook her head. She could do an entire presentation and it would still sound like nonsense. "I told you I fell into the river behind my building, right? I didn't fall. I was pulled. It pulled me in and kept me under until it transported me to this place where I saw my ancestors."

"That happens when they try to warn you. You experienced an ancestral dream?" said Heaven, surprised.

"But it wasn't a dream, it was a visit. I was *there*."

Heaven shook her head. "That's not possible."

"I'm telling you, I think they gave me visions or gave me back my visions or my 'sight' or whatever, because I've been seeing some *shit* this morning and I just want it to stop, but I don't think it'll stop until I find this comb and if I don't find this raasclaat comb . . ."

Alicia thought back to the vision within her vision: the rivers of dust and pebbles and boulders because the water in every stream, every pond, every creek that once belonged to River Mumma had dried up.

"I just need to get this comb," she said.

"What does a comb have to do with this?" asked Heaven.

Alicia couldn't respond because the noise had returned, but now Mars and Heaven heard the clanging too. Heaven clutched her chest and Mars bent down low, like he was expecting something to fall from the sky.

"What—?"

It sprung out of the trees. At first it looked as if a shadow had become animate and leapt into the middle of the park, then Alicia realized there was a form to the shadow. It was a bull, except it was monstrously large, the size of a small house, its hide black with an inky texture. Coiled around its neck was an enormous metal chain that dragged behind its body. It had no eyes; rather, fire flamed out of its sockets. It was living terror.

It was a Rolling Calf. Legitimately.

"Baxside," Heaven whispered.

There was an overall malice to the spirit, and it radiated an ill will that bored into Alicia with an intensity she'd felt only once before. Yet when she'd been looking at the white man in the tableau, she was the one simmering with hatred, not the one receiving it.

There was no time to think.

"Run!"

She and Mars took off at the same time, but when Alicia looked back, she saw that Heaven hadn't moved at all.

"Heaven, come on, let's go!"

She still didn't move. Alicia could see on her face that she wanted to but simply couldn't. She ran back for her as the bull charged toward them, the jangling of the chain making her squeeze her eyes shut against the noise. She snatched Heaven's hood, dragging her as she ran forward. As if yanked out of a trance, Heaven started moving on her own alongside Alicia. She tried to speak but couldn't form a full sentence.

Alicia yelled so Mars could hear her. "We have to get out of the park!" The information she'd just read was still fresh in her mind. "There's a Catholic school across the street!"

"So what?"

"Duppies don't like crosses!"

"That's vampires!"

Alicia yelled, exasperated, "Vampires don't have a monopoly on crosses, Mars!"

The sky continued to brighten slowly, readying itself for the impending sunrise, and the fence grew closer and closer. A dreadful wail pierced the air, and it struck Alicia with a terror that tightened her insides. She chanced a glance behind her. The Rolling Calf was galloping, but its hooves never seemed to touch the grass. The duppy reared its head. Alicia knew what was about to happen and she yelled—more a strangled cry than a word of caution. The duppy grunted, hard and long, and a jet of fire shot out of its nose.

"Get down!"

Mars dove to the ground, but Heaven turned around. Alicia grabbed her, tackling her onto the ground. The fiery stream blazed over both of their bodies.

Heaven put her hand to her mouth to muffle her screams and then started cussing when she removed it. "Nothing I've read— nothing I've heard—said a Rolling Calf could fucking shoot fire. This isn't right." She started getting frantic. "Nothing prepares you for this. Something isn't right."

She disentangled herself from Alicia and started getting up again. Alicia grabbed Heaven's ankle, tugging hard so that she fell back to the ground, barely escaping another surge of fire.

"No, I need to get out of here!"

Heaven scrambled to her feet and began running.

"Heaven!"

Alicia started to get up to follow her but then flattened herself when the duppy blew out another surge of fire, singeing the tops of her braided buns. The intensity of the heat made her cry out. Raising her head slightly, she saw Mars leap out of the way.

Alicia rolled sideways, out of the line of fire, gasping as bits of snow slid beneath her coat, under her hoodie, and into her jeggings. Her buns unravelled and her braids whipped against her face as she tried to stand up again but slipped on the ice. She flipped over on her back to see the Rolling Calf charging toward her, and went rigid.

No memories flooded her mind, no last wishes; she couldn't think of anything except that she was going to die unsatisfied and lost. She watched, transfixed in muted terror, as the Rolling Calf neared her.

Alicia was jolted out of her morbid reverie. Hands roughly grabbed her by the arms, pulling her up to her feet and pushing her so that she tripped forward. Alicia turned her stumble into a run and looked to her right. Mars kept stride with her, the anger in his expression outmatched only by the fear in his eyes.

"How are you going to make Heaven run and you're just straight sitting here? We should've booked it from *time*!"

The distance between them and the Rolling Calf had shortened. She could hear its gnashing teeth and crackling fire. The *clink-clink-clink* of its chain seemed to reverberate within the confines of Alicia's mind, and from the way Mars kept shaking his head, she was sure he shared in her suffering. She felt a sinister heat pass through her body, as if she couldn't help but draw it into herself. For a moment, she felt ill and then . . . dead. Like a corpse or a shell with nothing inside. Mars looked at her, his eyes vacant before a flicker of life returned to them.

Alicia screamed out to Heaven, who had made it across the street, leaning against the fence that bordered the Catholic school. "What do we do?"

But Heaven couldn't answer. She was clutching her chest, doubling over with the effort of trying to breathe. Alicia had never seen her so uncomposed.

The duppy cried out once more, and Alicia's stomach dropped; a new warmth brought on by panic overtook her. She racked her brain for the stories Winston had told her, the flippant warnings she had dismissed. Quickly, she took off her scarf, dropping it on the ground. Looking behind her, she saw that the duppy had slowed down and then halted in front of it.

"Start emptying your pockets," she said. "Whatever you have in your wallet. Anything!" When Mars looked at her doubtfully, Alicia unzipped her wristlet. "On God, it'll help!"

She dropped her lip gloss as she fled. Mars dug into his pocket for his wallet, opened it, and dropped a packaged condom. And then another. Alicia discarded her library card. He threw away a couple of mini Aero bar wrappers. She took out her pocket pack of Advil and scattered the few pills left before letting go of the little bottle. Mars released a few receipts but then yelled, "There were two fifties in there!"

Alicia saw him start to turn and she grabbed his wrist to keep him on track. "You want to go back and get merked?"

"OK, it's not, like, six bills, but a hundred dollars—"

"Means shit if you're dead, Mars!"

He cursed loudly, craning his neck to see behind him. "It stopped following us. It's just standing there."

"Duppies have to count whatever you put in front of them," Alicia said.

They made it out of the park and continued running across the street to the Catholic school, where they found Heaven in tears and repeatedly apologizing.

"I'm sorry. I couldn't think," she said.

Alicia moved over to the fence and held on to it, winded. "It's fine."

"I never blank on an exam, I don't get stage fright, but I just couldn't *think*!"

"It's fine," she said again firmly, almost like a snap. "It's over." Alicia was too exhausted to listen to Heaven work herself up into an emotional crisis. "Mars and I gave it some stuff to count. The sun will be up by the time it finishes, and duppies sleep in the day. We're good, it's all good, just done it."

Alicia sagged against the fence next to Mars, who was rubbing his head. She felt the pangs of her headache more intensely than before, though the pain was different now, a kind of swelling that made her head feel hot and slightly dizzy.

"OK, I have a question." Mars stood up straight. "What the fuck is wrong with you two?"

Alicia and Heaven blinked in surprise. They didn't get a chance to respond before Mars continued, "You two were legit just going to die. Heaven, fine—you froze. That's a physical response you can't control, I'm gonna let that ride. But, Alicia"—he turned to her—"you fall down once and you—" He started coughing, beating his chest with his fist. "And you just stay down, my guy? Are you serious?"

Alicia's shock momentarily dulled the throbbing in her temple. She'd never seen Mars this upset. In the six months she'd known him, she had never really seen Mars fazed by anything, even when customers swore at him for rejecting expired coupons or berated him for a slowly moving line at the cash register. Alicia never reacted to entitled customers out of sheer apathy for the job, but Mars was just good-natured.

"I didn't wake up to watch two people die today. That's so fucking selfish."

Alicia moved away from the fence and looked from Mars to Heaven and back again. She was going to apologize and tell them to leave, to run, to save themselves from the trouble of her responsibilities. Alicia looked directly at both Heaven and Mars, her face set with purpose and intent, parted her lips, and then vomited on Heaven's fur-trimmed booties.

VIII

WORK. MISSED CALL (3).
Alicia's phone stayed on long enough to display two texts: one from Pradeep informing her that it was 7:15 and her shift had started fifteen minutes ago, and the other from her mother, saying, "Be careful if you see a raccoon." Alicia was relieved when her phone died again and decided she could deal with the consequences of her no-show at work during her next shift.

Mars had thrown up a few seconds after she did, and they all decided to take a beat at the Tim Hortons by the twenty-four-hour car wash. Alicia sat at a window table while Heaven cleaned her boots in the washroom and Mars went outside to "get himself straight" by the drive-thru. She bounced her leg and slammed her hands down on the tabletop.

The few customers in the store carefully avoided looking at her, the way people do their best to ignore unpredictable strangers, but Alicia couldn't help her nervous energy. Even in the absence of the Rolling Calf, she could still feel its heat, and she didn't know how to make it all stop. There was no road map; she was, once again, utterly lost.

Mars came in through the front door. A sheen of sweat glistened on his forehead and his lips were chapped; there was even a shake to his step, interfering with his usual swagger. He sat in the chair across from her and rested against the window.

"I'm sorry about before," said Alicia after a few long moments of silence. "I didn't mean to just stay down when it was coming at me, but I wasn't thinking. Thanks."

Mars nodded but didn't say a word in response. Heaven walked out of the washroom, her makeup freshly reapplied, but her eyes were furtive and her movements jittery, as if she was wary of the chairs or tables springing to life and attacking her.

Looking at her friends, Alicia felt guilty that her unexpected drama had swept them into its current, but a part of her was also glad to have witnesses. Besides, she had no intention of involving them further. She owed them an explanation for what they had just experienced, but after giving one, she would leave and work on finding the comb by herself.

Heaven reached the table and sat down next to Mars. She looked like she was trying to contain her anger, and Alicia didn't know if it was because she had just been attacked or because the smell of vomit was still strong on her boots and had ruined her general sense of glam.

Finally, Mars spoke. "I'm really trying my best not to lose my shit, and I'm not doing a good job. So what's going on, Leish?"

Alicia looked around the store, at the eyes that were on them but not actually looking at them. "OK, first, someone has to order something or we're going to get kicked out."

"No one gets kicked out of Tim's," said Mars, leaning back in his chair. "Mans can hijack a bus, bring it to Tim's for a coffee, and still not get kicked out."

"Well, he had a knife," said Alicia.

"Fine, I'll go get something!" Mars got up from his chair, stumbling a little. Heaven and Alicia exchanged glances, and he cleared his throat. "I didn't mean to be that loud," he said in a voice that carried, alerting the other patrons to his contrition. He looked disoriented but shook his head as a way to focus himself. "One of you spare a likkle change, yah."

Heaven fished a bill out of her coat pocket and handed it to him before he went to the counter, then glanced at Alicia's hands, dry and cracked from the snow. Heaven reached into her bag and put a small tube of lotion on the table. Alicia smiled and Heaven smiled back, the offering sprouting a dim warmth between them, and Alicia opened the tube, quickly smoothing the lotion on her hands. Accepting the gesture seemed to prompt Heaven to talk.

"You know, my parents freaked out when I told them I was going to major in book and media studies? They thought it was pure nonsense. Didn't think I could get a real job with it, and trust, minoring in Caribbean studies and digital humanities did *not* make things better." She paused for a moment, biting her lip. "I had to give them a presentation on all the benefits of the degree, explained that there are internship opportunities. I even gave them *materials* to look over, fam." She laughed at what Alicia assumed was the memory of that day. "Eventually, they agreed."

Alicia wasn't really sure what to say. "That's a pretty cool story?"

"My point," said Heaven, "is that I have the answers—it's what I do." She shrugged. "I never thought I would freeze in that situation. Never. That's not me."

Alicia regarded her, feeling an odd mixture of sympathy and righteousness, which brought about a bit of shame. She'd never been as outgoing, but Heaven did remind Alicia of the self-assuredness she used to have Before, when she'd thought that her plans for the future were foolproof, that *she* was foolproof. Seeing Heaven unusually rattled assuaged Alicia's anxiety a little, and yet she truly didn't want her to feel as world-weary as she did. Nor did she blame her for temporarily losing her shit during the ambush.

She put the lid on the tube, handed it back to Heaven, and exhaled deeply, doing her best to channel the vibe of a sage mentor.

"Just 'low it," she said. "It's why I always say wait until you graduate, things don't always line up the way you think they will. I thought I'd be set by twenty-six. Like, *set*. Bro, I'm nowhere near set. Shit's different in practice."

Heaven was about to respond but stopped, taking her phone out of her pocket. She concentrated on the screen for a minute. "Jalyssa's blowing me up, mad that I didn't show up at the store."

"Damn," said Alicia.

Heaven put her phone away. "I'll get her a Starbucks the next time I see her or something. I don't have the capacity to think about that right now, because this shit, *our* shit—"

The thud of a yellow-and-red Timbits box hitting the table made Heaven flinch. Mars put down a medium-sized red paper cup and sat back in his seat.

Alicia chose not to press Heaven to explain what she meant by "our shit." Instead, she opened the box and took out a chocolate Timbit but didn't put it in her mouth. The thought of eating sickened her, but she needed to do something with her hands. She picked at the doughnut hole, letting the crumbs fall before she eventually put it down and clasped her hands together on the table, like her mother would do. She spoke as if she were giving a report.

"After I left your house, I had an encounter with River Mumma." Her eyes flicked up to Heaven. "*The* River Mumma."

Heaven's eyes shone with amazement, with an understanding of what such an encounter meant, which Alicia saw brought about a hint of fear.

"A tourist has taken her comb," Alicia continued, "and it's my job to retrieve it for her and I only have today to find it or else she will leave this world. She also made it very clear that attacks like the one that just happened are a consequence of this journey. Then I was pulled into the Humber River at Cruickshank Park and saw my ancestors, who, I think, gave me back my ability to see spirits."

Alicia cradled her head and waited for an outburst from the other two, for them to insist that they'd been seeing things when they faced the Rolling Calf. Mars lowered his head onto the table with an anguished groan, and Heaven wordlessly reached across for a Timbit. The silence was exacerbated by the ongoing din of the store around them.

"I want to say you got jokes," said Heaven finally. "But you were speaking in the voice you put on when you approach old white ladies in the store, so you're for real." Heaven nibbled on a glazed old-fashioned doughnut hole.

"Great. Now that we've established I'm telling the truth, I have literal hours to do the impossible, so—"

"I'm not done," said Heaven. "I have questions. What was River Mumma like?"

"Extraordinary. Terrifying." Even though she wanted to keep this conversation brief, Alicia found herself elaborating on her meeting, as if River Mumma demanded to be described. "I didn't want to cross her, but I also didn't want to let her down. It's hard to explain to someone who wasn't there."

Mars sat back up. "OK, so who or what is River Mumma? A goddess like the Greeks?"

Alicia muttered, "Not everything is like the Greeks," the same time as Heaven said, "No, not like the Greeks, not even like the orishas. It's spirits we're talking. They don't really have a pantheon or anything."

She said it offhandedly, like a reflex, and Alicia saw her eyes brighten with a kind of relish, as if she took pleasure in answering Mars with her usual authority. She then made a performance of her incredulity that Mars didn't already know the answer. "Bredren, do you really not know?"

"I know Anansi," said Mars, shrugging.

"Well, River Mumma is a spirit, or many spirits, depending on who you speak to or what you read, but she has power like a deity," said Heaven.

She continued to explain what she'd learned from different books and articles and stories from her Auntie Em that sometimes contradicted Alicia's knowledge. In a version Heaven was told, the golden table that River Mumma guarded was left by Spanish pirates; in an essay she'd read, River Mumma appeared only on moonlit nights and not when the river turned green.

Heaven edged forward in her seat. "And you're saying," she said to Alicia, "that she gave you no hints about who the person who stole her comb could be, that she only gave you a day to find it, and that she gave you no instructions on what to do when you have the comb, so that even after we hunt it down, we don't know shit?"

Alicia felt as if she was going to throw up again. "What is this 'we'? Heaven, we were just attacked and because of that my head is in so much pain it feels like it's about to explode. On the bus, I got this vision of women giving offerings to River Mumma, and one of them was my ancestor. Something probably happened in *my* lineage, and it's fucking up my shit now, like I'm being punished. So I have to deal with it, but you can go. I know you feel bad because you froze back there, but let it go. You have no obligations."

"No obligations? You're my friend."

"Jesus, where is your self-preservation? This is like a horror movie when the protagonist buys the haunted house even though they know it's haunted and then act mad surprised when they have to deal with a haunting. You get that, right? You get that you're acting like a main character in a *horror* movie?"

"I don't cut on my friends," said Heaven simply.

"We don't even talk outside of the store, Heaven; we are *barely* work friends."

Heaven raised her eyebrows while Mars said "Wow" beneath his breath, stretching out the short *o* as he looked at his phone.

"It's not like I don't try. How many times have I asked you to come to Sephora after work?"

"And I don't go." Alicia actively ignored the twinge of guilt in her chest—it was only a few minutes ago that they'd shared a moment, but this needed to be said. "I'm not trying to be an ass, I'm just saying, if you think you need to do this out of friendship, you're off the hook."

"Real talk?" said Heaven. "How delusional are you that you think after seeing what I saw, I could just walk away? I became involved the moment a legit duppy attacked me. Anyway, you can't do any of this alone when you have no leads, you have no phone, and you can barely sit up straight."

"So what, this is to satisfy your curiosity?"

"Sure."

Alicia opened her mouth to speak, but Heaven raised her hand to silence her.

"Mars, you looking up info? *Mars*," Heaven repeated. "Wah gwaan?"

"Nothing," he said. "Work tings."

"We don't have time for you to call in."

"I already called in. Nah, I'm talking about another gig," he said. "I do delivery sometimes. Hate riding my bike in the snow, but I'm by myself, and, you know, Instant Pay."

Heaven opened her mouth incredulously. "Are you actually saying you're going to *work*?"

Mars looked at her, his eyes bloodshot. "Yeah."

She put her hands together and then touched the sides of her fingers to her lips before speaking. "Let me see if I'm getting this. So Alicia is Frodo carrying the ring, right? And I'm like, 'Cool, let me be your Samwise whether you want me to or not.' And you can't offer your bow or your axe or your sword? Even the fucking Ents got involved."

"I don't know why you're so cheesed," said Mars. "I have nothing to offer. It's not like Alicia's going to die if she doesn't get this comb and me not helping accelerates her death sentence. You're not going to die if you don't deliver this comb, right, Leish?"

The thought hadn't occurred to her. "River Mumma didn't say that," she said, though she couldn't help but remember that River Mumma had quasi-drowned her the night before.

Mars shook his head. "Low stakes, fam."

Heaven hit him on the arm. "Are you kidding me with this myopic shit? Everything has to be physical life or death? A guardian spirit has threatened to leave the world if she doesn't get her comb, which would *have* to have a direct effect on the rivers. Water heals, water nourishes, water has power, and it would be a serious problem if the spiritual source of waters back a yaad was no longer in this world. Low stakes, my ass."

Heaven looked to Alicia for confirmation, but Alicia didn't want to encourage her self-appointed involvement by letting her know she was right.

"I don't get it," said Heaven. "I don't get how you can ignore everything that's happened in the past half-hour. Like, are you in shock?"

"I'm broke! I lost money in that field and not everybody lives with their parents; some of us have people counting on us." Mars did his best not to raise his voice. "Do you know how much money I have in my account? Just enough for end-of-month fees and OSAP. That hundred dollars was supposed to hold me over until payday. I can't even afford a three-dollar box of Timbits, fam."

Mars's furious whispering morphed into a coughing fit so intense it made him hunch over, and Heaven looked at him with concern. They were distracted, so Alicia thought now was the time to go, even though Heaven was right and she had no way of finding anything she needed before the day was over. She moved to stand, but the pain in her temple swelled to a throbbing heat and rooted her to her seat. It was her turn to rest her head against the window.

BAM!

A German shepherd banged the window from the outside, jolting Alicia back. She pushed out her chair and skittered away from the window, though standing up made her feel faint.

"I am so sorry!" the owner yelled from outside. "I don't know what's gotten into him! He's never done this! Let's go!"

The dog bared his teeth, with his posture low and his legs spread. He started growling, and Heaven jumped up from her seat, joining

Alicia, but Mars stayed where he was, closing his eyes against the sound. The barking drew the other customers' attention.

Heaven stared at the dog for a few moments before turning to Alicia, but she didn't speak right away.

"You said your head felt like it was going to explode?" she asked finally.

"Still does. It's like it's expanding."

Heaven looked to Mars, who was rubbing his temples, and then at the dog, who switched from aggression to fear and had now flattened his ears, tucking in his tail.

"Fuck, this is not good." Heaven covered her mouth with her hand, triggering an uneasiness in Alicia that she was quickly getting accustomed to feeling.

The dog slammed once again into the window, barking wildly as he threw himself at the glass, straining against his leash.

"This is not good," Heaven repeated.

IX

When Alicia was eight, she'd overheard Grandma Mabel gossip to her mother about friends who were sick with duppy. The three of them were gathered around Grandma Mabel's dining table. Alicia was at the far end with a cold glass of Milo and a colouring book, and her mother and Grandma Mabel sat next to each other in the middle, one drinking coffee, the other ginger tea.

"Theodora, listen, Miss Beth grudge Miss Palmer!" Grandma Mabel whispered. "She told me at Sunday service said she felt hot-like and then she dropped on the pastor him floor and writhe something bad."

"How do you know she wasn't just catching the spirit?" said Alicia's mother with a grin as she sipped from her mug of coffee. "Was she speaking in tongues?"

"She was in *pain*! God doesn't make you suffer for catching His grace."

"Of course not. Still, it could've been anything, Mummy."

Frustration quickly passed over Grandma Mabel's face, and she adopted a patient tone. "Dora, yuh nuh listen. I spoke to her two weeks prior, yuh understand? I told her not fi have her husband pick she up at church in him new Mercedes, because some people eye too red. But she want fi show off. And now look pon she. Haffi go fi get—" Grandma Mabel glanced around, as if they weren't in the privacy of her own home, as if anyone could be listening. "Now she haffi go get science done," she said in an undertone.

From what Alicia understood of the rest of the conversation and of Grandma Mabel's vague warnings to her mother through-out the years, duppy sickness was more like a curse than an illness, a spell that an enemy set upon you. Failed a test in a class you normally get 80 percent or above? Duppy must fi catch yuh. Car got towed, credit card declined, got reprimanded by your boss, all in succession? Obeah work yuh.

"You know I am a Christian woman," Grandma Mabel would say. "But all ah we haffi protect ourselves from bad mind every once in a while."

It was, then, a surprise for Alicia when Heaven took her by the wrist, grabbed Mars by the hood, and ushered them both out of the Tim Hortons to tell them that they, in fact, had contracted duppy sickness.

"And that's why you think the dog was going ballistic?" said Alicia, remembering what she'd read on the bus about dogs sens-ing duppies. "He could sense it?"

"It fits," said Heaven. "Both of you have the symptoms."

"It's winter." Mars looked on the verge of collapse. "People get colds in winter."

"I think we all know this isn't just a cold," said Heaven. "My auntie told me that when duppies bump into you, you'll get hot, the heat will make your head swell, and you'll feel awful. I'm not sick because I wasn't close enough to the Rolling Calf, but you two . . ."

"I didn't ask for any of this," Mars said.

"This wasn't exactly in my plans either, Mars," said Alicia. "But the sooner we get this fixed, the sooner you can get to work and handle your business. I mean, sure, you can go now, but I don't see how you're going to ride a bike when you can't stand."

He stood up, almost as if he was trying to defy her, but ended up putting his hand against the wall to steady himself. He said nothing for a few moments, and then he spoke again. "OK, so then what do we do? Where do we go? A hospital?"

"No. We need to get science done."

"'Science'? What do you mean, 'science'? What science?"

Alicia wasn't entirely sure. Neither Grandma Mabel nor her mother had ever elaborated on the concept, and her grandmother's apparent fear of it, combined with her mother's general dismissal of that fear, had kept Alicia from asking for any kind of explanation.

"It means we go to Oni," said Heaven.

Alicia sighed. "I don't have time for detours. There's a running clock on this thing, Heaven."

"And that's why you need to get better."

"Do you know for sure that Oni can help us?"

"No," Heaven admitted. "I don't even know if she does science; I think she's in the process of becoming a balmist or maybe a psychic mother, or her mom is the one who is a psychic mother."

Alicia rubbed her temples. "Fam, I thought she was your friend."

"There can be a lot of overlap with these things, OK?"

"This is a legitimate question: have you even gone to a balmist or a psychic mother or an obeah woman yourself? Or have you just read about them? Do you just like the idea of them?"

Heaven regarded her with a hint of steeliness in her gaze. "At least I find this worth learning about. You can't even listen to a podcast about spirituality. Bottom line, Alicia, I know more about this than you do and Oni knows more about it than me. So if I were you, I would listen to me."

"What's the difference," said Mars, "between"—he waved his hand—"all of that stuff?"

"You get science done when science happens to you," said Heaven. "Like if someone curses you with obeah, you need obeah to un-curse you. Or myal, but myal is a group effort that requires dancing and ritual."

That tracked, Alicia thought. Her mother had told her that when she was a little girl, Grandma Mabel would once in a while feel a "presence" or would dream that a black cloud was hovering over their heads. How she'd rub their bodies down with the fetid oils she got from a neighbourhood acquaintance, as protection from weaponized envy. "Be happy I never put you through that," she'd said. "The teachers used to ask if your grandmother ever bathed me."

Heaven said, "Balm is herbs, medicine, bush bath, ting to heal your spirit, suh, and psychic mothers, they can sense things about you, read you up. I don't know if they can heal you, though. I think some can and some can't. The essays I've read all have different interpretations, and my auntie doesn't really distinguish between the different things."

Alicia shook her head. "I'm hearing a lot of 'could be' or 'couldn't be,' nothing definitive, and I don't want to waste my time when I have so little of it."

"Alicia, can you think of a better option? Yes or no?"

She couldn't. It wasn't as if she could go online and search for an obeah man or a myal priestess or a balmist. She didn't know much, but she knew that wasn't how it worked. Grandma Mabel couldn't even admit to her beliefs publicly. She and all her friends would privately rely on traditional solutions to their problems. It was an open secret, but to actually admit to it was social suicide. It was all by word of mouth, and the only mouth Alicia knew that had any information was Heaven's.

She glanced at Mars, who shrugged, which she took to mean he agreed with the plan to ask Oni for help. Heaven looked faintly smug as the three of them waded over to the bus stop.

"I know time is a factor here but it's not going to take that long," said Heaven as they boarded the 89. "Oni doesn't live far away. She's on campus at UofT. It's a straight shot from Keele Station to St. George—it'll take us twenty minutes. We'll get there around eight, eight-twenty the latest."

When the driver neared the station and announced that there would be no train service until further notice, Alicia blamed herself for believing that getting anywhere on the subway would take less than half an hour. She had often wondered if the universe and the Toronto Transit Commission worked together to conspire against her emotional and psychological well-being, but today she truly worried that something supernatural was at play.

"Anyone know why there's no service?" said a man Alicia couldn't see.

A woman scrolling on her phone responded, "Fire at Christie!"

There was a collective groan. That should've been Alicia's first guess; each subway line had at least one problem station, and for the west end of the Bloor–Spadina line, it was Christie.

The bus approached the subway and waited to pull in to the platform. Keele Station was a brown-brick two-storey building. Either side had street-level bus platforms exposed to the outdoors, and the subway above was encased in an enclosure of ribbed concrete that, to Alicia, looked like a grey shipping container. Outside the entrance, the subway was propped up by six pillars, creating an underpass for cars to drive beneath.

Once the bus had let the passengers out, Alicia, Mars, and Heaven made their way to the front of the station. It was pandemonium. Calls into work, curses at the weather, questions about where to go all blended into a din of frustration.

Alicia slumped against one of the six pillars, holding her head in her hand as the sounds of the morning became echoes in her ears. A vibration began to build within her body. The throbbing in her temple sharpened, and Alicia closed her eyes. When she opened them again, she no longer saw Keele Station. The river she'd seen earlier in the morning returned to her vision.

X

The sun was setting over palm trees and craggy hills. There were women in the river, dressed in white headwraps and loosely tied skirts, hunched over clothing draped on rocks. Soapwood leaves in hand, they scrubbed shirts and dresses and trousers with the plant's thick, sweet-smelling suds, or beat the dirt out with paddles, singing in harmony.

Guinea corn, I long to see you
Guinea corn, I long to plant you . . .

One of the younger women brushed linen with a coconut husk, and Alicia recognized her as the woman who had stood between River Mumma and the familiar stranger in her first vision. She looked exactly like Alicia and her name was Alice. Alicia knew this because her consciousness was split so that she saw through Alice's eyes yet also saw everything outwardly as herself, though no one else seemed to see her.

Next to Alice's feet, nestled on the stones at the bottom of the river, was its gift—a wrapped piece of the toto her mother, Adelaide, had made. This was Alice's personal ritual. Moments after the midwife had bathed her mother—after, Alicia recalled, the river had foamed around her—Adelaide had given birth to Alice right on the bank, and so every time Alice went to the river, she brought with her an offering for the River Maid, like the coconut cake she'd given today.

Chatter had suddenly replaced the singing—*Look there, suh!*—and Alice stopped washing the clothes to see what the other women were excited about. They were all pointing at something floating down the river.

It was a dress. Drifting slowly downstream. The closer it came to them, the more the women yelped and tittered in astonishment.

Mi never see a dress like that so!

One by one the women reached for it, but their hands never got close, even if the dress drifted right by them, even if they momentarily abandoned their wash and walked through the river toward it. One woman finally succeeded in getting a hold of it, but it glided out of her grasp as if it were water itself slipping through her fingers. The dress evaded all attempts and efforts until it finally stopped by Alice, floating right beside her, unmoved by the current.

One woman cried, *Mi work so hard on mi dress for Jonkonnu and now it look like rag next to a dress so pretty!*

Alice said nothing in response. It was true. They saved their fanciest clothes for the Christmas festivities, the only three days in a row when they weren't toiling and picking and cooking and serving the buckra, boasting their outfits during the Jonkonnu masquerade, where they danced and feasted and used song to ridicule the buckra. And this dress was sure to win Alice the respect, admiration, and envy of the parish.

It was like nothing she'd ever seen. Dazzling. At first, she thought it appeared British in style, with its puffed sleeves and corseted bodice—a castoff from the mistress's wardrobe. But the hem was too short for a British dress, and the blue-and-white designs bright with beauty and regality were nothing like what the white women wore. Alice never knew colours could look like this, and the patterns invoked in her a sense of home she had never before felt.

With trembling hands, she picked up the dress. It was dry to the touch despite its watery journey, and the material was neither the muslin of the great house nor the cheap osnaburg they were given. It was a dress beyond any available definition, a dress that appeared appeasing but, like the songs they sung during Jonkonnu, which were jokey-jokey on the surface with the passion of resistance just beneath, this dress was intricate.

One of the women continued her lament. *All year mi a work!*

How you so surprise? The river always did favour her from when she was born!

Truth yuh ah speak!

Alice rubbed her thumb back and forth across the dress, feeling the soft material on her skin, and when she looked down by her feet, the toto was gone.

Without warning, the day changed like a scene; the colours of the sky, the river, the bank flickered like they were colour bars in television static, and Alicia found herself in the exact same spot, except the river was nothing but dust, its ground cracked, not a drop of water in sight. Neither Alice nor the washerwomen were anywhere near her. The surrounding grass was yellowed and brittle, and the trees were scorched. Alicia somehow knew the dryness had stretched on for months, parching the provision grounds where the people who came before her grew yam and sweet potato, plantain and coco, stifling harvest and striking hunger in bellies that compelled the taking of food from the great house, the taking of cane from the field—food they'd cooked, cane they'd toiled over, yet if they were found out, the thieving planters would accuse *them* of thieving. A dry climate that stirred rumblings of rebellion in secret meetings.

On the riverside stood a buckra—the same white man who infuriated Alicia whenever she saw him—scowling at the barren riverbed. His glare suddenly fixed on her, as if he saw her standing there with his two pitiless green eyes, and instinctively, she closed her own.

When she opened them, the chaos of Keele subway station struck her bluntly. She felt Heaven's hands on her arms. "Look at me. You good?"

"Yeah," she said weakly.

"Had another vision?"

Alicia nodded and tried to reorient herself. Now that she was back in the present, she was back to feeling the effects of duppy sickness. Mars was crouching by the pillar next to Heaven, scrolling on his phone.

"How long was I out? Please don't tell me I've wasted an hour or something."

"Nah, you weren't out of it long," said Mars. He sounded ill. "A minute, maybe."

"What did you see?" asked Heaven.

Alicia was quiet at first. "A history," she finally said. "A relationship between my bloodline and the River Maid. I saw River Mumma give my ancestor Alice a dress."

"A dress?" Mars repeated.

"It wasn't just a dress, like." She sighed. "Heaven, you understand. It was Christmas," Alicia stuttered, trying to articulate what Alice felt, what Alice knew. "Families who were ripped apart, sold to different plantations, could meet and gather on Christmas."

"Because of Jonkonnu," said Heaven.

Mars stood up and stretched. "The carnival?"

"Well—"

"Historically speaking, it was a carnival for the enslaved to vent," said Heaven before Alicia could continue. "To flass, you know? And people saved their best clothes to attend it, be out and stuntin' and all of that."

"Right, and the river gave Alice the prettiest dress," said Alicia. "It was a reward because Alice gave an offering every time she went to the river. River Mumma probably gave her more rewards or gifts throughout the years. She favoured Alice, and something must've went wrong. That's why she chose me to do this in a ridiculously short time. That's why she said I owe her."

Heaven didn't look convinced, but Alicia didn't have the time to address her skepticism. These glimpses into the past pressed upon her the importance of her task, but the burden of responsibility became heavier every time she learned something new. Alicia was sure Alice had done something to anger River Mumma and ruin their relationship.

"We just really need to get healed quick so I can find the comb and done it. Did you find a—You're on Twitter?" she said, looking at Mars's phone. "You're supposed to be trying to find a ride!"

"I mean, you're right, but look at this. Heaven already knows."

Under "Trending in Canada," Alicia saw "#attackthe6ix." When Mars tapped on the link, the first result was a tweet from @IvanJohnson416: "Yo WTF??? Get me John Boyega #attackthe6ix," under which there was a shaky recording.

At first, Alicia couldn't make out what she was looking at—the video was pitch black. But then, in the distance, fire blew outward in a stream, illuminating the surroundings as a park. Three faraway figures started running or dropping to the ground, and then the video looped back to the beginning.

Mars started scrolling, and Alicia's eyes passed quickly over the tweets:

DRAGONS in the 6ix?? Daenerys come get your kids #attackthe6ix

The captain of the spaceship trying to explain to the rest of the aliens that the GPS told him to land there and not the CN Tower #attackthe6ix

All these born in 2000s babies. IT'S THE TDOT #attacktheT-DOT #tdotforlyfe

The recording had even become a meme, some still photos and other GIFs of the stream of fire and Alicia, Heaven, and Mars on the ground with captions that read:

Wen di mandem verses r fire . . .

Warden's patties be like . . .

That last tweet had a bunch of replies. Someone had used the same meme but crossed out "Warden" and put "Islington," and that correction got a "yuh dun kno" and a "nah" and an "EEDIAT TING DIS. THEY'RE ALL THE SAME PATTIES." Another user crossed out both "Warden" and "Islington" and put "Wilson," and someone else wrote, "Just sleepin on Downsview patties. Disrespectful."

"This doesn't concern us," said Alicia.

"It *is* us," said Mars.

"Who *cares*? It's already eight o'clock, the TTC is down, we're nowhere near downtown, and"—Heaven showed Mars her phone—"check out these surge prices."

Mars laughed in horror. "Fuck that. A taxi is definitely our best bet."

"I'm glad we agree," said Heaven.

The three of them followed the horde of commuters in a sickly lumber, heading south on Keele Street toward Parkside Drive, past the yellow-and-red Money Mart sign, until they reached a red light at Bloor Street. There was a swarm around the bus shelter by High Park, with one or two people stepping into the road, braving honks from traffic, to check on the status of a bus.

They neared a condominium, red-bricked and glass-clad, with a trendy Italian restaurant on its ground level. A woman paced back and forth outside its entrance, looking at her phone, and Alicia stopped walking.

She moved to turn around the other way, but it was too late.

"Alicia? Alicia Gale?" The woman started waving.

Alicia inwardly reprimanded herself for forgetting the house-warming photos posted on Facebook. She felt herself slip into the persona she'd adopted throughout school, both grad and undergrad.

"Oh my God, Kennedy!" she said in a high, cheery voice.

She wanted to die. She was nowhere near her best—sweaty and harassed-looking and staving off a delirium that was bound to take over at any minute. In her state, she would've rather run into an ex than an old classmate, especially when that classmate was Kennedy Astor. She would've rather faced another duppy attack than see Kennedy Astor, with her sleek ponytail, Tiffany eyeglasses, Canada Goose parka, and general sense of put-together-ness.

"So do you live in the area?" Kennedy asked, after introducing herself to Mars and Heaven, who had apologized for the smell of her boots and even buried them a bit in the snow, as if that would mask the stench.

"Not exactly. I take the bus to Keele, but with everything happening . . ."

Kennedy looked over to the aggravated mob of commuters across the street. "It really is a hectic morning, hey? And now, according to Twitter, aliens are invading us? I try to take the subway as much as I can, you know? Minimize my carbon footprint. But I have a presentation at nine and I can't miss it, so I called a cab, which"—she glanced at her phone again—"should've been here ten minutes ago."

Just then, two short honks sounded from across the street. An orange-and-green Beck taxi stopped in front of the bus shelter, and the driver called out from his rolled-down window.

"That's my ride." Kennedy looked to Alicia. "Where did you say you were heading?"

"I didn't," said Alicia. "It's OK, you don't need to—"

"UofT," said Heaven at the same time.

"Our alma mater? Are you doing your PhD there? Are you teaching?"

Alicia forced a smile. "Just running an errand."

"Doctor," Heaven offered.

"Got it," said Kennedy. "I'm actually heading that way. We should just share the ride."

Heaven answered Kennedy before Alicia could speak, but she lost the thread of what they were saying. River Mumma's voice infiltrated her head: *Yuh nah know what mi disappearance gwine fi mean.* The others vanished from her vision, and so did her surroundings; instead, Alicia saw River Mumma suspended in deep water like a seahorse. Her tail was golden, her hair long and thick and big, and she wore a beaded necklace of white seeds from the Job's tears plants that grew along the riverbank. Her eyes were closed as if she was meditating, her arms outstretched, and Alicia could see a shining golden aura potent with power.

Abruptly, River Mumma opened her eyes. A vortex spiralled upward from her open hands, forming a giant, fast-moving whirlpool on the surface of the river. Alicia was able to see River Mumma and the effect of her actions simultaneously; she saw all the rivers, all the streams, all the falls slowly drying up, the waters rushing into River Mumma as if she were calling them all home. Her aura brightened, a blinding golden light, and then she was gone. The island was dry. Not a drop of water in sight. And Alicia knew she'd seen what her ancestors had warned her against.

XI

Alicia came to with a loud gasp, as if awaking from a nightmare, and found herself in the back of a taxi, Mars squished between her and Heaven, and Kennedy in the front passenger's seat.

The driver had his turn signal on and was waiting for an opening in the bumper-to-bumper traffic. The cab smelled like pine freshener and vinyl and vomit from Heaven's boots, and the combination odour churned Alicia's already sensitive stomach. She opened a window.

Mars shifted his weight uncomfortably between her and Heaven before resting his head back against the seat, muttering how he should be working now.

Heaven looked at Alicia and spoke in a whisper. "Rough vision?"

Alicia buried her face in her hands. "I can't afford to be sick. I can't afford to lose any time."

Mars closed his eyes—some sort of silent statement of his unwillingness to get involved—but Heaven leaned forward.

"What happened?"

Alicia glanced to the front to see if Kennedy was listening, but she was looking intently at her phone.

"River Mumma left and there were no rivers, no streams, nothing, and that's what's going to happen if I don't get the comb in time," Alicia said quietly. "She's going to take the rivers with her."

The taxi jerked to an abrupt stop when a black Dodge Ram cut them off, keeping them from merging into the traffic. Alicia thrust her hand out to avoid colliding with the back of the driver's seat and saw the large blue eye looped around the rear-view mirror swing violently. She couldn't believe they hadn't left their parking spot yet—nothing was moving at the speed necessary for the deadline she had.

The cab driver honked his horn in a loud continuous beep. "*Manyak!* What's wrong with you, eh?" he muttered and then apologized to Kennedy.

Kennedy nodded along with the driver's tirade before giving him her destination, and then she turned to the back. "Is Bloor and St. George OK?"

"Perfect. Thanks again for letting us catch a ride."

She started to mention splitting the fare but was interrupted by Mars's groan. He tried leaning forward to put his head between his knees, but then sat up again. Alicia understood. The heat made him want to crawl out of his own skin. She rolled down the window further.

"Is that helping?" Heaven asked.

"A bit," he said. "At least if I was on my bike, there'd be wind to cool me down."

Alicia rolled her eyes but said nothing. She was in no mood to indulge Mars's whining; her recent vision had increased her nervousness as an after-effect.

"Sorry about the window," she said to Kennedy and the taxi driver.

"It's fine, I'm not feeling anything in this coat," said Kennedy. "Normally I wouldn't wear it," she continued quickly, "the coat— you know, Canada Goose—but I got it when I didn't really know any better, and it's *freezing* today."

Alicia didn't want to engage in small talk. Kennedy's cellphone rang before she could continue. "Sorry." She picked it up. "Hello . . . Yes, I'll be there on time, ten minutes late tops . . . The traffic is absolutely ridiculous. I'm in a cab, the TTC is down . . . Yes, again."

Alicia listened to Kennedy on the phone with a passive envy; the call sounded important, she sounded important on it. She sounded like she was at the place she thought she'd be by this time in her life.

"OK, so what exactly is our timeline to—" Heaven glanced to the front of the car, but Kennedy wasn't listening. Her voice was rising slightly.

"It's not my fault. Have you never taken the subway in this city?"

Heaven started again. "How much time do we have to find the comb?"

"Why do you sound excited?"

"Well, don't you think it's a little exciting?"

"Bitch, no!" Alicia yelled in an incredulous whisper. "Part of me still hopes that I'll wake up and the worst thing I'll have to do today is clean the employee bathroom in the store. You're on some Don Quixote shit."

Kennedy moved her ear away from her phone and spoke to the driver. "Excuse me, sir, is there any way we can go faster? A side street we can turn down?"

The driver shrugged his shoulders and gestured to the traffic in front of them.

"Just tell me the timeline," said Heaven.

"I was told sundown. What is that, like, four o'clock?"

"We basically have the workday. That's a doable amount of time."

Mars scoffed. "If the roads are like this all day, you're fucked."

Alicia looked out to the traffic in front of them. He wasn't wrong. They weren't nearly as far on Bloor as they should've been, given the amount of time they'd spent in the cab.

"Don't put that out into the universe," said Heaven. "Positive vibes return positive results."

"Not today," said Mars. "When you say nothing bad will happen, then the opposite will happen. If you just accept that *everything* bad will happen, then you can at least plan for all contingencies. Just look out the window: I have never seen the morning look so dark, even in the winter. Are you sure sundown is four o'clock today?"

"No one asked you," Heaven said. "Especially when you're saying such foofool nonsense about a mission you're not even helping us with."

Alicia rubbed her eyes, exasperated. "It's a *mission* now? Look, planning doesn't do shit, and hoping for the best does even less. Whatever's going to happen is going to happen. Nothing matters."

"That's kinda dark still," said Mars.

Alicia caught Heaven's unimpressed expression. "What is it?"

Heaven shook her head and then shrugged. "OK, I'm just going to be honest: I don't really get why she chose you. You don't even see the importance—"

"I don't see the importance?" Alicia thought about what she'd just seen: the whirlpool and the vanishing waters. Just thinking about it allowed the vision to continue and expand to the aftermath of such a departure. A viral video of a protest and an elderly man on a country road, addressing whoever was recording.

"All ah we up here, nuh have no pipe for water, not for years, something like sixteen, seventeen year. Wah some ah we haffi do is ride for miles to this here stream to fill up jugs. But this stream here gone! Dry out! Ah wah mi supposed to put inna the jug now? Mmm? Dirt?"

Comments beneath the video:

So 98% of the cities here have running water and that drops to 88% when we get inna country and now rivers and streams are just DISAPPEARING??

HOW ARE RIVERS JUST GONE?

When the vision left her, Alicia looked at Heaven and laughed incredulously. "The importance is raising my fucking blood pressure, Heaven."

"This is my point—you're acting like it's a burden, you don't see this as a privilege."

"And what, you do? Is that what you're saying?"

"I'm saying that if this *was* happening to me—"

"But it's not," said Alicia. "She said I owed her. This is my mess."

"And it just doesn't make sense. Like, on the real, your ancestors are not the only ones who revered *her* and gave her offerings. I—"

"I don't know, Heaven. Maybe she wanted someone who wouldn't choke when she saw a duppy."

Heaven glared at her. "That's fucked up," she said, raising a finger. "I'm just trying to help."

Alicia shrugged, conceding that her words were a little harsh, but she didn't back down. "Maybe, but you're also trying to make this about you."

"Bullshit," Heaven muttered.

Alicia's phone vibrated. She struggled to get it out of her coat pocket, wondering if it was one of the Google Alerts she'd set, but it was just another text from her mother.

MOM: Go to coral after work.
Wdym coral?
MOM: What's wdym?
Idk what coral is.
MOM: What?
"Oh my God."
Mom what's coral?
MOM: That hair store. It's right by the mall.
You mean Cloré???
MOM: Whatever. Get me another wrap.

Alicia closed her eyes in frustration but then found herself drifting into another vision. This time the past. She was in a red-walled, mahogany-floored dining hall that felt airless and confined despite its size and the breeze that blew in through the open windows. The same buckra man sat at a long table surrounded by four couples, drivelling and prattling and gorging on an excess of meats laid out on silver platters beneath a chandelier. The scene left Alicia's sight, and she bit down on her lip and focused on the back of the driver's seat until her mind settled. Visions so close to each other made it difficult to root herself in the present, and Kennedy's insistence on small talk didn't help matters.

"I'm still reeling, though. It's just so wild running into you, Alicia."

"Yeah, that's the thing about Toronto, it's just so—"

"—connected."

"—incestuous." Alicia paused. "'Incestuous,' 'connected'—practically synonyms."

Kennedy laughed, taking off her gloves. "You haven't changed."

Alicia nodded. "So what it's like living in your area? Do you like it? It was . . ." The sickness and delirium made it difficult for her to speak, and finding the right word, "graduation," filled her with a sense of accomplishment. "It was a graduation present from your parents, right?"

"Well, they helped a lot with the down payment." Kennedy said it as if the distinction made all the difference, but Alicia didn't understand how what she'd said needed correcting.

"But yeah, I can't complain. There isn't much to do here yet, but I can just hop on a train downtown for a good bar or restaurant."

"I'm sure a brunch spot will open up around the corner."

"Oh, definitely, but until then, gotta make do, you know?"

Alicia realized Kennedy wasn't responding to her facetiousness with her own sense of irony and was in fact serious. She opened her mouth to say something else, but Mars stopped her.

"Whatever you're going to say about brunch spots, leave it alone. Things are supposed to change." His words started slurring. "Does it really matter if the convenience store becomes an artisanal bakery that sells French pastries? I fucking love French pastries."

"Mars," said Alicia, "what the hell are you talking about?"

"I'm talking about how you always rant about the SkyDome being called the Rogers Centre or the ACC being called Scotiabank Arena. They're just names. It's like harping on the closing of BiWay at Eglinton and Dufferin. Who cares?"

"First of all, names definitely matter. It's history and . . ." She lost her train of thought. "Second of all, you *should* still be mourning BiWays. The fact that there are no more BiWays is a tragedy. That shit was essential, OK? Like Zellers."

"Leish," said Mars, "you're saying that if you could afford a condo in a—"

"Don't be an asshole and say 'up-and-coming neighbourhood.'"

"I didn't, you did. But you're saying you wouldn't buy one

because of some moral code? Nah, I don't believe it. You would live there *same way*."

"Well, that rhetorical is pointless because I can't even afford—" Alicia glanced at Kennedy for a second time and sighed. "The point is that it shouldn't be one or the other, Mars."

"You're too sentimental about this city."

"I'm not sentimental about anything," said Alicia flatly.

The last thing she heard was Heaven. "Maybe you should be, maybe that's your problem," she said.

And then Alicia let the delirium take over.

XII

Alicia woke up on fire.

It was as if she were drowning in heat. She didn't even realize that the taxi had stopped until she felt as if she were being crushed. It was Mars. He leaned across her to force open the door, and then he pushed her out just in time for him to throw up on the ground.

Everything was off-kilter, out of balance, because Alicia was walking on unsteady feet, half a step away from falling. She didn't know where she was going. A voice was calling out to her. It sounded like Heaven, it sounded like she was yelling "Stop!" So she did.

Alicia could hear snippets of conversation, panicked exchanges, muffled as if she were eavesdropping from beneath a pool.

"I would help you if I wasn't already so late."

"Don't even stress." Had to be Heaven. "I've got this."

Alicia blinked in her surroundings, dimly recognizing that they'd made it to an expansive round field encircled by a paved street and continuous sidewalk. King's College Circle was known as the University of Toronto's front campus, which meant a few

Gothic buildings stood behind the sidewalk, creating an Ivy League look that movies like *Cocktail* and *Harold & Kumar Go to White Castle* had taken advantage of when filming for cheap. The last time Alicia had been here was for her graduation at Con Hall—the domed rotunda outside of which the taxi now idled.

Six years ago, she was one of many marching happily across the green field to the impressive round building, to a future she thought would mean something. Her mother had taken two hundred photos (really, Alicia counted) of Alicia and her degree that afternoon, directing her to strike every pose imaginable, encouraging her to wear her gown for the rest of the day, clapping each time a stranger congratulated her on her accomplishment. Before leaving the campus, they'd even drunk a couple of Kola Champagnes on the Con Hall steps, pocketing the bottle caps as a way to celebrate the convocation with Grandma Mabel.

The memory triggered a deep sense of betrayal—an icy shock to Alicia's overheated body. She was overtaken with anger directed inward. She was furious with herself for believing in any of it, for plunging into further debt for a graduate degree like it mattered.

You stupid, stupid bitch!

That thought wasn't in her voice. It was a foreign, angry shout that was somehow also a physically cold sensation. She didn't know where the voice came from—she felt invaded, tapped into; the voice brought about thoughts she'd cloaked in derision and off-handed bitterness for the past few months so that she felt them all keenly, without the armour of irony. She had to move again.

"Alicia, *where* are you going?"

She wanted to answer Mars, but it was hard to explain—the voice was pulling her to an exact location, but there was a warning in her head too, an instinct that alerted her to the need for caution, that became a chorus of voices, different from the intruder, all distinct and yet in perfect unison, as if a singular person was speaking in different tones. The voices brought with them a familiar warning: *A nuh ev'ryting soak up water a sponge.* A saying Grandma Mabel used to tell Alicia's mother when she was younger.

Alicia thought she could hear Heaven screaming at her to run, but it was too faint a warning, just another feeling added to her internal storm.

She neared a round grey-brick tower topped by a turret and covered in snow. A small colonnade with a roof of three dormer windows connected the tower to a large Romanesque building: University College. She was approaching the Croft Chapter House, a place she'd never once set foot in during her undergraduate years. The only time she'd spent in UC at all had been for end-of-term exams in classrooms that took forever to find in the winding halls of what Alicia used to call Bootleg Hogwarts.

She stopped walking. A thin ray of sunlight beamed through the clouds. It did nothing to brighten the sky overall, but it materialized a . . . She blinked several times until she realized what she was seeing. Delirium hadn't caused her to hallucinate. A ghost, a few feet in front of her. A ghost that was the translucent figure of a broad man wearing a straw boater hat, appearing in the light as if projected onto the ground from a movie about the Victorian era. The ghost was looking toward Croft House, so its back was to her. It looked like an imprint.

As the figure turned to face her, Alicia noticed the wound. The ghost was wearing a partially ripped shirt that exposed a hole in its chest, thin but gaping, oozing blood in translucent white gushes. Then she took in the rest of it: a gnarled face with large features, some of which were obscured by a beard; a thick brow that gave it a menacing expression; hands as big as mallets. Its eyes were the only opaque things about it.

It was terrifying. Not because of the wound, which was gruesome even in vapour, but because its misery infected everything around it. A deep hatred radiated from the phantom—it was the beacon that Alicia's own emotions had responded to. She wanted to leave Croft House, but it was as if the ghost was keeping her trapped where she stood.

"You see me? Even in light?" Its voice was raspy, like it was struggling for air despite being dead. "No one ever sees me. Not in day. Not even in night. They hear only my cries."

She realized she didn't share the ghost's incredulity; seeing it only confirmed that she had been regifted her second sight. But if this renewed ability brought her only interactions like this one, like the Rolling Calf, like the thousands of barren rivers she saw in her mind's eye, she wanted her ignorance back.

"Why did you bring me here?" she asked.

"Bring? No, you came here. Because you . . ." Its expression didn't change, but Alicia had the horrible feeling that it had reached an epiphany. "Susie, it is you."

"No." She didn't know who that was, but she knew she didn't want to be her if the ghost wanted her. "I don't even know who that is."

"I am right!" it insisted. "I feel it. Your shame, your humiliation. So strong, these feelings you have. Because you feel guilt for what you have done. Your guilt brought you back to me!"

"No, I—"

Alicia thought she heard Heaven shouting from a distance. She turned around while her feet remained planted. Heaven wasn't as far away as she expected her to be; she was crouched next to Mars, who was hunched over.

"What do you see? Alicia, who are you talking to?" Heaven called out.

The ghost demanded that Alicia's attention return to it. "Look at me!"

She did.

"Susie, it is me—Reznikoff, your soon-to-be husband. Your rightful husband. You are finally back at my side!"

"You've got the wrong person. Let me go, release me, whatever." She put her hand to her forehead—the duppy sickness intermingling with everything else.

"You not remember your human life? You not remember—"

With every word Reznikoff spoke, Alicia saw his memory:

University College partially built—scaffolding criss-crossing stone walls, heaps of bricks and stones piled outside the entrance, toiling men hammering and heaving. Reznikoff in the flesh, as a human, black-haired and red-faced, swinging hammer against stone, brazen gulps from a hip flask. Several paces away, a pale, dark-haired waif of a man Alicia thought was reminiscent of that actor all the white girls loved—Timothée Chalamet— was meticulously carving with such concentration that sweat remained on his brow instead of being wiped away with the back of his hand. Not a word was said between the two of them, yet the mutual animosity was felt even by Alicia. A curly-haired, red-headed woman in a puffy-sleeved dress walked onto the site, a paper bag clasped in both hands. Some men ogled. Some men took off their caps. The waif gazed, awestruck, and averted his eyes when Reznikoff met them with his own glare.

"This is no place for a woman, Susie," Reznikoff chastised while taking the bag all the same. "When we are married, I will not stand for such things."

She left him but remained on the site, in a faraway corner, to be joined moments later by the waif, who took her in his arms.

"What if he did not believe my excuse? The risk—"

He stopped her speaking with a passionate kiss. "I do not care," he said. "You will not suffer him anymore. We leave tonight."

She nodded. "Tonight."

"Do you have the money?"

"It is somewhere safe, but, Paul"—she pulled away from him— "Ivan is a drunkard, a brute of a man, but he saved this money for our wedding. It seems wrong—"

"It isn't!" He clasped her hands with his own. "If you ask me, you earned every cent by enduring his crude presence. Meet me here at half past midnight. Say you will meet me here."

Susie nodded, earnest, excited.

"—but you did not know that I had suspected your treachery for months. That—"

It was dark now, the worksite empty. Reznikoff lurked behind trees, intoxicated. With drink. With rage. He spied Diabolos standing by the UC building. The man who dared to carve a gargoyle with Reznikoff's face, who dared to call him a baboon, who dared to make a cuckold out of him.

He showed himself.

"Reznikoff." The disgust in Diabolos's tone contorted his entire face. "Where is she?"

"You will not take her!"

Reznikoff lunged. The two shuffled and jabbed across the grounds, brawling and clashing, a violent dance that brought them to in front of Croft House. Reznikoff cast around and saw an axe. He dislodged it and swung at Diabolos and missed. He cursed with each failure. Swing and miss. Swing and miss. Diabolos taunting with every dodge.

One swing nearly struck home. The fear lit in Diabolos's eyes, his frantic reach for the dagger concealed in his boot, fuelled Reznikoff's lust for his blood. He charged and Diabolos sought to hide in the colonnade outside of Croft House, but Reznikoff followed, backing him against the door to the tower. Triumphant, he stepped back to deliver the fatal strike, but Diabolos swung the door outward and the axe connected with the wood instead as the two of them fell to the ground, wrestling and choking and striking each other. Diabolos broke free from Reznikoff's hold and ran into the building, quick and light on his feet. Reznikoff's pursuit was a lumbering shuffle through the unfinished corridor, up the stone steps.

Diabolos pounced from a flight above, dagger in hand, the blade piercing Reznikoff's chest. He spluttered and gurgled, convulsed, and then died. Through his spirit's eyes, he watched Diabolos heave his body over the railing and down the stairs.

"I have been here ever since."

Alicia touched the spot on her chest where Reznikoff had been stabbed on his, trying to overcome the sensation of death.

"You are not Susie," the ghost said finally.

Alicia nodded, grateful for the realization. "Exactly, I—"

"But you must stay here. With me."

The ghost moved, a teleportation. Alicia jumped.

"You came to me. No one comes to me. I feel it, your pain. You are adrift. If you stay here, with me, you will be fixed to the spot. You will have a single purpose."

The response was unexpected in its appeal to Alicia's sensibilities; she was wrong-footed and speechless, and a part of her was acquiescing to the offer—would it really be that bad? In that moment, it kind of felt right—poetic, even—to spend an eternity haunting an institution that had been haunting her since she'd left it. No other thoughts, no other pressures, no other expectations, just her and another ghost rooted to one spot for eternity.

A moment was all that was needed.

Reznikoff's ghost seized Alicia's consideration and disappeared into her body, smothering her with its presence. She clawed at her throat until she was too tired to lift her hands. Reznikoff made her even weaker than before, blanketing her with fatigue. The ghost was like a parasite, siphoning her energy, emptying her. The more it drained her, the more her vision blurred into whiteness, smearing out parts of her surroundings like finger smudges on a screen. Reznikoff incanted: *Me and you together forever, forever me and you together . . .*

Heaven running toward a building entrance was the last thing Alicia saw before the white overtook her vision.

Me and you together forever, forever me and you together . . .

This was it. This was how she was going to die. There was no angelic light; this was brightness without warmth, a cold and inhospitable gateway to limbo. She wished she'd understood the implications sooner. It was in every movie, every book; as a child she'd even asked her mother what it meant after hearing it in the '95 movie *Casper*: "unfinished business." Being rooted to one spot for eternity would not bring about a single purpose; it would leave her to exist in a state where purpose would elude her eternally.

Alicia had begun to resign herself to this bleak inevitability when the same chorus of voices that had warned her away from Croft House returned to her. Now they filled her head with singing:

Done baby, done cry, yuh mother gone ah fountain.
Sweetie water never dry, yuh get it down ah fountain.
Milky water never dry, yuh get it down ah fountain.

The voices sang the song over and over, and with each repetition, what felt like kinship surged throughout her and gradually returned life to her bit by bit. The melody, the words, they planted a seed of strength that didn't belong to her but that she had claim to, like an inheritance. In the voices, she started hearing Adelaide and Alice, as well as voices she'd never heard before yet recognized, like the voice of Joycelyn, and her mother before her, and her mother before *her*—the other women at the waterfall.

The ghost hadn't let go of Alicia completely—it didn't want to leave, not now that it had named her its companion—but its grip had slackened. Suddenly, the white dulled and there was a third presence, one that was comforting, one that was physical—a silhouette in the distance, shimmering black like crushed velvet against the blazing whiteness. The silhouette moved toward Alicia, getting bigger with each step, bringing a warmth that Alicia yearned to fill herself with. The larger it got, the more the whiteness shrank and the louder the voices chanted, encouraging the shadow, while Reznikoff's hold redoubled, resisting the living's claim on her.

Alicia blinked in the sight of Oni in grey flannel pyjama pants and a Wakanda sweatshirt with Chadwick Boseman's face, her hair wrapped in the kind of satin scarf Grandma Mabel would tie around her neck for church. There was a jar in her hands filled with water and a leaf.

The singing grew louder. Oni walked even closer to her, holding out the jar, muttering beneath her breath, and Alicia felt a sudden release. The slackened grip on her was now nonexistent. Reznikoff was gone. The white was gone. The voices were gone. Just like that. For a second, Alicia could see her surroundings clearly. She saw the aura curved over Oni like the night they met; the two of them locked eyes, the intensity of Oni's gaze sending a tremor of warmth through her. She then saw Heaven behind

Oni, running out of the entrance she'd run into what seemed like ages ago, and then the world started to tilt. She could hear Heaven's screams, see her run toward her, see her try to break her fall—

XIII

Alicia was, once again, both in and out of her body. She could see everything—Oni, Heaven, Mars, the campus—from a vantage point below them, like she was sitting in the front row of a movie theatre, craning her neck to look at the screen. She was privy to their thoughts too, an odd sort of omniscience, yet she could also feel the hard ground beneath her body, the snow chilling her skin. The dissociative experience wasn't unfamiliar, but Alicia didn't understand why she seemed to be watching everything from a place underground, connected to the earthly world but not really a part of it. She didn't understand the reason for the split in consciousness at all.

Oni was standing beside her and Heaven was crouched next to her body. Mars sat against a tree a few feet away, his eyes halfway open, his face covered in sweat. His thoughts were the ones that pulled to her the most. She saw them rather than heard them— quick, disparate images that raced through her own mind. Mars pulling her up before the duppy could attack her. Mars as a little boy swimming back to a beach while holding on to an unconscious toddler—his brother. "Sam! *Samuel!*"—the adults splashing toward them from the shore. The anger she'd seen in his eyes when they'd started running again. The fear as he remembered his brother's near death. The memories of the beach, of the Rolling Calf became jumbled and distorted by the pain Mars felt, and he suddenly visualized the symptoms of his duppy sickness, so Alicia saw his head literally on fire and now heard his interior moaning: *It hurts, it fucking hurts . . .*

Oni was deep in thought. She had heard the voices, sensed the power of the chanting, the power of the women those voices belonged to. It made her wonder whether Alicia was possessed by spirits, but then she remembered that when the spirits worked through someone, the vessel was animated, convulsing and speaking in tongues, while Alicia was catatonic.

Alicia didn't feel like she'd been taken hold of either; she still felt like herself. What she did feel was a sort of hangover from the chanting; there were no voices or singing like before, but she still felt the lingering presence of her ancestors.

"Help me take her to my room. It's exam time and campus is quiet, but people still like to walk through here." Oni looked to Mars. "I need you fi carry this for me."

Heaven was nervous. "Can't you come back for the water later?"

"If I could just leave the water anywhere, then I would've left it back upstairs, nuh true? Ah *consecrated* water this. It has the leaf of *life*."

Alicia could sense Heaven's confusion—the leaf in the jar didn't seem like anything special; it looked pretty regular: thick and elliptical, with red scalloped edges. Heaven still wasn't clear why Oni couldn't just leave it.

"I think if you—"

"I thought you knew all this," said Oni. She gestured to Mars. "Duppy," she said. "A duppy means—"

"I know what 'duppy' means." Heaven's embarrassment turned to indignation, which made her tone sharp. "Did *you* know that it originated from a West African word? A Twi word, specifically: *dupon*—"

"Them love off water but them hate life, understand?" said Oni, speaking over Heaven. "Death is the opposite of life."

She handed the jar to Mars, who took it from her with both hands and immediately pictured it falling out of his weakened grip and shattering into pieces.

"The water draws the duppy them out, but the leaf keeps them at bay, it makes them go back to where they from. So no mi cyaah left the water."

Heaven gritted her teeth in frustration; she knew this. The name was in every text she'd read about bush medicine, about spirituality and traditional religions, but having never actually seen what *Bryophyllum pinnatum* looked like in person, she hadn't recognized it in Oni's hands.

"Hurry before people start coming."

Oni grabbed Alicia under her arms, Heaven clasped her by her ankles, and they lifted, her body hanging like a hammock.

Heaven motioned to Mars with her head. "Grab on to me so you don't fall."

Mars cocooned the jar in the crook of one arm, then put his other hand on Heaven's shoulder. The three of them shuffled through the quad until they made it to an entrance Alicia had never seen before—a black door that was labelled "Palmer-Hall House." Mars took Oni's keys and unlocked the door, holding it open for Heaven and Oni to carry Alicia inside.

They started climbing the staircase and stopped when they heard voices from above get progressively louder and closer.

"So aliens come to Earth and instead of destroying this late-stage capitalist hellscape, they were like, 'Let's just, I don't know, hang out in *Toronto*'?"

"Maybe they're capitalist aliens. Maybe they don't have a concept of what capitalism is."

"That's so basic. What alien breathes fire? Obviously, it's a seraph."

"It was shooting fire, not *made out of* fire—"

Two girls stopped their debate when they saw Oni and Heaven on the landing. They looked at Alicia and then exchanged glances but said nothing as everyone manoeuvred their way across the landing, though Heaven and Oni could hear the rest of their conversation as they continued to Oni's floor.

"I want you to kill me if I ever get that drunk."

"You *have* been that drunk."

Oni's room was noticeable right away: it was the one with a bunch of eggshells in front of the door.

Alicia felt Heaven's need to get something right. "That's to ward off spirits, right?"

"Just the unfriendly ones," said Oni. "In a place this old, you can never be too careful."

"Your don doesn't make you clean it up? Everyone's good with it?"

"They think it's wicca, so they think it's cool."

Oni's room was spacious and more greenhouse than dorm. There was a twin bed with a window behind the headboard, and right across from it, a standard desk and a standard bookcase. On the windowsill were water lilies in glasses, and over the bed there was a shelf displaying Mason jars stuffed with herbs, above which hung a large Jamaican flag. Each bookshelf housed a potted plant, and the desk was crowded with vases of poinsettias and desert roses. There were even vining jasmines climbing the wooden trellises on the walls. The room was like an oasis.

The minute Oni and Heaven had heaved Alicia onto the twin bed, Heaven rushed over to Mars and led him to the wooden swivel chair by the desk. He leaned forward and hurled; this time the vomit was reddish.

Oni put her hands to her mouth—she was way out of her depth. She needed guidance. She grabbed her phone from the desk and opened the video chat on her WhatsApp. After a few rings, a woman in a tie-head appeared on the screen, eating from a plate of ackee and saltfish and boiled banana. There were bushes and trees behind her, like she was sitting outside.

"Oni?" she said between bites. "Why yuh badda wid me this morning?"

"Mummy? Yuh see me?" said Oni, her accent getting heavier. "Yuh hear me?"

"Yes, mi see yuh fine, but why yuh ah call?" said her mother, pushing out her mouth as she rubbed the front of her teeth with the tip of her tongue. "Yuh have exams, nuh true? Hang up the phone and tek up yuh book!"

"Mi need fi beg yuh something." Oni tried to appear calm. "I have two client here, catch duppy sickness bad. They crossed a Rolling Calf."

Oni's mother put her plate down. "Who told dem fi ramp wid Rolling Calf?"

"It's not like we meant to, Ms.—"

"Barrett," said Oni in a low voice.

"Ms. Barrett." Heaven rushed to Oni's side so that her mother could see her. "It just came out of nowhere."

"Mi never hear of Rolling Calf inna Canada, enuh. Someone grudge you bad, eh?"

"We need help, please," said Heaven.

"Let me see."

Oni turned the camera off selfie mode and walked over to Mars so her mother could get a better look at him.

"Mm," she said after a few seconds. "Next one, next one."

Oni walked over to Alicia. Her mother studied Alicia's body. "Bring it up to her face. All right, put me down before mi get sick."

Oni put the phone on the desk so that it was standing upright. Ms. Barrett was sitting up straight. Her face was all business.

"This here is spirit work and balm, yuh understand?" she said. "So wah you gwine fi do is draw two baths for him and for she. This will clear their spirit and rejuvenate them. Him nuh too bad. Him just need some frankincense and myrrh."

Oni opened a desk drawer and took out a large wooden box, putting it on the floor. Inside were dozens of small corked bottles with brown labels tied to them. She took out one bottle with a liquid that looked almost like honey and another filled with a liquid that was reddish brown, then put them on the desk. Alicia was surprised—when she heard "frankincense" and "myrrh," she hadn't expected to see bottles of essential oils. Her mind had gone straight to the Three Wise Men. So had Heaven's, but she was trying her best to look unsurprised.

"He's set. And her?"

"Mi see that it nuh just one duppy she brush against, so she need a whole heap ah ting. Plant, herb, everything. Yuh have jack'na bush?"

"See it here." Oni reached over to the shelf and picked up a jar of what looked like wood chips but earthier, then put it down on the bed next to Alicia's feet.

"What else do I need?"

"Wild rosemary. Donkey weed. Shama macka."

Heaven thought the donkey weed looked kind of like thyme and the shama macka looked like thorned twigs and stems and leaves.

"Some chocho," said Ms. Barrett.

Heaven furrowed her eyebrows at Oni. "Chocho like that green squash thing?"

"I don't have chocho," said Oni, turning around to look at the phone.

Ms. Barrett folded her arms. "Why yuh nuh have chocho?"

"It's a vegetable," said Oni matter-of-factly. "I couldn't bring it over from yaad."

"Ah wah Canada nuh have vegetable, then? They nuh call it chocho over there. Ah wah they call it? Chayote."

"I know, but I have a meal plan," said Oni, picking up the four different jars and balancing them in her hands. She dropped them unceremoniously onto the desk. "I don't really buy vegetables if I'm not going to cook."

"Yuh need chocho—"

Oni opened her mouth to speak, trying to find an opening. "OK, Mummy, but—"

"—not just fi cure duppy sickness. Chocho good for the inflammation—"

Oni nodded, trying not to show her impatience. "Mm-hmm."

"—blood pressure, *stress*!"

"I understand, Mummy, but is the bath going to work without it?"

Ms. Barrett looked like she wanted to continue chastising Oni, but she answered her instead. "It will work, but it nuh be as strong.

Yuh still need fi get oil and salt. Then you mix it up, boil it, and put it inna the bath. But first, she must drink from it. And then yuh need fi—"

"Wait, wait," said Heaven, putting herself back in Ms. Barrett's line of vision. She took out her own phone and opened the Notes app, typing furiously. "OK, go on," she said.

"Yuh need fi burn a white candle when she bathes and before she even bathe—" Ms. Barrett stretched toward the screen like she was trying to see more of the dorm room than the phone would allow. "Where your Bible deh? Every time mi ah call, you have the Bible front and centre, right pon the dresser for me fi see, and now mi ah call you off guard—"

"I called you, Mummy." Oni rushed to the dresser and opened a drawer. "I put it *in* the dresser fi keep it safe," she said, holding a small Bible out to the phone.

"Mm-hmm," said Ms. Barrett, unconvinced. "Read a psalm over the bath before she goes in it. Then when the bath finish, yuh must balm her, understand? Rub her body down wid the oil. Then yuh must get a pigeon—"

"Wait, draw brakes. A pigeon?" Heaven immediately stopped typing and looked up from her phone to Oni. "Why?"

"Fi beat the girl's body wid it."

Absolutely the fuck not, Alicia thought.

"Nope." Heaven shook her head—she did not remember reading that. "Nope, we're not doing that. Oni, we're not doing that."

Ms. Barrett threw up her hands. "Ah you who call me for instruction, enuh! Fine, don't do it. But yuh must work fast now. Last thing, that girl there, does she have sight or gift?"

"Sight, maybe," said Heaven. "She gets visions. Why? Is that important?"

"From what mi can tell, her spirit gone ah journeying."

Oni glanced at Alicia on the bed. "What do you mean?"

"Journeying!" Ms. Barrett repeated the word as if it were an explanation in and of itself, and when Oni and Heaven continued to look blankly at her, she kissed her teeth. "When yuh spirit goes journeying, it leaves yuh body and travels," she said. "Her spirit was called away, nah know where—sometimes the spirit journeys back to Africa, sometimes it journeys to the ancestors, sometimes it journeys time. But journeying can be ten minutes or four hour, no exact science to it. So yuh must fi do the bath but she may not wake up right away, understand?"

That her spirit was travelling to different places and times made sense to Alicia. It explained why she'd felt within and without herself all morning, why she'd felt like she was visiting the places in her visions rather than seeing them. But it didn't explain her current situation. She saw nothing but the world around her and felt nothing but the faint hum of that continued presence.

"OK, thank you, Mummy." Oni hung up the phone and walked over to her closet, bending down.

"So wait a minute," said Heaven. "Alicia won't wake up right away?"

"Might, might not." Oni took an electric kettle from the bottom shelf and, seeing how small it was, realized she was going to have to boil everything in batches.

"But we have a deadline." Heaven checked her phone, and Alicia saw that it was nine thirty. Commuting really was an enemy to her today. "We don't have time for this."

"Let's focus on the bath first, OK?" said Oni. "The only three things I don't have that we absolutely need are olive oil, salt, and a candle."

Heaven looked at Oni incredulously. "You have something called donkey weed, but you nuh have oil? Or salt?"

"Go see if there's any in the kitchen." Oni unscrewed the cap of the spray bottle and poured the water into the kettle. "I'll check if anyone has a white candle."

Heaven hesitated. "Just regular olive oil? Or is there some consecrated oil from the motherland?"

"Regular olive oil, Heaven."

"Ah so yuh say." She started walking toward the door but then stopped and looked back, eyeing the kettle. "Is this going to work?"

Oni plugged the kettle into the outlet. "We're going to find out."

XIV

Heaven was about a half-second away from losing her shit. Alicia could hear her cussing in her head. The kitchen was proving to be unhelpful, with only a stack of mismatched plates and a few grubby-looking glasses in the cupboard. There was some plastic cutlery in the top drawer along with condiment packets, and she pocketed all the salt she could find. But no olive oil. There wasn't even a frying pan or a pot in sight.

She thought about asking a student to go to the dining hall, but finding someone willing to help her would take too long. Galleria, the closest supermarket, was at least ten minutes away, and they needed every second of the six and half hours they had until sunset.

Heaven pushed the urge to scream back down her throat and opened the fridge—a last-ditch effort—revealing shelves packed with takeout and Tupperware, bottles of Dasani, expired milk. On the middle shelf there was a clamshell container inside a clear bag with "Bowl Bros: The Freshest Salad in the 6ix" typed on it. On top of the container, she saw two sauce cups filled with viscous yellow liquid.

"You've got to be shitting me."

Her phone vibrated with a text from Oni: "Get Saran wrap too."

When Heaven returned to the room, Oni had brought in another swivel chair, with a white candle and a matchbook on the seat. She'd gone to a few neighbouring rooms searching for the needed supplies, and when one guy asked if she was going to do a seance, Oni had just laughed, not bothering to explain that if she wanted to contact the dead, she'd need lots of rice, some drums, and way more candles.

Heaven put the box of Saran wrap on the chair. "Fam, your kitchen makes no sense," she said. "Couldn't find one likkle bokkle of olive oil and there was no salt, but there was Saran wrap in the bottom drawer? Foolishness."

Oni put the chair in the hall and stepped back into her room. "We don't have any salt or oil?"

Heaven reached into her pockets and took out what she'd got from the kitchen. "This is all I could find. Is it enough?"

Oni didn't know but she didn't say that and just took the condiments out of Heaven's hands, replacing them with the bottles of frankincense and myrrh.

"Take Mars to the washroom, Saran-wrap both the bathtub them, then you haffi come back and help me."

Heaven didn't move for a second; a part of her expected some kind of acknowledgment for having found what she did find in such an unstocked kitchen, but she told herself to get over it. She shoved the bottles into her pockets.

"Why do I have to Saran-wrap the tubs?"

"The two of them bathtub *dutty*," said Oni, putting the condiments on the desk. "No point in cleansing if the containers for the cleansing aren't clean." Oni started opening the jars she'd pulled from the shelf and poured the herbs into the water-filled kettle. "No one is going fi trouble you because no one goes to the bathtubs fi wul a fresh; they only use the showers."

"Then why weren't we—"

"It's called 'bush bath' not 'bush shower,'" she said, channelling a bit of Ms. Barrett in her tone.

Oni opened a couple of salt packets, emptying them into the concoction. She tipped a few drops of olive oil into the kettle, then plugged it in and pushed the button down.

Heaven put the box of Saran wrap on Mars's lap before wheeling him to the doorway. He started mumbling. Oni closed the door after they left, but not all the way. She picked up a vase of bright yellow flowers from the bookshelf and took them out, dashing the water into the little trash can before putting the flowers in the vase with the roses. She placed the empty vase next to the kettle and then sat down on the bed beside Alicia and looked to the glass jars on the windowsill. Each one contained a white water lily. She bit her lip, considering the benefits of the water the lilies were floating on, and then reached forward, picking up a jar. She put the rim to Alicia's lips but stopped herself from tilting the water into her mouth.

"This water is from a spring back home where a few people drowned," she said. "Everyone said it was haunted, said that the drownings happened because treasure would tempt you and River Mumma would drag you down to the bottom."

Those words pulled all of Alicia's focus to Oni. She didn't pay attention to Heaven in the empty washroom down the hall, lining the first of two grimy bathtubs with plastic, cursing about how unsanitary it was without latex gloves.

"When I was six, I nearly drowned in the spring and I did see River Mumma for a moment too, you know, with her big, big hair like a nimbus," said Oni, her eyes glazed. "I also saw something like gold at the bottom of the spring, but mi nuh bother with it, mi just want fi live. She must've felt gracious that day, because she saved me, pushed me ashore. My mother did teach me bush, but River Mumma gave me something extra. From when she saved me, mi never get sick, mi never feel pain too long."

And to give thanks, Oni had looked after the spring. Alicia saw her giving River Mumma perfume and jewellery, sometimes makeup—pretty offerings, since River Mumma was one to like nice things, her now-lost comb an extension of and another physical symbol of her beauty. Alicia recalled the lace and the coins the women by the river had left for the mermaid, and the beaded necklaces she had seen her wearing.

"When I came up here to foreign, my mother warned me, said that the gift might leave me. Fi true, sometimes I get a cold in winter, but I can still read people through the cards and . . ."

River Mumma had dreamed Oni a week ago; she'd come to her in the form of a woman rather than a mermaid. The two of them stood on a beach at sunset. Oni was in her pyjamas, but white fabric criss-crossed River Mumma's breasts like a halter and fanned out to a blue skirt that flowed and rippled, becoming the ocean's waves whenever there was a breeze. In the distance, a house stood on the water—Heaven's house—as if the ocean were solid, and Heaven stood in front of it in her grey sweater-dress, beckoning to Oni. Jumping in and out of the water was a blue fish that glowed from within, and River Mumma spoke to Oni silently: *Follow the fish* . . . And Oni dove into the water, swimming toward it.

"The day after my dream, Heaven invited me to her party." Oni blinked and freed one of her hands, gently touching Alicia's forehead. "Where I met you."

Alicia saw herself at the party but through Oni's eyes—she had a glow around her like the fish in her dream, like the aura she had seen around Oni.

Oni cleared her throat and then looked down at the jar. "Water from River Mumma can heal. I don't know if it will work. When I go back a yaad, I still give my offerings, but I don't know if you need fi drink it from the source. But drinking it can't hurt you more."

She put the jar to Alicia's lips again and tipped some of the water into her mouth. The moment it made contact with her tongue, she felt a tingle on her skin and the presence of her ancestors intensified. The buzzing made sense to her as summoning, inviting her to them, and Alicia realized she was what was keeping herself earthbound; she was afraid of what they might ask of her and couldn't seem to find the will to finish her journeying, to go to them.

A quick snap. The kettle was boiling and the button clicked up, indicating that the herbs were ready. Oni put the jar back on the windowsill and walked over to the desk to pour the mixture into the empty vase.

By the time the second batch finished boiling, Heaven had returned and she and Oni heaved Alicia onto the swivel chair, putting the candle and matchbook in her lap. Heaven pushed her down the hallway and Oni followed with the vase, leaving it on the floor in front of the bathtub stalls and telling Heaven to get started, then running back to her room for the kettle.

Heaven decided to start with Mars—his bath was easier and she'd already helped him into one of the stalls, sitting him on the little bench before she'd run back to Oni's room. She turned on the spout and took the frankincense and myrrh out of her pockets. She emptied both bottles into the tub and then helped Mars take off his jacket while he leaned forward and unlaced his boots. Heaven stepped out of the stall, closing the door behind her, when Mars started to undress. Oni returned with the kettle in one hand and her Bible in the other.

"Why is the smell so overpowering?"

Heaven frowned. "I didn't know how much to put, so I just put it all in. Seemed safest."

"Rhatid," said Oni beneath her breath.

She took the candle and lit it in the stall, setting it down on the bench next to the bathtub. Heaven had the vase in her hands and waited for Oni to turn on the water before inching by her and pouring the concoction into the tub.

"Mars, you good?" she called out.

"Blessed!" His voice sounded stronger.

The tub was nearly halfway full when Heaven poured in the second batch and Oni chose a psalm to pray over it.

"OK, let's get her into the bath."

"Really?" Heaven couldn't hide her disappointment. "That's it? You just—you just read it like normal?"

"Ah wah yuh want? Fog and confetti like a Beyoncé concert? Be serious."

They put Alicia's arms over their shoulders and stood her up, inching her toward the bench next to the tub, then stripping her down to her underwear.

Heaven poured the oil into Oni's hands and Oni went over to Alicia and rubbed her arms and legs with intention and purpose, her touch skilled and careful as she glided her palms over Alicia's stomach, trying to get as much of the oil on her skin as possible, and in her place, Alicia saw Adelaide in the care of the midwife and the river.

When they finally lowered her into the bath, it was like the water was searching to seep into her skin, into her blood. It was getting harder to stay rooted—the voices beckoning to her grew louder and louder. The bush bath soaked into her, unearthing truths she didn't even know she was keeping. Truths about her resistance to leave, about how it was not fear of what they would ask of her but fear that she wasn't strong enough to carry out whatever duty she must.

Oni was speaking. Her voice was like a faint echo. "We forgot to give her some to drink."

"Shit. Well, is it too late now?"

Oni picked up the vase and tilted Alicia's head back, pouring the last few drops of the mixture into her mouth. The liquid felt like air being breathed into her lungs and she exhaled sharply, her eyes snapping open for just a moment, barely a moment, before she sank down into the bath, the water enclosing her face.

XV

What Alicia noticed first was that the stream she emerged from was extraordinary. It ran through a narrow valley between looming cliffs curtained by hundreds of waterfalls, but the stream didn't want her in it; she could feel the currents beneath her pushing her upward as opposed to pulling her down. What she noticed second was that she no longer saw herself outside of her body—she didn't even see the bathroom anymore, as if her spirit had finally fully untethered itself and journeyed to its destination.

"The stream is not meant for you."

Alicia knew that voice, and as soon as she heard it, she found herself at the top of the waterfall, standing in the river that plunged over the cliff's precipice into the gorge she'd just been in. Waiting for her, knee-deep in the water, was a woman in white, her grey twists framing a high-cheekboned face.

Her body trembled with emotion too tremendous to express yet too powerful to contain. She couldn't move from where she stood, she could barely breathe, but she didn't have to. Grandma Mabel closed the gap between them and held her. Now that Alicia was in her arms, she could do nothing but shake with the magnitude of the circumstances. When she stilled, her grandmother touched her face, then her braids, her fingertips gently stroking her scalp until she naturally started fixing her hair, parting her braids in half.

"You haffi dead fi cross that river," said Grandma Mabel, taking half of Alicia's braids and weaving them together in a single French braid.

Alicia looked down to the stream and saw women adorned in beads or jewellery flowing atop a current no human would survive, journeying peacefully through rapids and whirlpools and under-tows to what she assumed would be their final resting place.

"You come find me beneath the earth where the spirits do live, but yuh nuh dead so yuh cyaah journey the stream fi get to the spirit *world*."

That must've been why the river had expelled her.

"We're meeting halfway."

Alicia nodded but found herself unable to speak. There was so much she wanted to say that she couldn't say anything at all. Grandma Mabel fondly put her hand on Alicia's shoulder, and Alicia knew Grandma Mabel knew everything, felt everything she couldn't express. She finished braiding Alicia's hair and touched the side of her face with a tenderness that made Alicia afraid she was leaving so soon after appearing, and she held on to her in an effort to keep her grandmother by her side.

"Yuh nuh wash pickney belly, yuh wash them back. Some things you haffi figure out yourself, and some things you need your family fi help you." Grandma Mabel smiled and took Alicia's hands in hers so she could kiss the wrist that used to bear the bracelet she'd bought for her. "Mi have another gift for you now. Your spirit came to me fi help, so I gwine fi guide you so you can understand. I will be right here."

And then it was as if Grandma Mabel multiplied into the different women from the very first waterfall, all of whom stood behind her in a line. Alicia's skin began to hum, a vibration started to build within her—a feeling she came to recognize as the telltale sign of a vision. Scenes unfolded, each a memory belonging to a different woman but all seen through Alicia's eyes and experienced as if they were from her immediate past. She lived through each recollection simultaneously—regardless of chronology, regardless of time, regardless of place—the feel of Grandma Mabel's presence, of her hand on hers, the only constant through her journey.

Alicia found herself in a group of people dancing and drumming; she was among them as Adelaide. Her feet moved quickly, body jumping and swaying with the others in the circle, kinetic and alive, responding to the songs and the chants. They danced on the riverbank and there was rum and honey, flowers and coins, fowls and even an ox, all prepared as gifts, all prepared for River Mumma. Their exaltation for the mother of water, the source of life, shivered through the circle, binding them together in unshakeable community, a spiritual bond that tightened and intensified with each hop, each clap, each sway.

Now she was inside the red-walled room she'd had a vision of earlier in the day, the window open to a vista of lush hills and blue waters. She, as Alice, along with the other enslaved, followed the silent instructions of Thomas, the head servant, pulling out chairs for the white folk to sit on, placing tureens and platters on the long table, taking off lids to reveal the turtle and the fish, the mutton and the turkey, the chicken and the ham they had spent the entire day preparing and cooking. Then they left the white folk to feast on snapper and snook, tearing the fish with their knives and forks, gnashing the flesh between their teeth, their wet chewing, gluttonous moaning, and shrill titters adding to the weight of the air that, even now, Alicia felt choked by, the sensation made bearable only by the feel of Grandma Mabel's hand holding her own.

The buckra of the house regaled his guests with the history of their meal, how he'd thought it'd be a treat to add some zest to their dinner and told his boy to procure fish from the river that hosted those silly gatherings from time to time; how he'd had to strike him for backchat and threaten him with a lashing if he didn't get the others in line and insist on a catch from that river.

To emphasize his point, he summoned Thomas and Alice back to the dining room, and when Alicia briefly caught Thomas's eye, she felt a recognition that radiated through her sight as a passenger to the past, all the way to her bones, to the future, which was her present, and it shook her. In his place she saw Mars, and in Mars's place she saw Thomas, the images of both men flashing between each other until she realized they were kin.

The buckra demanded that Thomas explain the apprehension around the meal, and when he spoke, Alicia saw him as Mars.

The fish them belong to the River Maid, he said to the delight of the guests.

The river maid, can you believe it? A water goddess, like in a children's story! Tell them what else, boy!

Thomas's neutral tone was contradicted by his hardened eyes as he responded. If you eat the fish them from the river, the river will dry up.

The buckra spat tiny bones onto small saucers as the others belly-laughed at the superstition, at the simple-minded slaves— oh, the *savagery*. And then he told Alice to bring in dessert.

Drought had come now, scorching trees, hindering the growth of yams and dasheen, potato and breadfruit, bringing starvation that took lives, some of which Alice still saw as wandering duppies. Alicia, as Alice, crouched in the barren riverbed, putting her hand flat on the cracked ground, feeling the dirt beneath her palm. Then the buckra appeared on the bank, glaring out to the barren river, and when his cold eyes landed on Alice, Alicia averted her gaze.

At night, there was chatter in the village: Buckra nuh listen and now the river dry up!

Alice, who had such an intimate connection to the river, who had felt its sandy remains earlier in the day, knew only another offering would set it right—one of blood. The right blood. And she would be the one to get it.

Another dance. Another ceremony. Dressed in white, a woman whom Alice knew to be one of the spiritual leaders in the community whirled around in the middle of the circle, enlivened with energy until she collapsed onto the ground in a fit, calling out orders that were sure to be followed.

The next gathering Alicia saw was made up of men and held by a tiny stream that struggled to flow with so little water. They'd told the buckra they wanted to congregate for prayer, but after the spiritual leader's revelations, they had come together to organize, to choreograph, to swear oaths.

A pot hung over some burning wood and a tall, broad-shouldered man boiled a fowl he'd killed, rubbing the water on the faces of the men in the circle. They'd made a Great Swear, pledging to be faithful to their mission, to be faithful to each other, to die rather than betray their plans, then had sealed their loyalty by drinking a concoction of rum, grave dirt, and gunpowder. The broad man finished the ritual by rubbing wild sage on everyone's faces, promising spiritual armour to all who participated and a spiritual death to whoever abandoned their oath.

Alice worked close to the same stream, though on the other side, having taken a copper pan from the kitchen to hold the juices from a cassava plant she'd squeezed, leaving it out in the sun to breed insects, which she then ground into a powder. In the night, she mixed that powder into the buckra's brandy and served the drink to him after his supper of pigeon pie. When he told her to leave, she insisted on staying by his side to ensure his comfort. Soon he cried out in pain, holding himself in his bed, yelling for help, and as she watched him writhe in agony, those who had made the oath and armoured themselves in spirit set the plantation ablaze.

Rebellion. Revolution.

Alice slit the buckra's throat moments before Mars as Thomas (or Thomas as Mars) ran into the room to investigate the strangled noises coming from it. When she asked him for help taking the white man to the riverbank, he ran from her instead, flying into the night, neither betraying her nor helping her. Alice could not haul a dead body by herself, so the next best thing would have to do—she ripped off some of the bedsheet to catch the blood she'd spilled.

Once she was outside, friends she'd danced with, family she'd picked herbs with helped her race undetected to the riverbank, where she threw the sheet into the riverbed, urging the River Maid to take their offering. The water returned in the space of a blink, as if it had never gone.

Not too long after this night and nights like it across the island, gatherings would be prohibited by law, as would drumming, as would the possession of feathers and eggshells, rum and broken bottles—all items of obeah, all punishable by death. The ways would still be practised but in secret, becoming less and less common, forced out of everyday knowledge with each passing law, with each connection made to the devil, until only remnants remained, trickles passed down through the line of Adelaide and Alice until they had become a whisper, actions done in the background that no one explained. Alicia caught a glimpse of Granny Joycelyn drawing crosses outside of her house to keep spirits at bay, tensing as if she could sense Alicia's spirit.

Not you, said Joycelyn. You're OK.

Then Grandma Mabel loosened her grip, releasing her hold on Alicia, saying farewell: *Now you understand—*

Thrashing. Disorientation. Alicia woke up not knowing where she was in space and in time. There were different voices telling her she was safe, begging her to calm down, assuring her everything was OK. A touch on her arm focused her and she processed that she was in Oni's room, though it looked a bit different: some of the jars of lilies were on a blue towel on the floor, along with the white candle, a few herbs and plants, and a bowl of frozen berries. Alicia was on the bed again, wrapped in a towel and then in a comforter.

"Alicia," said Heaven, "you OK?"

It was the hardest question of her life. She tried to answer it, but her body heaved with the weight of such an impossible inquiry into her well-being. After everything she'd just seen, she was more than OK and yet not OK at all. Her shuddering turned into gasps for air, becoming quicker and quicker, too intense for her to even begin admonishing herself, to even begin to think of getting herself under control. The hyperventilation gave way to sobs for the cruelty she'd witnessed and the resilience, the honour she'd felt— loud cries that seemed like they would never end.

Heaven sat on the bed and hugged her first, and Alicia put her arms around her without any thought. Only a few seconds later did Mars sit behind Alicia and hold her, and Oni touched her shoulder, leaning down and pressing her lips to the top of her head.

XVI

10:00 AM *MOM: Apparently raccoons are particularly vicious this year.*

Attached to the text was an article about a spike in raccoon attacks over the past year.

10:30 AM *MOM: Did you get the wrap from C L O R É?*

10:35 AM *Don't forget to go to the store.*

10:40 *We also need oxtail seasoning.*

10:50 *Why aren't you responding?*

There was also a long text from Pradeep that Alicia didn't read fully, getting the gist of the message from words like "unprofessional" and "write up" and "short-staffed." She focused on her mother. She had just started to text her back when the phone died again. She squeezed it, imagining the plastic and silicon breaking apart in her hand, and then she tossed it to the side.

No one else was in the room, which now smelled like blownout candles. The others had left her to get dressed as soon she'd stopped crying and convinced them she was OK, but after they went, she stayed sitting on the bed, shuddering in silence. She wanted to get up and rally—she'd spent much longer at UC than she'd intended. It was already eleven o'clock and she still had no way of finding the comb—but her body hadn't finished processing the knowledge her ancestors had decided she should experience first-hand in order to acquire. It was a peculiar thing to feel such a profound sense of pride in the resistance, in the will to live of the people who came before her, and to feel personally lacking in the face of that ability at the same time. She had done nothing with her life. When tasked with a duty, the same kind of duty they'd carried out, she resented the responsibility. Heaven was right. She wasn't the right person for this job.

Alicia touched her hair, half hoping that it was somehow still in two French braids, as a kind of physical token of what she'd seen, what she'd taken away from her last conversation with Grandma Mabel. When she realized her braids were not in the style her grandmother had fashioned, the lack of tangible proof that she'd seen Grandma Mabel didn't bother her as much as she'd expected it to, as much as it probably would've before. The experience was what mattered, not evidence that it had actually happened.

There was a knock on the door.

Instinctively, she knew it was Oni. She turned her head, almost as if she was drawn to her presence on the other side. She quickly got dressed and called for her to come in.

Oni entered, a textbook under her arm. She closed the door behind her, saying nothing, but kept her focus on Alicia. The silence between them was both comfortable and charged. She caught herself looking for the title of the course reader and realized she wanted to know more about Oni.

"Urban geography reading," Oni said, putting the reader on her desk and pulling out the chair to sit on. "Exam's on Monday."

"I keep forgetting it's exams. I didn't mean to cut into your studying. And I took over your room for almost two hours."

"Alicia, it was an emergency. You and Mars needed to recuperate, and Heaven—"

"What about Heaven?" said Alicia, panicked. "She's OK, right?"

"Yes," Oni assured her. "She was busy while you were sleeping and Mars was resting."

"Why? What she was doing?"

Oni glanced toward the floor and Alicia didn't need her to say anything else. What Heaven had been doing was clear to her. Although she wasn't able to draw on the same omniscience she'd had an hour ago, her sight had heightened her intuition and she saw that while Oni sat with Mars in the common room, Heaven had stayed here with her, attempting a ritual to connect with River Mumma for help. She'd referred to one of the many blog posts she had bookmarked on her phone and set up a makeshift altar—there was no blue tablecloth in the room, so she'd used a towel and had laid down lavender and the jars of lilies, offering some frozen berries she'd seen in the kitchen freezer and filling a bowl with water.

Sitting cross-legged, she'd apologized for the haphazard state of the altar—whenever she'd pictured forging communication in her mind, it was never so improvised. She'd begged River Mumma to receive her, only for a minute, a few seconds, so she could be useful. If Alicia had been trusted with a task so spiritually significant, Heaven thought she could at least do that. But all she received was maddening silence.

When Oni had dropped in to retrieve her course reader from her desk, she'd looked at Heaven and said, "You haffi *listen* for her, Heaven. Stop and listen."

Heaven hadn't understood.

"I'll clean this up—" Alicia began to say.

"Nuh fret it," said Oni, shaking her head.

Alicia was sheepish. "'Thank you' feels insufficient for everything that you've done."

"'Thank you' is plenty."

Alicia did her best to keep looking Oni in the eye. "OK. Well, then, thank you," she said. "And your mom too."

"No problem."

"Well, I—"

"Stay here a minute," said Oni.

Alicia hesitated. "I'm on a deadline."

"I'm aware," said Oni. "Heaven filled me in. She and Mars are in the common room. Mi nuh ask yuh fi cease and sekkle, just to sit down for a minute. Looks like you need it," she added.

Alicia laughed—out of either nervousness or relief, she wasn't sure—but she sat back down on the bed.

"How was your journey?"

Alicia contemplated her next words. An unuttered cry swelled in her chest. A cry that turned into a tremble in her voice.

"I was wrong," she said simply. "I was just wrong." Oni's silence prompted her to continue. "I thought this whole thing was happening because River Mumma was punishing me for something, or because I had to rectify a mistake from the past or pay a debt owed by my great-great-great-great-grandmother or something. But it's not debt, it's"—Alicia gestured, as if the movement would help bring out the word—"legacy. It's unfulfilled legacy. Today, for me, is about continuing their work. Mars is . . ."

For a moment, Alicia was no longer in the room; she was seeing it all again, hearing it all again: images of Thomas reappeared in her mind, and they became entwined with the moments throughout the morning when Mars had insisted on leaving.

"My spirit journeyed to the past and I think I saw him there, saw one of his ancestors who just wanted to stay out of everything. I don't know, maybe he's the one with the historical debt, the one who needs to make things right with her. But I don't really know how to do what I'm supposed to do for her. I'm just at a loss, you know?"

Oni didn't say anything at first and only moved from the chair to the bed, sitting next to Alicia and touching her hair, running her fingers down her braids.

"Out there, I heard them singing to you: 'Done baby, done cry, yuh mother gone ah fountain,'" she said.

Alicia nodded.

"It's a lullaby. Actually, my mom sang it to me when I did small."

At that moment, realization sparked within Alicia. Truthfully, she had no recollection of her own mother singing the lullaby to her, but she knew that it'd happened, that she had been simply too young to have a memory of it. And she also knew that Grandma Mabel had sung it to her mother when she was a baby. That was where the familiarity came from when she'd heard it in the courtyard—it was a lullaby that was passed down through her family. It was about comforting a scared child. *A weak child*, Alicia thought. She let out a "hmph." It seemed fitting.

"I asked Mummy what it meant once," said Oni. "She said that it meant the baby should stop crying because her mother was spiritually fulfilled, in touch with the fountain, the boundless source of everything mother and child could ever need. Doesn't sound like weakness to me," said Oni, for the second time responding to Alicia's unspoken thoughts. "Sounds like encouragement."

Alicia could still feel how the words had seemed to nourish her back in the courtyard, how they'd seemed to feed her, how she'd felt strength grow within her, keeping her from falling into Reznikoff's despair. She flexed her hands with the phantom sensation of the ordeal.

"I think you know what to do just fine. It's like that quote about a woman's spirit. I think Maya Angelou said it, mi cyaah remember, but trust. It suits you. You'll be fine."

"I'm glad she dreamed you and led you to me." Alicia paused, considering something. "Or me to you," she said. "When I saw you at Heaven's, it was like you were a beacon or, I don't know, but there was pull, there was a . . . well, you were there."

Oni smiled, amused.

"You said that there was this energy or vibe ting happening," Alicia continued, getting more and more flustered. "And then there was the tarot and the reading. All of that was to open me up to this"—she motioned with both of her hands—"quest. Get my mind open enough to accept it. Right?"

"Something like that," she said. "But we can still hang out after this. I don't have to come into your life just to help you and then leave."

Oni reached over to her desk and took a pen out of her course reader and then lightly grabbed Alicia's other hand.

"Heaven said your phone's mash up." She started writing her number on Alicia's palm. "Old-school ting here," she said. "Text when you reach your deadline."

"Bet."

When Oni had finished, Alicia looked at the number that bedecked her palm. Finally, she stood up from the bed again.

"Walk good, eh?" said Oni.

Alicia smiled. "And seriously, study—that's my bad."

Oni moved back to her desk and opened her course reader with a flourish. Alicia walked to the door, tracing the numbers on her palm like they were a talisman that would bring her good luck.

XVII

When Alicia stepped out of Oni's room, a bunch hangover cures were clustered at the door like an altar of recuperation: a bottle of Gatorade, a bottle of water, and a bottle of Advil, with a note that said: "Drink this—Heaven." She picked up the Gatorade before wandering the halls to find Heaven and Mars; she wasn't hungover but the electrolytes couldn't hurt.

It didn't take long to make it to the common room. There were upholstered armchairs and tufted sofas and antique rugs to match the antique candleholders mounted on the walls. Heaven was lying on one of the chairs, her legs on the armrest, and Mars sat in one next to her. It wasn't until Alicia saw them that she realized she was glad she was no longer privy to their thoughts and emotions or their memories—they had the right to keep anything they wanted to themselves.

"I'm not going to lie, it was a pretty wack altar for a deity. Maybe I offended her," said Heaven. "Or maybe I didn't do it right, but I thought I'd get *something*, like I'm a spiritual person, right? Oni told me to listen, but I *was* listening! Fam, are you even listening to me?"

"My bad. This dude at my IT job asked me to take his night shift tomorrow."

"You know, I didn't realize you had, like, four jobs," said Heaven.

Mars didn't say anything right away. "My brother, he's got big Parisian culinary school plans. Scholarships don't cover every-thing. He needs Paris money."

Alicia headed over to them, her steps making the floorboards creak. Mars looked up from his phone, and when Alicia caught his eye, she saw Thomas in his features the way she saw Joycelyn in her mother's. Alicia thought Mars saw Alice in her and knew she saw Thomas in him, because he was the first to look away, and he kept his eyes on his phone. The affection that he had expressed when she'd woken up emotional and confused was now replaced by a distance he seemed committed to keeping.

Heaven also seemed committed to not letting Alicia know she'd tried to get in contact with River Mumma.

"Great, you're OK, so now we need to talk about what's really important." She paused. "We're internet famous, bredren."

Alicia blinked. "What?"

"That video from this morning is everywhere. Theories are wild, man," said Heaven. "And the patty debate is still going strong, when it's obvious who has the best ones."

She said "Islington" at the same time as Mars, without looking up, said "Bathurst," and the two of them looked at each other, disgusted.

Heaven broke the silence first. "What foolishness is this?"

Mars closed his eyes and assumed the expression of someone who'd been through this argument too many times.

"Bathurst patties are lit," he said. "They're flaky on the outside and warm and juicy on the inside."

Heaven scoffed. "If by 'flaky,' you mean crusty and old, then yeah, you're right—"

"Wow, chill—"

"Islington got that seasoning on lock."

Alicia watched Mars and Heaven argue without really listening to them, simply glad to have something to focus on as she took quiet but deep breaths to keep herself from shuddering again.

"Anyway!" Heaven raised her hands. "How are you, Alicia? Honestly."

She didn't say anything right away—she was picturing the barren river of the past and remembering the bleak vision of the barren rivers of the future, River Mumma's threat echoing in her mind.

"When I was journeying, I saw a time when River Mumma was defied and rivers disappeared, drought came." Alicia swallowed hard, though her voice still came out somewhat choked. "A lot of people died." She looked at Heaven. "One of my ancestors made it right with her." She explained what she'd seen with Alice, the poison, the bloodied cloth, her murder and the murder of others for rebelling. "I think that's why River Mumma chose me for this.

"I know I'm not the only one who has a family history with her, and I may not deserve to be the one she chose, but we *are* very connected."

Heaven nodded, saying nothing; she looked both amazed and confused. "Your spirit went journeying," she said finally. "I can't argue with that."

"We're still right where we were before this, though," said Alicia. "No address, no name, nothing that indicates who has the comb. I'm missing something."

At that, Mars cleared his throat and Alicia turned to him look at him. "OK, so there might be. I'm not sure." He'd stopped typing on his phone but still looked at it, remaining quiet.

"Well?" said Heaven. "Speak, nuh!"

"When I was in the bath . . ." He shook his head like he didn't believe his own words and then looked at Heaven apologetically. "I saw her. River Mumma."

Heaven kept her face neutral, but Alicia sensed her incredulity. Mars still wasn't looking at Alicia, but she could tell from the shift in his tone that he most likely had the same faraway look in his eyes that Oni had in hers when talking about River Mumma—as if the mere mention of her name enchanted him, and his recollection of their encounter would keep him forever ensnared. Alicia could see the way River Mumma had come to him too: rising from the water, bedecked in a crown of cowrie shells, this time with a white tail and white patterns on buttery brown skin. The memory didn't come from Mars—it flashed before her eyes like a particularly short vision and felt like it came from River Mumma herself, showing Alicia the various ties they had to each other.

"I was at a dinner table floating on a river and she just kept whispering 'reggae stylings,' 'reggae stylings' over and over. Her voice became a part of the water somehow. I don't know what it meant; it just felt like it meant *something*." He glanced up at Alicia before lowering his head again once they'd made eye contact.

"I've heard that somewhere before, I swear. Recently too. Like in the past two, three days." Alicia started to pace.

Heaven took out her phone, seemingly desperate to once again prove her usefulness. "I just typed it in—it's a restaurant."

"Yes! My mother sent me an article about it last night," said Alicia. "Something about authentic Caribbean cuisine."

"Yeah, yeah, I got it right here." Heaven began to read out loud: "'Caribbean cuisine is all the rage these days, with chefs and restaurateurs of all backgrounds getting in on the hot new trend. Sidney Roy is one such restaurateur, with her much anticipated bistro Reggae Stylings opening on King West later this month.' "I just wanted to combine sophistication with a food I admire and bring it to customers with elevated palates," said Roy.'"

Heaven stopped reading to pretend to gag.

"'Roy continued, "Authenticity is also really important to me, of course. I even went to the island earlier this year and brought something back to hang on the wall." When pressed to reveal what the object was, Roy just gave a mysterious smile. "All I'll say is that it's shiny." Reggae Stylings has already received some celebrity attention. Its biggest investor is Toronto rapper—'"

"That's the place!" said Alicia. "It's got to be the place. River Mumma said it would be something like that."

Heaven's face lit up. "So you're saying that this is where you have to go next?"

Alicia nodded. "Finally, something to work with."

"I'm glad I could help," said Mars. "I'ma head out now—" He stood up, but before he could even take a step, Alicia spoke.

"I don't think so. You're a part of this."

Her tone wasn't forceful but it was authoritative, and Alicia could tell that it surprised Mars. But she couldn't let him go.

"Leish"—Mars said her name like a plea—"I said from the jump that I was not getting involved in this."

"It's too late for that," she said.

Mars scratched his head. "Since when do you care if I come along or not? Two hours ago, you were dead telling Heaven to fuck off. And now it's 'us' and 'we're doing this together'?"

"Before, I looked at this like it was some kind of obligation, but it's not—it's an opportunity to do something."

"I'm glad you saw the light and all that, but my situation is still the same. Don't look at me like that," he said. "I thanked Oni for everything she did, but now I gotta do me. Like, I'm sorry about what's happening—or what's going to happen or might happen—but I haven't been to Jamaica since I was ten. That's, what, sixteen years?"

Alicia shook her head. "You are literally named after Marcus Garvey, one of Jamaica's national heroes. Your parents clearly wanted you to have a connection."

Heaven looked up from her phone. "*That's* why your name is Marcus?"

"A connection?" said Mars. "I didn't grow up the way you two did, OK? No cousins or aunts or grandparents or neighbours or whatever told me stories about duppies. I didn't go there every summer. I was born here, like—"

"Chattin' bare shit," said Heaven, irritated. "Are you actually saying that because you're a Toronto mans, you have no stake in this?"

He shrugged. "I don't know. Maybe."

"If that were true, why did River Mumma dream you about the restaurant and not me?" Alicia asked.

"Or me, for that matter?" said Heaven.

"I don't know. I don't care." He tried to move past Alicia toward the exit, but she stood in his way.

"That wasn't the only thing you saw or heard, Mars. I know you saw me. That's why you can't even look at me. I know you saw through Thomas's eyes. It all makes sense. Why would you tell me what your name meant? You told me that on the first shift we ever worked together. Why am I the only one who gets to call you

Marcus? You're the only one who calls me Leish. It's because we've been connected from *time*. You're supposed to be here because of what wasn't done back then. Thomas chose not to help, and OK, he did what he thought he needed to so he could survive, fine, but . . ."

Mars held up his hand. "I nearly fucking died because of this shit."

"I nearly died twice. A ghost sucked out my freaking life force." Alicia touched her throat with an unsteady hand. "I can still feel how that felt."

"And that's fucked up, but I plan on living, Alicia. This is your quest, your duty, your problem. Why would I continue to put myself in danger for something that has nothing to do with me? 'Where is your self-preservation?' Remember when you asked that? Well, I'm showing you mine."

"This isn't just about me, fam. OK, you want to forget about ancestral ties—let's do that for a minute and focus on now. No, seriously," she said, standing in front of Mars, continuing to block his way. "Can I talk to you for a second? Like legit. What's your favourite spot to eat at?"

He sighed. "You know this."

"I know I know this."

"Albert's."

"Albert's what?"

"Albert's Real Jamaican Foods, OK?"

"And what's the song you listen to non-stop when we clean up the store?"

Mars rolled his eyes to Heaven, but she shook her head and encouraged him to respond. "Answer, nuh."

"'Ting-A-Ling.'"

"Classic," said Heaven.

"Yes, thank you, Heaven," said Mars, irritated.

Alicia gesticulated as if she'd made her point, and Mars shook his head. "That has nothing—I mean, it's—let me explain, I—" He opened and closed his hands. "It's different."

"Bredren, how?" asked Heaven. "Half the things you say, half the things you like have Jamaican roots."

"Just 'low me, man," Mars said.

"Fuck that. You are connected," said Alicia. "And you know it. You got off the bus."

"What does the bus—?"

"You ran after me, and you literally didn't have to. You could've just been like, 'Alicia's trippin'. I'll text her later to see if she's good. Let me mop these floors and get these coins.' Even the fact that you're here now when you could've left after you were cured."

"What's your point, Leish?" Mars closed his eyes. "Alicia."

She took a deep breath and spoke in a measured tone. "My point is you already offered me your axe, so just . . . *offer* me your fucking axe."

Mars looked at Alicia properly, and she allowed him to see the extent of the emotions that threatened to leave her numb: the fear about the comb, the sorrow about the past, the beginnings of a feeling she couldn't quite pinpoint. It was not unpleasant but had the potential to overwhelm. She let him see it all.

In turn, he lowered his eyes. "OK, but it's a sword, though."

Heaven snorted and muttered under her breath, "Mans always want to be Aragorn."

"Broke-ass Aragorn," said Mars. "You're going to have to spot me, Heaven."

"I already said I would."

Alicia held out her hand for him to take and he did.

XVIII

After they'd figured out that Sidney Roy had the comb, Heaven suggested they do a bit of recon. They found her Instagram reel, which played a series of photos to a Taylor Swift song about strength and perseverance. The first photo was of Reggae Stylings on fire, the second of the restaurant's burnt and blackened skeleton. (Mars laughed in disbelief. "It burned down? Are you sure this deity isn't just fucking with us?") The third photo was of a flood in what looked to be Sidney's condo unit—she'd captioned that photo, explaining that because the water could have electrocuted her, she wasn't allowed back inside and had to watch her belongings get destroyed.

Mars felt bad. "That's a lot of bad luck in a week."

The reel continued with a picture of the Fairmont Royal York and then moved on to a photo of an old-fashioned elevator that said "Fairmont Gold 19th Floor Express." The fifth image, of a reception area, was captioned "Private check-in." And a fairly large and luxurious hotel room appeared as the final image.

Alicia didn't share Mars's sympathy. "I think she's doing OK. What was her latest post?"

Sidney had uploaded a photo of a nook with a blue armchair at a polished black desk looking out to the city below. On the desk were her laptop and some papers. Beneath the photo were the hashtags #goldlounge, #beastmode, #strength.

"If the comb burned with the fire—"

"We don't know that for sure, Heaven." Alicia refused to believe that River Mumma had dreamed Mars only for the information conveyed to be useless. "We'll find Sidney and ask about it. Looks like she's on Live," she said. "Check it out. Might see where she is."

Sidney looked severely different from the photo Alicia had seen in the article her mother had sent the night before. Now Sidney had a drawn, emaciated face and sagged skin beneath her eyes. She was swathed in a white robe and sitting against an upholstered cream headboard.

"And I don't usually do this, but it's just hard because instead of focusing on everything that I've been through in the past few days, they're focusing on bullshit and it's just—" She shook her head, her face flushed red. "I have no home, no business. I can't even sleep to get away from all the negativity because I've been having these *horrible* nightmares."

For a second, fear seeped into Sidney's expression, as if she were reliving the terror of her dreams, which Alicia knew in her gut were River Mumma's doing, much like the restaurant fire and the flood.

"I'm coming undone, you know? And then this article comes out about how my restaurant would've been 'appropriative'? It's fucked up." Her voice grew shrill and thick. "Anyone who knows me knows I'm not a bad person. I wasn't trying to *appropriate* a culture. I just wanted to share with a certain clientele something I find so interesting, so fun, so exotic. What's so wrong about that?

Like, I can't believe I'm even talking about this now when I'm literally homeless."

Comments popped up at the bottom of the video:

You are literally at a 5 star hotel.

Certain clientele = 2520.

Everyone's so sensitive these days.

It's literally just food! Food is meant to be shared!

You're doing amazing, sweetie!

We're still saying exotic?

"But I'm just going to do my best, get dressed, get into beast mode, and come up with the next thing, because life keeps going, right?"

Sidney stopped streaming, and Alicia, Mars, and Heaven agreed to make their way to the hotel to try to find her. But first, Heaven asked if she could buy a new pair of boots.

"We know where we're going now and it's not even noon yet. This wouldn't even be a detour, it'd be an errand," she said. "I'd just go to the H&M by Yonge. It shouldn't take more than ten minutes. Please? Because I smell like barf and I *cannot* live like this anymore. I refuse."

They said their final goodbyes to Oni and then left the UC dorm, heading up to Bloor Street and walking east toward Yonge Street. Heaven put several different alarms on her phone to mark the rest of their journey. She walked slowly, absorbed with her phone, typing in her Notes, calculating the amount of time they'd spend at each place so she could get a handle on the deadline. Alicia and Mars walked quickly, partly because of the cold, which they now felt more keenly because of their lack of duppy sickness. They passed by the skinny, leafless trees decorated from trunk to branches with holiday lights that were off during the day but a golden orange at night, making Bloor look like a street illuminated by two rows of torches in the dark.

Her mind still turning over Oni's words, Alicia hit Mars lightly on the chest with the back of her hand. "Let me check something on your phone."

He hesitated but dug into his pocket nonetheless and passed his cell to her after unlocking the screen.

"I didn't even have to beg you for it," said Alicia.

Mars shrugged. "Part of the team now, right? A couple hundred years later." He didn't say anything else. Alicia watched him retreat briefly into himself, distant yet focused, and wondered if he was sifting through the new-found memories that they both shared, if he was thinking about Thomas.

She laughed, shaking her head. "Nothing is loading."

Mars blinked. "Oh, my fault." He took the phone and turned the mobile data on, and when he passed it back to Alicia, she googled the words "Maya Angelou," "quote," and "spirit," which led her to a Goodreads page:

A woman in harmony with her spirit is like a river flowing. She goes where she will without pretense and arrives at her destination prepared to be herself and only herself.

—Maya Angelou

The quote inspired a yearning in Alicia that she didn't know how to navigate. She reread it multiple times, and each time she did, she willed the words to resonate with her, to see why Oni would say she reminded her of this sentiment. But that understanding escaped her despite how much she wanted to achieve it. She had woken up from her memories with a clarity and a humility that put her current circumstances into perspective, transforming an obligation into a quest, but harmony was an accomplishment that seemed unattainable.

It wasn't until her chin was wet that Alicia realized she was crying. She quickly wiped her face and was grateful to Mars for pretending not to notice when she handed him back his phone. The three of them crossed the street, passing the Gothic Revival church with the three arched doors on the corner of Avenue Road, and continued on Bloor. As they neared a white-and-black-accented Louis Vuitton store, a woman walked out of the entrance, coming face to face with them. Alicia stopped where she stood. It was as if all the air in her body had been snuffed out. Heaven and Mars didn't ask about her reaction because they too were stunned.

"I want to be her," Heaven whispered to no one in particular. "Who is she?"

The woman was magnificent. The bottom half of her was dark green: dark green miniskirt, dark green fishnet stockings, dark green thigh-high boots with skinny heels. Her royal-blue box braids were bright against the shaggy black jacket she didn't wear but let hang off her shoulders, nowhere near covering her sheer black blouse, which exposed a black bra. The woman carried various coloured shopping bags, each hue representing a different designer brand from Tiffany blue to Cartier red—the entirety of Yorkville was gripped delicately in her hands.

River Mumma.

Besides Oni's dream, Alicia never knew River Mumma to don legs and walk among humans, but then she remembered that one version of the legend said once a year, she could walk the land, though that story specified she did so only on a moonlit night. Then again, no retelling of the Rolling Calf mentioned its ability to shoot fire from its nostrils.

In an instant, a crowd gathered around River Mumma, even though there'd been hardly anyone on the sidewalk moments before. Phones were stretched high above heads as everyone snapped photos and whispered their burning desire to take selfies with this sure-to-be celebrity, though no one had a name for who they thought River Mumma was. No one approached her or tightened around her or even shouted anything. The circle of people stayed several feet away, giving River Mumma considerable space; she inspired an awestruck intimidation in the adoring crowd, and all they could do was admire from a relative distance. All except Alicia.

She drifted closer to River Mumma in a sort of daze, and the people even parted for her, as though they knew without knowing anything at all that River Mumma wanted her in her proximity. When Alicia was a few feet away from her, she felt a deference that was now weighted by personal history.

"Who do they think you are?" said Alicia.

River Mumma shrugged coyly. "Different for different people. A dancehall queen. An influencer. An athlete. They all have their ideas, but they all think I'm a somebody. It's the only way they can understand why they take to me so."

Alicia glanced at the bags clutched in River Mumma's jewelled yellow-black-and-green fingernails. "You seem to be having fun."

"Never mind my fun, you have the comb?"

"I know you know that I don't." Alicia heard the irritation in her voice, but when she tried to quell it, the desperation in her tone just became more apparent. "I still don't understand this. You made her restaurant burn down and drove her from her home. Couldn't you just *take* the comb?"

"Consequences for crossing me follow anyone anywhere—even sleep can't protect you—but that doesn't mean that I know where you are."

"Then why are you only giving me until sundown? I have just over four hours."

"That's plenty of time."

"Not in this city," said Alicia. "Seriously, why such an impossible deadline?"

"Deadlines are all you know. You don't forgive yourself when you don't meet the deadlines you think you should, even if you are the only one setting these deadlines, nuh true?"

Alicia furrowed her brow. "So it's not real? If I'm late, you won't leave?"

"I never said that, enuh."

"Of course," said Alicia, frustrated that she'd momentarily thought she would get something remotely close to a straight answer. The frustration made her bold. "And you also never said why you're punishing so many people for one person's ignorance."

River Mumma looked at her sharply, and Alicia instinctively shrank into herself.

"I have felt the world change, understand? Felt toxicity seep into my veins as companies foreign to my land, to my waters, spring up here, spring up there, mining and fouling, poisoning my children for red gold."

With each word River Mumma spoke, Alicia could hear a fury that seemed somehow ancient and yet freshly felt.

"I saw how the material started obscuring me, and I saw how knowledge of me and my ways was twisted for profit. You know what them say? They say that if you catch my spirit in a stone and you put the stone inna water, the water will have 'curative power.' Ah nuh lie they tell. You did drink from my water and it helped heal you, helped bring yuh home, helped yuh find your roots. But false people like fi pretend that any old rock is a mermaid rock, and a false mermaid rock they like fi sell or like fi use to get money. Or they take my comb. They only think of me as story and no longer respect tradition. I am *tired*."

And Alicia felt it. Her body was suddenly leaden with a fraction of the exhaustion River Mumma felt, but before it became unbearable, she was released from its heaviness.

"So you took a vacation." Alicia nodded, gasping slightly. "Makes sense."

"This is not a vacation," said River Mumma, lifting her bags slightly. "Mi cyaah be curious fi experience mi competition? Experience what people would rather do than honour me?"

"So what's it like for you?"

River Mumma looked from Alicia to the throng of people around them, scanning each person again, but this time her eyes had a shrewdness to them rather than a charismatic sparkle.

"Mi nuh care for it," she said simply.

She dropped the bags to the sidewalk and gestured toward them, as if silently telling the crowd "Have at it!" before leaving them there, the snow soiling the paper bottoms. River Mumma walked toward the people, who wordlessly parted to make a path for her as she sashayed away with ease, despite her thin heels and the icy ground. There was a beat in which everyone looked at each other, trying to process what had just happened, and then chaos erupted. People started running toward the bags, pushing and shoving and knocking against each other, yelling out which label they had dibs on.

Alicia didn't think and just picked up the bag closest to her and walked away swiftly, with Heaven and Mars keeping pace.

XIX

Mars and Alicia sat on a green bench in Bloor subway station while Heaven walked along the edges of a green diamond pattern on the platform in new boots. Bloor Station had white and mint-green walls, and fluted steel pillars that matched the corrugated ceiling.

Alicia stared up at the black information screen that had the news on mute (a segment on the "viral alien video sensation" was currently playing). At the bottom of the screen, there was a black bar with the number of the subway line and the minutes they had to wait for the next train, which had gone from five to seven to ten and back to five.

"I can't believe I didn't recognize her," said Heaven for what had to be the tenth time.

"How would you recognize someone you've never even seen?" said Mars. "I didn't even recognize her and I'd just seen her in my dream or vision or hallucination or whatever it was, because she looked like a whole-ass different person."

"I knew that altar pissed her off," said Heaven.

Mars threw his hands up in the air, fed up with trying to talk her down.

"Well, I'm sorry," said Heaven. "But this just isn't how I thought it would go if I ever met her. I don't know what I expected, but it wasn't this."

"I think it went well," said Mars, shrugging. "She left us gifts. Mad expensive gifts."

"Will you keep your voice *down*?" said Heaven, panicked. "We've got, like"—she lowered her voice—"at least ten grand in this bag." She gestured at her shoulder bag, which contained River Mumma's purchases of a sapphire ring, a rose gold bracelet, and a tassel necklace of pearls. "That's my tuition plus books. We've got my *tuition* in this bag."

"Your tuition plus salt," said Mars. "Can't forget the salt. Or the switchblade."

When Heaven stored her old boots in a locker at the back of a convenience store, they'd picked up the salt and the knife like they were picking up weapons for war. Duppies didn't respond well to either item, and they wanted to be prepared in case of another encounter.

Alicia switched her attention from the clock to the bag hanging off Heaven's shoulder. She wondered if she had been wrong for snatching up the Tiffany bag in the first place. The act was instinctual; she saw the crowd about to rush, and she just picked up the nearest bag and walked away. Maybe a bigger person would've walked away empty-handed. It felt like a test now—a test that Alicia had failed.

"What would I even do with a pearl necklace?" she said out loud.

"So that's what you're taking?" said Heaven.

"Pawn that shit," said Mars. "That's what I'm doing with mine. Always wanted to go to Oliver's." He started singing the song from the Cashman commercials, and Heaven joined in.

"What right does she have?" said Alicia, throwing up her hands.

Heaven glanced at Mars, who slightly shook his head. "Leish, we don't know what you're on about."

Alicia stood up and pointed at Heaven's bag. "I don't know what it means that I took this," she said. "I don't know what it says about me. I don't know *if* it's supposed to say anything about me." She started pacing a short length of the platform. "She was carrying on, yuh know, gwaanin', talking about money and humans losing our way or whatever, but like, she gets offerings, enuh?"

"True," said Mars.

"She likes jewellery and perfume, so why isn't she materialistic and we are? . . . I am? Am I not supposed to want material things? Am I a bad person if I want a job and I want to make money and just, I don't know, *live* in this society that requires me to have these things just to operate?"

Alicia was speaking so quickly she started hyperventilating. Heaven took her by the arms and held her gaze until her breathing calmed.

"Is that what she told you?" she asked after a moment. "Like word for word, that's what she said?"

Alicia sighed. "No, that's not exactly what she said; I just want to know if that's what she meant. If I'm doing this whole thing wrong, if there's some sort of epiphany I'm supposed to be having by now that I'm not having, because then I would just make it happen."

"Yeah, I don't think an epiphany is something you can force, sis," said Heaven.

"She's just so hard to read. Her moods shift in a second. Even the stories about her are the exact same and also completely contradictory. The first time we met, she literally drowned me, but it's also how I saw my ancestors. I don't know, it's all mix up, mix up."

"That's a god thing, though," said Mars. "Or deity, whatever. They're usually mercurial."

"'Usually mercurial'?" Alicia repeated. "What, like you have experience?"

"I do now," said Mars with a grin. "Where's the train? We've been waiting here for a minute still."

"There's really no way to tell when it's coming," said Heaven. "The train is Godot."

"I hope not—that bitch never showed up," said Mars.

Just then, Heaven's noon alarm went off, officially giving them four hours to complete the mission, and they all stilled with the knowledge, looking at Heaven's phone like it was a bomb. She turned off the alarm.

"Next one is at one," she said quietly.

"We're almost there." Mars sounded like he was trying to be hopeful but bailed halfway through the attempt.

"Well, the good thing is, we can go to the eighteenth floor without key cards or anything," said Heaven. "Website said an elevator will take you straight up to the private check-in. Lounge is on the same floor. It should actually be pretty easy to get to Sidney."

"All right, bet," said Mars.

The train arrived ten minutes later—Heaven timed it—and started crawling toward their stop, Union Station, moving a few paces before braking, the torturous inching forward because of "train traffic."

Heaven clutched her shoulder bag. Mars shook his head.

"You're being mad bait," he'd said.

"Did I ask you anything?"

Alicia shifted between bouncing her leg and changing her seat and swinging around the pole. Now that they were close to finding the comb, she was jittery with the type of restlessness that came with being so close and yet so far from finishing something. The anxiety spread through her chest like branches. And the train was taking long. Too long.

When she sat down again, Mars sat next to her.

"Can I ask a question? What's going to happen when you actually get the comb? How are you giving it back to River Mumma?"

Alicia didn't respond. It wasn't like the question hadn't occurred to her, but she kept pushing it off as a "next step" issue; she still had to solve the problem of this step, which was getting the actual comb.

"It's a good question," said Heaven. "The stories say that you have to return the comb to the place that you found it, and we're not getting to Jamaica by four o'clock, so . . ."

"Well, she isn't even there, she's here," said Alicia.

"But *where* is she here?" Mars asked. "Like, is shorty up in a hotel? Did she give you a contact number?"

Alicia narrowed her eyes in disbelief. "Did you just refer to an actual deity as 'shorty'?"

"Deity or not, she's a criss ting still," he said. "Never seen a woman that beautiful in my life."

"*Anyway,*" said Alicia, "we can have this conversation once we actually have the comb."

"You were just with her and you didn't think to ask about it?" said Heaven.

"Even if I did ask, she doesn't give direct answers," said Alicia. "Sometimes she doesn't give any at all."

Heaven shrugged. "I'll take your word for it."

Alicia spent the rest of the ride staring at Heaven's phone, watching in agony as the digits on the clock changed, taking away more and more time. The train ride should have been fifteen minutes at most but took twice the time. When they walked out of Union Station, they saw that it had started to snow, and Alicia and Heaven complained about not being properly dressed.

Mars shook his head. "Your fault. I know you two like fi gwaan with your Jamrock pride like you're real yaad mans, but you're Canadians and it's winter, you should know better."

"Did you forget I was dragged into a whole-ass river last night? In my winter coat?"

"And I didn't exactly wake up knowing I'd be going on a quest today, Mars."

"Excuses," he said.

They crossed the street to the hotel. Alicia had never thought the Royal York looked real, she thought it looked like one of those architectural models or an expensive collector's item maintained by the kind of wealthy men who built ships in bottles. It was a châteauesque hotel that loomed over the city, a limestone building of peaked green roofs and dormers and pointed-arch windows, a historic site that overshadowed the modern skyscrapers around it. The large flags mounted above the entrance billowed in the wind, but Alicia's eyes went to the topmost roof, where a neon sign across the front spelled "Fairmont Royal York" in cursive. Even though night hadn't fallen yet, the sign was switched on, radiating a red light in the dark grey sky.

She'd only ever stayed at the hotel once. In high school, she'd joined the prom committee and suggested the Fairmont as a venue. When the budget wouldn't allow for it, her mother eased her disappointment by booking her a room as a graduation present; she'd spent the two nights before frosh week in luxury, with room service, a king bed, and a view of the waterfront.

They crossed the street and pushed through one of the revolving doors, walking up the steps to the main lobby.

"I feel like I've walked onto a Baz Luhrmann set," said Heaven.

Alicia knew she was thinking of *Gatsby*. The lobby screamed art deco—the geometric sconces and chandeliers, the ornamental ceiling, the mosaic flooring, the jewel-toned furniture, even the golden-hued lighting made everything seem gilded and glam. Wreaths and garlands decorated the mezzanine above, and a brightly lit Christmas tree stood on a dais at one end of the entrance hall. Heaven looked around like she was decorating for her future house.

People milled around in the bar by the clock tower or at the check-in, or they sat on the various benches and armchairs. But there weren't as many as Alicia expected for December. The lobby was fairly empty, so she didn't know why she heard chatter and laughing as if there were hundreds of guests. The clinking of ice in glasses. The shuffling of chairs, of feet. The music changed too. Instead of Jefferson Airplane, Grace Slick crooning about Red Queen from the bar, Alicia heard pianos and saxophones, trumpets and drums, loud like the band was playing right in front of her. She looked around, dread making her stomach squirm. Nothing she heard matched what she saw.

Until the room changed.

Crystal chandeliers and ceiling drapery, marble pillars and round and square tables beneath white tablecloths. Alicia found herself walking through an event hall full of people who weren't dressed for this time of day, or this time of year, or this year at all. The band was on a stage at the far end of the room. Women in evening gowns, satin or fringed, and men in black tuxes were together on the dance floor doing the foxtrot. Waiters in bowties glided through the maze of tables, holding trays of drinks and tending to those who'd stayed seated. Alicia ambled through the spectral vision like she was the one who was a ghost, incongruous though invisible until she reached the centre of the room.

The laughter and the music stopped without warning. The silence fell hard, and Alicia started to panic. Every single person in the ballroom turned sharply toward her, the quick movement in perfect unison. Everyone focused on her, their faces blank, their eyes glowing red, bringing back the memory of the Rolling Calf. Alicia's hand flew to her chest.

"Leish, what are you doing in here? Elevators are that way."

She turned and saw Mars behind her. Heaven looked nervous. She didn't realize she'd left the lobby and had walked into the Imperial Room, which now had no one in it except for them.

Heaven touched her shoulder. "Should we be worried?"

Alicia looked around the hall and thought of Oni, how she protected herself from the history of University College with eggshells, a precaution to keep unwanted spirits at bay. The Fairmont was nearly a century old. Alicia was bound to run into some history that haunted it, and she had to get out before its ghosts attacked her.

"We should be quick."

XX

The elevators weren't too far away, and gold lettering above the first one indicated that it was an express to the floor they needed to go to. Mars pressed the button. They didn't have to wait. The door opened right away, revealing a group of people in suits and tulle dresses with white gloves and gold confetti in their hair and champagne flutes in their hands. Alicia knew right away it was another spectre, another glimpse into the past; this time, it looked like the 1950s. She closed her eyes, and when she opened them, the people were mangled corpses crushed on top of each other, their blood splattered all over the elevator walls, pooled on the floor around their disfigured bodies. She gasped, but before she could do anything else, they were all gone, replaced by Heaven and Mars standing in the cab.

"Coming?" said Mars.

She joined them in the elevator after a moment's hesitation. Heaven pressed the button for the eighteenth floor.

"I'm seeing things. Not right now," said Alicia as she looked around at the wood-panelled walls with geometric designs along the brass trim. "But"—she tuned in to the unease she felt—"be prepared for the potential of some bullshit."

"If this is another Reznikoff situation, should you just wait outside?" said Heaven. "Mars and I can talk to Sidney alone. We've got this."

"We don't know it's another Reznikoff situation," said Alicia. "But even if it is, waiting outside wouldn't matter; whatever is in here would just draw me inside the way Reznikoff did."

"Nothing's happened yet, so let's not think about that," said Mars. "Let's just think about how we're going to broach the subject with Sidney."

"If we find her," said Heaven.

"Weren't you the one who told me to stay positive?" said Mars.

The elevator stopped and the doors opened to a blue-and-white carpeted hallway with white chairs. No one was at reception, and Alicia, Heaven, and Mars walked past two white marble desks into a lounge that had the same velvet and leather jewel-toned furniture as the lobby, a marble fireplace in the middle of the room, and large windows that looked out to Toronto's many condos.

"Well, that was easy," said Heaven beneath her breath.

"Yeah, barely an inconvenience," said Mars.

No one seemed to be in the lounge, but Alicia could hear laughter, echoes of unseen children squealing with excitement, their feet pitter-pattering across the floor. She let out a deep breath, channelling her focus on finding the living and ignoring the racket of the dead.

They found Sidney in the same nook she'd taken a photo of the night before. She had a messy bun and was aggressively tapping the power button of her laptop, alternating between cursing beneath her breath and begging the computer to turn on.

"Sidney, right?"

She looked up from her laptop, and Alicia thought she looked even more worn in person. River Mumma had definitely made sure she felt her wrath.

"I'm Alicia, this is Heaven, that's Mars."

Sidney looked from Alicia to Heaven to Mars, her expression wary. "OK . . ."

"Now that we're all introduced, we can get right to it." Alicia explained everything as concisely and matter-of-factly as possible. "You took a comb on your last visit to Jamaica, and we need it back. It'll be in your interest to give it back because everything that's happening to you, the fire, the flood, the nightmares"—she gestured to the laptop—"your computer, it's because of that comb."

"Is that a threat?" said Sidney.

Alicia raised her eyebrows. "I don't see how. Can you make someone have nightmares?"

Sidney shifted in her seat. "I'm sorry, who are you?"

Heaven answered this time. "People who want the comb back."

"It didn't burn in the fire, right?" said Mars.

"I don't know how you know about the comb, but I'm not going to give you something that's clearly valuable just because you ask for it."

"We don't want it for us," said Mars. "We want it for the rightful owner."

"What rightful owner? I found it on a rock."

"That logic's faulty," said Heaven. "If you forget your phone on this table, is the phone no longer yours if another person comes by and takes it?"

Sidney opened her mouth, searching for a retort, and when she couldn't find one, she narrowed her eyes. Alicia's skin started to prickle with the anticipation of another journey. She needed answers now.

"Look, you took something that didn't belong to you for a restaurant you had no business starting," said Alicia firmly.

Sidney put her hand over her eyes. "Not this again."

Mars hit Alicia lightly across her shoulder. "Really, Leish?"

She rolled her eyes. "You're so predictable, Mars."

"What? Do I care that she wanted to open a restaurant? No. She says that she appreciates the food, and that's good enough for me. I'm all about intercultural, global sharing—that can gwaan in my book. But that's not the point. We're just here for the comb, not for you to get sanctimonious."

Sidney spoke directly to Mars. "Thank you. I do have to say, I'm feeling a little attacked right now."

"Relax," he said, putting up his hand.

Alicia leaned forward. "I'm just trying to explain that you're dealing with consequences."

Sidney shook her head, unwilling to hear any more. "I don't know what this is, but it's time for you to—"

"Your nightmares are about a mermaid," said Alicia. "Always about a mermaid. You've been having them for weeks. They're relentless because she's relentless."

Sidney looked like her heart had skipped a beat. Her eyes started to well with tears. "How do you know—?"

"Because she came to me last night demanding I get her comb back, and we have . . ." Alicia turned to Heaven.

"Three hours and fifteen minutes to get it," said Heaven. "She's not going to stop terrorizing you until you give it back."

"I don't have it," said Sidney finally. "I gave it away."

"Bless, it didn't burn," said Mars.

Alicia felt both relieved and annoyed. On the one hand, the comb hadn't melted in the fire, but on the other, there was yet another hurdle in the way of getting it.

"You gave away a solid-gold comb?" said Heaven.

"My investor was really taken with it. I gave it to him as a gift."

Alicia remembered that the article about Reggae Stylings mentioned that Sidney had a celebrity investor, and her stomach dropped. "You're not telling us that you gave it to him?"

Mars caught on right away. "Raas." He threw his head back and closed his eyes in disbelief.

"Get it back," said Heaven desperately. "If she doesn't get the comb back, there will be greater consequences that affect more than just you—they will affect thousands of people. You can't even begin to understand what and who you have crossed."

"I don't know what to tell you. The comb isn't mine anymore. If it's that important, I'm sure you'll find a way to get it back. Now, I have to get back to what I was doing, which was *trying* to prepare documents for an arson investigation. We all have problems."

Sidney turned back to her laptop, but Alicia couldn't speak. A journey was coming, she could feel it, like a gravitational pull to the unseen.

Heaven was talking, but she sounded far away. "Can you give us his number or his manager's number? Anyone we can get in contact with?"

"Look, I work in IT," said Mars. "I can help you with your laptop if you just—"

Their voices disappeared altogether, and Alicia was no longer in the lounge. She was pulled through a white space until she reached the source of her dread—a towering tree with buttress roots long and thick, snaking outward from a straight trunk the width of a small car, out of which sprouted massive branches that twisted in every direction, bearing fruit enveloped in cottony clouds and oval-shaped leaves.

Hung on one of the branches was something odd and foul-smelling that Alicia couldn't make out at first but soon, to her horror, discovered to be wrinkly skin the length of a human body. There was a duppy that could do that—shed its skin. In the day, it masqueraded as an old woman, and at night, it hung the skin on a tree and turned into a ball of fire, soaring through parishes, sucking the blood of children, before returning to its resting place in the roots of a cotton tree with all the other duppies. Ol Higue, that was what it was called.

Winston had told her about this legendary duppy when she wouldn't go to bed on a visit to Jamaica. "Ol Higue is what comes for rude pickney who nuh listen!"

Ol Higue had chosen this tree to rest in, which meant—

A slit opened to reveal a fire burning in the hollow trunk, red flames licking the sapwood, wild and yet contained within the tree, descending to the roots—a malevolent blaze that Alicia wanted to pull back from, but she hadn't seen what she was supposed to and drew closer. Red eyes appeared from within the fire, the same red eyes of the guests in the Imperial Room, the same red eyes that had bored into her as the Rolling Calf charged at her. They transformed into soulless green eyes she also recognized, green eyes that made her tense, made her conjure up every vision she'd had before now. Then they returned to the menacing red and she was struck with a cold epiphany that brought her back to the present.

She bent over, hands on her knees, breathing rapidly. Heaven was in the middle of arguing with Sidney but quickly stopped and leaned over Alicia, rubbing her back.

"What's going on? Where did you go?" she whispered.

"I saw a cotton tree and I saw the Rolling Calf," she said. "It's him."

Sidney looked at her like she was dangerous, and Heaven and Mars guided Alicia away from her to a corner of the room.

"What do you mean?" said Heaven.

"Alice killed her slave master, right? The Rolling Calf is his spirit. That's why it's after us—it doesn't want us to get the comb back, and I think it's going to get other duppies, other ghosts to come after us. Rolling Calves are particularly evil, right? I think it could do that."

A realization dawned on Heaven. "And you've been seeing things here. There are ghosts here."

Mars started picking up on what they weren't saying. "So that means—"

"That means we need to get the fuck out of Dodge," said Alicia.

"What about—?" Mars pushed his mouth out toward Sidney, who had gone back to trying to turn on her laptop.

"She's not going to help us. We'll have to figure it out."

They left the lounge, saying nothing else to Sidney, and waited for the elevator in the hallway. As they stepped through the doors, Alicia mulled over everything that had just happened. She knew they wanted to formulate some sort of game plan, but they'd have to wait until they left the hotel, when the threat wasn't so high.

Suddenly, the elevator plummeted down in free fall. Heaven stumbled backward and Mars swore, slamming his hand against the wall to brace himself. Alicia hurtled toward the button panel, pushing the red emergency button to no avail. She started smashing other buttons on the panel, but none of them lit up.

The elevator jerked to an unceremonious stop, making Alicia and Heaven collide into Mars, pushing him face first into the wall. The door clanged open and they all toppled out onto the eighth floor, falling onto a lavish Victorian rug. Alicia hit her head on a

lacquered table that displayed a potted plant, and Mars acciden-
tally elbowed Heaven in the face.

"Fuck!"

"Shit, my bad," said Mars. "You OK?"

"I'm good. But, Alicia, you're bleeding."

She stood up, gingerly touching her head. "I'm fi—"

Suddenly, all the elevators dinged open at the same time, and a
high-pitched drone sounded as the doors opened and closed like
they were jammed. Before anyone could react, the power went out,
swallowing the entire hallway in unnatural darkness. The exit
signs illuminated the hallway in flickers of red light, the ruddy
glow briefly exposing their expressions of dread and panic before
the shadows obscured their faces again, like quick snapshots.

In a flicker, a silhouette emerged, making them all jump. It was
a grey-haired man with a gnarled face wearing a purple waistcoat.
A ghost. Alicia thought its eyes were red, but it disappeared before
she could be sure. Mars and Heaven stayed still, tensed and alert,
and Alicia tried to make out as much as she could in the brief red
glow produced by the exit signs, and then—

The vase on the table hurtled toward them. Everyone ducked.
As Alicia stood up again, the table came flying at them next,
breaking apart when it landed on the floor. In the brief light, Alicia
could make out the ghost seizing an armchair at the other end of
the hallway, and they all ran the opposite way, the chair smashing
into the wall just behind them.

Metallic clicks sounded throughout the hall; dozens of door-
handles turned up and down as guests tried and failed to get out of
their rooms. Thuds followed as futile attempts were made to ram
down the doors. Alicia could also make out muffled yells for assistance. The same laughter she'd heard in the lounge rang throughout

the hall, and the echoes of pitter-pattering feet trailed their running footsteps. Alicia, Mars, and Heaven were nearly at the stair exit when they skidded to a stop. Mars and Heaven looked behind them.

"What is it?"

Three children—two boys, one girl—had materialized in front of Alicia, the boys in pinstriped pyjamas, the girl in a pink nightie. All of them had red eyes and small smiles that warped their faces into eerie expressions. They started laughing—terrible high-pitched giggles that conjured an image of hyenas circling, cornering her—and Alicia took a few steps back.

"Nope," she said, shaking her head, but the door to the stairwell burst open and she was thrown forward, her chin cracking on the ground, as Mars and Heaven were flung backward.

Abruptly, she felt a grip on her ankle, yanking her toward the doorway. The ghostly children grasped her feet and dragged her into the stairwell, speedily pulling her up the stairs. She cried out and watched as Heaven screamed, running after her with Mars.

The stairwell was dark, but Alicia stretched out her hands anyway, reaching for Mars, who threw himself forward to hold on to her. Their fingers touched briefly before Alicia was dragged beyond his reach. Another door was flung open and the children tugged her down another dark hallway. Heaven and Mars followed, calling out to her. Alicia could hear more slamming and thuds as guests on this floor also tried to force their doors open. She turned her body in an attempt to flip on her back so she could at least try to use her hands to free herself.

An overhead light crashed to the floor, narrowly missing her and landing in front of Mars and Heaven. They sped up as another light fell, and another. Heaven kept screaming Alicia's name, and Alicia screamed back until her voice was devoured by silence. The unlit hallway still in view, the cotton tree returned to her vision, its trunk splitting open, folding outward like a book. The fire inside streamed down the thick roots, the flames taking the shape of hands crawling toward her, those red-then-green-then-red eyes looking out from within, and Alicia knew that it was coming for her spirit.

Another door opened. Up another stairwell, lit only by a yellow neon sign that spelled "Honey" across a pink rose wallpaper. The children hauled her outside, across the gravel, and Alicia could see snow-covered apiaries and a bee sculpture. She could see a green wall bordering the roof. The intention was clear—a fall to the death, a permanent separation of spirit from body so it could dwell in the tree forever.

Alicia tried to wriggle out of the ironclad grasp that was dragging her, her body flailing and undulating, her feet kicking. The duppies wanted her with them, but she wouldn't resign herself to that fate, even if it was inevitable. She would put up a struggle, she would cling to life with all the strength she had, physical and spiritual. Alicia didn't know how close to the edge she was, how much time she had; she reached her hands out to hold on to something, her nails scratching against the stone path laid in the gravel, grateful for the pain in her fingers, in her legs and jaw, the physical sensations that reminded her she was still a part of this world.

Heaven ran onto the roof, Mars behind her, and sprinted toward Alicia. When she was a few feet away, Heaven drew back her arm and shot her hand forward like she was pitching a baseball, throwing a burst of salt above Alicia. Some grains fell into her eyes, stinging them, but her leg dropped. The grip on her was released, and Heaven and Mars rushed toward her, falling to their knees, holding her, demanding to know if she was OK.

Alicia spat out some blood. She couldn't speak to them. Not

yet. She had to see. Holding on to Mars, she stood up and walked her once-again aching body toward the guard wall.

He looked worried. "Let's just go back down."

She didn't listen and moved a few steps closer.

"Alicia . . ."

She peered below to see what the drop would've been if the ghosts had succeeded in throwing her off. The cars on Front Street looked like tiny dots from this height. Chunks of snow from floors several storeys below fell through the air, disappearing from view. She shook with adrenaline, and the split-second intrusion of *what if?*—of imagining a successful push or throw from the roof—made her throw her head back with her eyes squeezed shut.

The ghosts had been repelled by the salt, and the cotton tree, the Rolling Calf, were no longer a current threat, but Alicia addressed them anyway. "I am getting that *fucking* comb!"

She looked around at the city, at the CN Tower, at Union Station, at the crops of steel-and-glass buildings, all blanketed in snow beneath the grey-blue sky. Her eyes settled on the lake stretched out to the Toronto Islands, and the words her mother had spoken that morning came back to her: *If yuh want good, yuh nose haffi run.* The words blurred into memories of Grandma Mabel, and Alicia screamed with a ferocity that felt new yet not unrecognizable to her.

"Small axe cut big tree!"

She turned around from the railing and bent forward, breathing heavily, then allowed Mars and Heaven to usher her away from the edge.

XXI

There were two hours left until the deadline. Alicia wanted to keep moving, keep up the momentum, but when they'd left the hotel with a crowd of confused and horrified guests, the adrenaline had left with them.

Alicia and Heaven crossed the street and sat on some building stairs on University Avenue while Mars went searching for painkillers in a nearby Shoppers Drug Mart. Swelling had started to form around his left eye, a bruise had darkened Heaven's chin from the kick she took to the face, and Alicia ached everywhere. Scrapes from rug burn pained her stomach and her fingernails were raw, and yet she felt a determination that only yesterday had seemed like nothing more than a vague memory from a past life.

She winced as she took her phone out and stared at the black screen that was now cracked. The soreness made it difficult to move but wasn't what demanded she rest for a bit; she kept picturing herself on the roof, so close to falling; in the university quad, so close to slipping away; and she needed to take a pause. She willed her phone to power on for even a few seconds, just enough time to text her mom "I love you," but it didn't turn on.

After putting clean snow on her chin, Heaven took Alicia's hands in her own and put some on her fingers to give her a bit of relief. Alicia's breath caught in her throat and then she exhaled, looking at Heaven appreciatively.

"How did you find snow so clean?"

Heaven smiled mysteriously. "I have my ways." She put more snow on Alicia's fingers. "So this whole day has been pretty fucked."

Alicia chuckled. "Not the whole day. I mean, true, a lot of shit has happened, and two hours ago I was thinking, 'I didn't ask for *any* of this,' but . . ." She shrugged. "I don't know, I don't think I've ever felt so connected to anything."

"I saw that," said Heaven. "On the roof? You had a whole-ass revelation, girl."

"Yeah," said Alicia, laughing. "It was terrifying."

"Nah, I don't do well with terrifying things," said Heaven.

Alicia looked at her. "Well, who does?"

"You," said Heaven. "And, surprisingly, Mars."

"If this is about how you—"

"It's not," said Heaven, shaking her head. "I kept reading about all this stuff—obeah, folk medicine, spirituality—even after I was finished my assignment because I wanted to fill in the gaps, get to the root of the different stories or the little things my family does but can't explain, you know? The things that kind of feel like rituals or aspects of rituals tied to other things?" She paused a bit before explaining herself. "Today was the first time I actually tried to do something I'd read about. I tried contacting River Mumma when you were gone journeying. It didn't work. I thought it was because the altar was kind of bullshit, but I also thought she'd just 'low it because all this knowledge I have made me deserving of summoning her."

From that sentiment alone, Alicia could see why River Mumma wouldn't appear to Heaven—she'd think of her as too bright, too haughty. But Alicia didn't tell her that; she didn't think she needed to either.

"You said I was trying to make this search for the comb all about me, and you were right. I felt like, out of the two of us, I was the one who deserved the responsibility, but even when I thought that, it was still all theoretical. 'If this were happening to me, I would do *this* instead of *that*.' Then I saw what this whole thing happening to me would look like. I'm watching you go through it, and I'm realizing I wouldn't actually be ready. I like reading about this stuff because I believe in it, but it's not *real* to me, which is a comfortable place for me to be in, and I don't know if that makes me a coward or a hypocrite or—"

"Heaven"—Alicia held on to her hand—"you're the furthest thing from a coward. You're just good with where you are in your life right now, and that's cool, fam. Trust, you'll—"

"Get it when I graduate?" said Heaven, arching an eyebrow.

"Something like that."

Heaven sighed and leaned her head on Alicia's shoulder. "I just realized you're actually trying to look out for me when you say that."

"Partly," said Alicia.

"I'll make sure we find the comb, OK? I got you."

Alicia rested her head against Heaven's. "I know," she said. "I believe you."

When Mars came back with a bottle of water and some Advil, Heaven explained that the TTC was too unreliable and it would be best to take an Uber to North York. There was no better time. Rush hour was about to be upon them but the prices hadn't surged yet and Heaven thought Alicia should rest her body as much as possible.

"It's a good thing we have this, eh?" said Heaven, tapping her bag with River Mumma's jewellery. "Because this fare is half the money in my account right now."

"I'll e-transfer you my part when I get the chance," said Alicia.

"No need, I'm stacked," said Heaven. "I put in the Glendon campus as the drop-off. It's twenty minutes away, seemed the least sus."

"Good," said Alicia, popping a pill in her mouth.

Mars gagged. "Why do we need to look like we're not suspicious? What are we doing, a heist?"

"I don't know, Mars. I'm thinking of all possibilities," said Heaven.

"All what?" He took out his phone and, after a few swipes, showed Alicia and Heaven a picture of a mansion. "How are we supposed to infiltrate this? It's a fortress."

Heaven looked at him. "A fortress, though?"

"OK, let's say we do pass the twenty-foot trees and climb the wall and the fence and get into his house undetected by all the man dem post up at his place—how the fuck are we going to get out?"

"I don't know, we're just going to have to figure it out as we go," said Alicia.

"Because that's how every successful break-in starts," said Mars.

"Well, think of a better plan."

Their ride came in five minutes—a paint-chipped Honda Civic that seemed held together by duct tape.

"How is it even legal for this to be on the road?" said Alicia.

When the car pulled up and Heaven confirmed her driver, she looked at Mars and Alicia, hesitating before opening the door to get in. They really didn't have time to be picky. It was after two o'clock now and that meant the sky could instantly go from its overcast grey to pitch black. Alicia nodded and they squeezed into the back seat, Mars insisting on getting in first this time, spreading out his legs a bit.

"You look pretty messed up," said the driver, eyeing them in the rear-view mirror. "Get in a fight or something?"

Alicia ignored the question. "We're just kind of in a hurry."

The driver made a gesture with his hand as if to say he understood. He turned sharply onto Front Street, tires screeching, and then blew past a red light onto Lower Simcoe, drumming his hands on the steering wheel and making noises like he was trying to beatbox. He sped along different streets, riding the bumpers in front of him, braking suddenly and often to keep from hitting the cars he tailgated or the pedestrians he saw just in time.

"Did you see this?" He held up his phone. It was the recording of the Rolling Calf breathing fire. "Fucking pandemonium. All these people saying it's, like, angels or aliens."

Alicia, Heaven, and Mars didn't answer. They were too busy holding on to the seats in front of them.

The driver hit Lake Shore Boulevard and had to slow down, then stop driving altogether. The traffic to get onto the Gardiner Expressway kept the car idle. Alicia looked out the window to the congestion beneath the concrete bents of the underpass and felt a flare of panic—they could literally be there for an hour; she'd once spent twice that time waiting in the car with her mother to get onto the Gardiner.

"So," said Alicia in a low voice, "how do we know the comb is even in the house he has here? He probably has houses all over the freaking world, it could be in any one of them. Maybe he doesn't even have it, maybe *he* gave it away as a gift."

"Well, if it's in his Toronto house, we'll find it," said Mars, swiping through his phone. "There are bare photos of mans' compound on the internet. Videos too. It won't be hard to spot. It'll just be impossible to get in."

"He doesn't show his entire house, though," said Alicia.

Heaven was scrolling. "He shows enough of it."

Alicia glanced over as Heaven swiped through photos of spiked chandeliers and black marble tubs, jersey collections, white marble kitchens.

"He love off him marble, eeh?" said Alicia.

"Luxury shit."

Mars barely got the words out before their driver moved into the left lane, passing the line of cars inching toward the on-ramp. Picking up speed, he swerved back to their original lane, narrowly avoiding a median strip and cutting sharply in front of a truck. The Gardiner was still congested, and the driver slammed the brakes to avoid crashing into the car in front of them. Everyone started honking.

"Bredren!" Mars shouted. "Calm down!"

"You said you were in a hurry."

"Yeah, we want to get there quick, not dead!"

"I felt safer on the roof," said Alicia, pressing her hand against her chest.

"You know?" said Heaven in agreement. She'd dropped her phone in the mayhem and bent down now to pick it up.

Heaven tapped Alicia on the shoulder and gestured for Mars to lean in even closer to her. "I found it," she whispered. "It is in the Toronto house."

"Say word." Alicia took the phone out of Heaven's hand, and Mars leaned over to get a better look. She started scanning the photo—she was looking at a lounge, all bronze and yellow with a gemstone wall and a black ceiling. It took her a minute to find the comb, but her eye finally caught it resting on one of the many shelves along the walls; it was encased in a vintage frame sitting among various action figures.

"Holy shit, it's there for true," said Mars.

"DM him," said Alicia.

Mars made a noise of disbelief. "Do you know how many DMs he must get, like, every second? He's not going to pay attention to that shit."

"You don't know that."

"Heaven's right," said Alicia. "If River Mumma has been terrorizing Sidney for not giving her the comb, it only makes sense that she'd be doing the same thing to him, since he has it now. If we all DM him about it and say the same thing, it might get his attention. We just have to be specific."

"What exactly am I supposed to say? 'Ay, boss, wah gwaan? Your head all mix up? It's that comb ting still'?"

Alicia shot him a look that said "Why not?" and Mars sighed and started typing.

Heaven sent a quick message and then offered her phone to Alicia. When she logged into her account, she mulled over the different combinations of words that could explain the situation in the succinct detail needed, and images from the past, both distant and near, sprang into her mind: the waves of rivers, a flash of gold, chanting, dancing, a face of indescribable beauty that both changed and remained fixed over the years.

The mermaid is not one to be crossed. She wants the comb back. If you want the nightmares to stop, if you want to know peace again, you need to hand over the comb Sidney Roy gave you. Think of your last few weeks. Fiyah deh a mus-mus tail, him tink a cool breeze.

"And now we wait," said Alicia.

They'd taken the Gardiner to the Don Valley Parkway and were inching their way to the exit they needed. Alicia started nibbling on her thumb, looking out to the steadily darkening sky. "Hold on," she willed the sun. "Just hold the fuck on." She looked back at Heaven's phone, staring at her private messages with the same kind of intensity, willing a response to her message. The clock said it was two forty. Alicia had to admit that their driver was getting them where they needed to go as quickly as he could.

The phone vibrated and Alicia elbowed Heaven, showing her the single line of text: *How do you know about the dreams?*

Heaven nudged Mars. "Check your social," she said.

"Already on it," he said. "*Woi*, yes, I got the same thing."

"OK. OK." Alicia tried not to get too excited. "Let's say that the dreams concern us."

Almost as soon as they'd sent the message, there was a response.

"'Could you please specify exactly how they concern you?'" Alicia read out. She shook her head. "We don't have time for this round-and-round ting."

This isn't really something we can discuss via DM or text or what-not. It would be better to do this in person, so can we arrange a meeting today? This is time-sensitive, and full disclosure, we—that is, me and the two other people who have sent messages about the dreams—are on our way to his residence. It would be beneficial for everybody involved if we could just meet there. Thanks.

"We legit come off like stalkers," said Heaven.

"Look, we have to be clear. I don't need them saying we have to go to an office in, like, the fucking west end when what we need is in that house," said Alicia.

Mars read out loud: "'Take photos of yourselves for identification.'

On the day we look mash-up? True." He shifted in his seat as he prepared to take his own picture.

"We'll just do a selfie," said Alicia, opening the camera app.

Heaven moved closer to Alicia and turned her face slightly to the side, lifting her shoulder.

"Bitch, are you actually posing right now?"

"Just because circumstances are dire doesn't mean I have to take a picture like a mugshot. I'm too cute even with this bruise on my face."

Alicia grinned, shaking her head, then took the picture and sent it. She received a QR code in response. "Did you get—?"

"Yeah, I got one," said Mars.

Alicia looked at the code. "It's like we got tickets to his house, like his house is an event we're going to. Like it's the Emerald fucking City."

"I mean, it kinda is," said Mars. "So wait, then who would we be?"

"Heaven's the Lion and you're the Tin Man," said Alicia matter-of-factly.

"Obviously."

Heaven looked at her. "Is this just a nice way of you calling me a cowa—whoa!"

Their driver had tried to exit but needed to swerve back into the lane as the car he'd cut off at the ramp flew past them, the driver honking and giving them the middle finger as he passed.

"Fuck that!" Their driver turned wildly and took the exit, passing over a solid line and driving through the gore area, barely missing the barrier. He followed the other car down the curve to Bayview Avenue, honking and swearing, driving along the shoulder in an attempt to catch up. Alicia, Mars, and Heaven yelled at him to stop or pull over, to calm down, to let them out, but when they started driving on the main road, Alicia stopped screaming.

Something was happening.

Something was off. She could feel it. It was like a rolling or a shaking, and it was making the car vibrate.

"Do you feel that? Hi! Hello! Do you feel that?"

The car was shuddering, except it wasn't the car; it was the street beneath them, rumbling like it was about to break apart.

"Everyone shut up!" She screamed so loudly, the entire car fell silent. "Do you feel that?" she repeated, emphasizing every word.

"I do," said Heaven.

"It's not the car," said the driver.

"I know," said Alicia. "But something is happening."

Mars spread out his hands like he was trying to get a sense of the situation. "What is—?"

Suddenly there was a massive swell beneath the road just in front of them, like a wave beneath the surface. The snowy street split open and a giant spurt of water shot out from underground, exploding high above the trees and streetlights, gushing up and out, pouring through the pavement with such ferocity that Alicia pictured the car getting swept away like a bottle in a flood. The driver swerved to avoid ice and debris, and to keep from plowing through the fountain of water. Alicia, Mars, and Heaven screamed and the driver honked frantically as he drove over the concrete median strip and veered into oncoming traffic. Other cars swerved to avoid them and then swerved to avoid the massive jet of water that was spilling onto the road in gallons. The driver turned sharply back into his lane to dodge an advancing van that kept honking at them to get out of the way. The wheels skidded against the pavement, and the car crashed headfirst into a streetlight.

XXII

Alicia couldn't stop laughing, and Heaven and Mars were concerned. No one was hurt, but she'd been in hysterics since the impact.

The crash happened just behind the Loblaws grocery store, and when the driver realized that everyone was unharmed and his car had suffered a relatively mild dent, he cancelled the ride and sped off—but not before Heaven checked to make sure that all the jewellery was in her bag. They rested at one of the concrete traffic barriers separating the parking lot from the road, several feet away from the watermain break, but it wasn't the best place to settle. Everything was chaotic. There was honking from drivers, and pedestrians kept stopping to see if Alicia, Heaven, and Mars needed anything, which kept them from having any real conversation, but they couldn't leave. Alicia had collapsed onto the ground, laughing, the instant they reached the traffic barrier, and that prevented Heaven and Mars from trying to move her.

"I think it's the adrenaline," said Heaven.

Alicia rocked back and forth, crying with the force of her laughter, as she listened to the hiss of the burst pipe and watched the water gush forth and flood the street. She felt like cursing at it or begging it, as if it were a channel of communication that could deliver her struggles to River Mumma. As if River Mumma didn't already know.

"I think she's just snapped," said Mars.

She continued to cackle. Maybe she had lost it. Maybe adrenaline was a part of it too. But mostly she was laughing because she had fumbled her way through the day in a cold, sore, terrified, and semi-wet state to reach a deadline she would be just short of making, a deadline that was an hour away. Yet that knowledge did nothing to quell her sense of urgency. She could feel her familiar defence beckoning to her: the numbness she'd cocooned herself in for months. How easy retreating into apathy would be for her, but she didn't want to. She had to at least try to beat sundown, even if it was impossible; she had to see the task through.

"OK, I'm done," she said, standing up. "Heaven, pass your phone."

"Want to fill us in?" said Heaven, unlocking her phone and handing it to Alicia.

"I'm going to send a voice note."

Heaven and Mars started protesting at the same time.

"Ah yuh head nuh good?"

"You don't know him like that, fam. That shit is off-putting."

Alicia waved at them to stop talking and then pressed down on the microphone icon. "To whomever it may concern, uh—"

Mars cringed.

"This is Alicia Gale," she continued. "Which I guess you can see from my IG handle. Anyway, the car that we were in was involved in a, uh, a tiny, *tiny* crash, and to . . . expedite matters, I guess—I *suppose*—it would be beneficial to perhaps have someone bring us to the meeting? Like, someone from your camp or your detail—I don't really know what to call it . . ."

Heaven mouthed at her. "Hang. Up."

"But you would be providing the transportation. OK, that's it. Bye. Or bye for now."

Alicia took her thumb off the microphone icon and took a deep breath.

"Wow," said Mars. "You know, when you finally have an office job, you're going to have to work on your phone etiquette, because damn."

"Oh look, a response," Alicia said smugly. "They said to drop a pin."

Mars shook his head. "When this is all over, you're going to be insufferable."

"Count on it."

Alicia sent the details of their location and they walked over to the front of the Loblaws on Moore Avenue. In twenty minutes, a white Nissan arrived to pick them up, and Alicia felt oddly disappointed.

"Well, what did we think, he was going to scoop us up in a Maybach?" said Heaven.

"Yes," said Alicia and Mars at the same time.

The car pulled into the parking lot and a man dressed all in black got out of the driver's seat. After he scanned the QR codes, then searched Heaven's bag and Alicia's wristlet (confiscating the switchblade), he gestured for them to get into the car. He didn't speak to them as he drove through residential streets until he reached the main road, passing building complexes and car dealerships and a forest of dead trees in the snow.

Mars leaned over to whisper to Alicia and Heaven. "OK, 'low me but"—he paused to think—"I know everyone knows where he lives and ting, but the way this whole thing is going down, it just feels like one of those situations where you get a bag over your head so you don't see where you're going."

"I'm actually a little disappointed that they didn't do that," said Heaven.

They'd made it to the Bridle Path, but it was practically dark by the time they entered the street of palatial manors and mansions partially obscured by tall fences and trees. Snow seemed to fall differently up here, the way it blanketed roofs, accented wrought-iron gates, adorned the lawns and evergreens—not a speck of brown—it was almost like an enchantment that turned the neighbourhood into a true winter wonderland. It was pristine. Yet Alicia was uneasy.

The feeling of impending doom weighed in her gut. The car pulled into the driveway of a house that had two of the largest red wreaths Alicia had ever seen hung on double black gates that opened automatically, ushering them into the compound.

The driver idled in front of the entrance steps, where four men stood as if unaffected by the falling snow.

"Are they here for us?" Heaven asked as she opened the car door.

"When you go to see the bossman, he lets you know he's the boss," said Mars.

The moment Alicia exited the car, she heard barking and music that seemed to be coming from within the house yet still a distance away. There was another noise too, like the crackling of twigs, that filled her with a familiar dread. She looked around at the looming arborvitae trees that enclosed the property, trying to suss out the source.

"Leish?" said Mars.

She pointed to the trees. "I heard something over there."

"It's probably the wind."

"I don't like the way that dog is barking," she said.

"Not every barking dog is a sign of something, though."

"Maybe. But today?" said Alicia. "I'm catching a vibe, Mars, and not a good one. Same one I had on the bus this morning, same one I had last night, same one I had at the hotel."

"We'll explain the situation, get the comb, then cut, OK?" he said.

She nodded, trying to convince herself it would be that easy. They joined Heaven at the bottom of the front steps, and one of the four men on the landing, a tall bald man in a black suit, nodded at them.

"We have NDA forms for you to sign, and we will be confiscating your phones," he said.

The three other men, also dressed in black, walked down the steps and held out tablets with pens for Heaven, Mars, and Alicia to use for signing.

"I thought he only did this for parties," said Heaven.

"You are welcome to leave," the bald man said.

The three of them went through the documents, signed them, handed over their phones, and then entered the house.

The foyer was black-and-white marble and probably bigger than Alicia's entire apartment, with a ceiling so high it was as if they were in a cathedral. She allowed herself a split second to acknowledge the grandeur of the space. She could still hear the barking, like a distant echo, and was unsure if it was a phantom noise in her head. She looked down the hall to see if there was a dog around. Instead she saw multiple rooms with various couches and various people milling around. She took a step forward, but the head of the security detail moved with her, blocking her from venturing farther inside with a smoothness that was neither abrupt nor impolite. He stretched his arm out to the side.

"Please join me here," he said.

He waited until they turned left into a room of plush couches and floor-to-ceiling windows framed by mauve curtains.

Alicia and Heaven sat on the edge of a couch. Mars checked out the Andy Warhol painting on the wall and then looked around at the polished desk.

"I'm trying to be on this level," he muttered.

"Are certain people designated to certain rooms?" asked Alicia.

"Certain meetings are, yes."

"OK, and what kind of meeting is this?"

He looked at her steadily. "That's what I'm trying to determine."

"So an undetermined meeting starts in the foyer—"

"This is hardly the foyer—"

"—and then once it's determined, we can move to the lounge or the great room? Like levels of a video game?" Alicia could still hear the dog. She didn't know how much time she had. "Can we skip all that and head straight for the lounge? Because what we need is in there. Sidney Roy gave a gift—"

"Sidney Roy has been in contact with us. She said three people paid her a visit earlier this afternoon and she felt the energy of the conversation was rather threatening."

"Threatening?" Heaven repeated. "Is this a joke?"

"Ms. Roy said—"

"What she said doesn't matter, because obviously, *we've* said something of interest. I mean, you picked us up and we are in this house, right? Which means you haven't deemed us a threat."

"A threat, no," said the man. "A waste of time, I'm still not sure. Unless you provide more details, I'm going to have to ask you to leave."

"Look," said Alicia, standing up, "you're acting like this is *The Sopranos* and we're asking for a sit-down with a mob boss, so we have to go through the proper channels or some shit. It's just one gold comb; he's not going to miss a gold comb. I know he spent at *least* a million dollars on this room alone." A throbbing pain stabbed her temple and she felt the same trepidation she had when she heard the dog barking. "I know this doesn't make sense to you and it sounds like I'm spouting nonsense, but it will make sense to him."

The man was unmoved.

"You're right, Leish," said Mars. "This isn't the mafia, but boss-man, he's the don, right?" He looked at the security guard to agree with him. "What kind of don is he going to be? Vito or Michael?"

"I'm afraid I don't follow you," the man said.

Another voice spoke, unhurried and vaguely contemplative. It came from the left side of the room.

"In the opening of *The Godfather*, an undertaker, Bonasera, asks a favour from Don Corleone on his daughter's wedding day, which he grants. In *The Godfather Part II*, when Michael is now godfather, Pentangeli—who is a capo of the Corleone family—has to beg to see him, his own don, over business that affects him. One godfather is a man of the people, the other is purely a man of business."

Everyone turned around. A bearded light-skinned man was standing in the entryway that connected the room to another. He looked the kind of casual that only wealth could buy, in a black sweatshirt and joggers, all slick and glossy, yet he seemed tired, almost slightly emaciated. His expression was focused and distant at the same time, as if part of him was intently listening and the other part had wandered off and was somewhere else entirely.

"That's what you meant, right?" he said.

Mars didn't answer right away, and when he did, he could only nod.

The bearded man shrugged and then leaned against a wall. "OK, you've got me here. Say what you need to say."

XXIII

He led Alicia, Mars, and Heaven into the great room, deeper into his mansion. Mars had taken it upon himself to engage in pleasantries, and Alicia and Heaven trailed behind, staying close together as they walked over marble floors, following the gold veining in the tile like a road map.

"You're not losing your shit over this"—Heaven pointed to the man leading them—"even a little? Look at where we are!"

"Heaven, I met an actual deity."

"OK, true."

They were the only ones in the great room; the people Alicia had seen milling around when they first came in seemed to have moved on. It was an expansive space with a grand piano, black like the giant marble bar across the left wall. He invited them to sit on a sofa with chinchilla throws and purple cushions but didn't sit on the couch across from them; rather, he remained standing, resting his elbow on the bar.

In a matter of seconds, a woman, also dressed in black, entered the room holding a tray of three deceptively plain-looking glasses and a bottle of Fillico. She put the glasses of water on the table, and Heaven picked one up, taking a sip and leaned back on the sofa like she'd slipped into a life that was waiting for her.

Mars watched the woman leave. "So is there, like, a dress code for your house or something?" he asked. Alicia glanced at him and he shook his head. "Not what we're here to talk about."

"What *are* you here to talk about? You"—he pointed at Alicia— "why'd you send that quote?"

Alicia was about to answer when the barking she'd been trying to ignore turned into a loud whine.

"Am I really the only one hearing this dog?"

"I apologize. Her breed doesn't bark much, so this is pretty irregular. She's been a bit skittish. She's not in the house anymore, so I didn't think anyone inside could hear her."

Those words confirmed for Alicia that trouble was indeed coming, and she could tell by Heaven's and Mars's expressions that they were thinking the same thing. They didn't have much time and it would be easier to explain everything unfiltered.

Alicia sighed. "Can we just talk?" she asked. "Like, can we *talk*?"

He stared at her for a few moments before moving his hand from his chin and gesturing in a motion that said "Go ahead."

"Bless. OK, so no word of a lie, we need the comb Sidney Roy gave you. Full stop."

"But why, though?" He walked over to the couches. "You haven't told my people any details, and that's mad sus, you understand?"

"I assume you've heard of River Mumma." When he shook his head, Alicia scoffed. "Really? With all your collabs, all your visits, you've never heard of her—one of the most pervasive urban legends in the country?" He shook his head again. Alicia then glanced at Heaven, who understood that she would help her explain the situation they were all in.

"Short version is she's a mermaid," said Heaven. "The mother of rivers in Jamaica, although some people say there are multiple mermaids in multiple rivers. If you eat fish from a river she's known to inhabit, the river will go dry. She also guards treasure at the bottom of the river—many people have drowned trying to take items, particularly a golden table."

Alicia couldn't tell if he was listening intently or drifting into sleep with his eyes open. Now that she was close to him, she could see the extent of his fatigue—wrinkles; dark circles beneath his eyes; dull, pale skin. She picked up the crash-course education.

"It's said she can be seen combing her hair on a rock, and if she realizes a human has seen her, she dives back into the water, sometimes leaving her comb behind. If a human takes the comb, she'll appear in a dream asking for it back, and reward them for doing so. If people don't bring the comb back . . . well, she'll terrorize them until they do. Nuh ramp wid she, understand? She visited me last night and tasked me with getting the comb back today and showed me what would happen if I didn't."

He took a cell out of his pocket. "Run that name again?"

"River Mumma."

As soon as Alicia said her name, she saw all the dried rivers again in quick, disturbing flashes. The barking became more insistent, intensifying her anxiety. It wasn't just danger she sensed but doom, and that made it difficult for her to concentrate.

"You have water that's, like, two hundred dollars a bottle and you're offering it to guests. This is a multi-million-dollar house with multi-million-dollar finishes," said Heaven.

He glanced up from the phone. "What's your point?"

"You can afford to look rested, fam. You have the resources to get a good night's sleep, but you're tired as fuck and it shows, because wealth is no match for a deity. You have something of hers, and this is the consequence of that," said Heaven. "Sidney hasn't slept in weeks, she's pretty much cursed. I'm guessing it's the same for you."

"Bare facts," said Mars. "This is the OG ting. Traditional. It's"—he gestured for emphasis—"*spiritual*. She's not of this world; trust me, I've seen it. If you have something of hers, you just give it back."

He looked skeptical and Alicia became agitated.

"I am not exaggerating," she said. "If we don't get this comb to her, she's going to leave and take every body of water she guards with her. Do you know what that would mean?"

"OK, OK." He leaned back in the sofa. "You tell me this is a spiritual thing, I believe that. For real, like"—he stroked his chin and his eyes went distant—"I know what it is to be exhausted, but this shit goes beyond that, you know? It's dead, like, in my soul, but truth? River Mumma"—he pointed to the phone—"she's opened a whole other door for inspiration."

Heaven blinked. "You're saying you want to stay like this?"

"I get a nightmare, I see her, and mans has to write, you know? I can't help myself. Beautiful dark skin, she's got the kind of face your heart can't recover from. She's got that wild heart, wild temper, she's a blessing to my pen."

"What are these, lyrics?" said Alicia.

He shot her a look and shifted in his seat. "I'm just saying, she's got me up and working. That's what I was doing when your messages came through, just in my studio straight grinding."

Heaven kissed her teeth. "So you're saying fuck any real-world consequences as long as you've got your muse?"

"I respect your craft," said Mars, "but, like . . ."

He looked up at Alicia, and when he caught her eye, a recognition passed between them. Alicia knew they saw each other, saw

Alice and Thomas, saw their present together, as well as their shared past.

"Recognize her game too." He pointed at Alicia. "Because she's been through it today just to get here. No lie, we nearly died—she nearly died *three times*—to get this comb. And I'm not talking about a figure of speech, eh? We've been dealing with things you couldn't imagine, fam: fire-breathing fucking monsters, ghosts from back ah time. And I was just going to leave, you know what I mean? Because I don't need that stress, but"—he licked his lips—"we have a responsibility, and she's just trying to carry that out."

The man said nothing in response, descending instead deeper into quiet contemplation.

Heaven got up from the sofa and sat down next to him. "Can we at least see the comb?" she asked. "Just *see* it?"

He didn't say anything. When he got up, they instinctively rose too. He led them through his marble hallways, where other people stopped briefly to give him props or ask a question; one man delivered the message that someone was waiting for him back in the studio.

"I'm on the other side of the house, it's going to have to wait," he said.

"Did he really have to build a mansion the size of a small island?"

"Leish, 'low it," said Mars.

"I'm just saying, you know, like, are we there yet?"

They turned a corner and stopped short. A white cat sat in the middle of the hallway. Its eyes were too big for its face, absent pupils; they were clouded orbs that looked like two moons nestled in sockets.

He took a step back. "Whose cat is this?"

"It's not yours?" said Mars.

He shook his head. "I'm getting bad vibes. Like, bad, *bad* vibes."
The cat then smiled widely.

He gestured at it. "Like, why the fuck is it grinning like that? Can cats even smile?"

The cat turned its milky eyes to Alicia and her stomach churned; a faint heat skimmed her skin but also caused goosebumps to erupt. At that moment, a high-pitched tone invaded the entire house, as if it had taken over a central intercom: *Whoop! Whoop! Whoop!* It almost sounded like a voice, but it wasn't human enough to belong to a person. Everyone started looking around as if they could find the source of the noise right in front of them.

The unease simmering in Alicia's gut had now bubbled up, causing a bitter taste in her mouth. The cat. The barking. The noise. Something was about to happen, or was already happening.

Whoop! Whoop! Whoop!

"I know this noise," she whispered.

"Yeah," said Heaven, her eyes darting around.

A group of people came out of a single room. Some were still holding glasses of liquor, a couple had blunts between their lips.

"What's that noise?" said one of them.

"It's good, it's cool. Security is on it," he said, taking out his phone. "You should probably get back in—"

Suddenly a woman clutched her hair, raised her head to the ceiling, and screamed. It was so shrill, the image of vocal cords shredding popped into Alicia's mind. Another woman grabbed the first one by the shoulders.

"What's wrong? What is it?"

Whoop! Whoop! Whoop!

The woman didn't speak but just continued to scream. The other people started getting nervous, some staring at the cat, others looking around, everyone flinching each time a whoop sounded. A couple of security guards charged down the hallway, making their way to their asset.

"I'm good," he said. "But I don't know what's going on with her. Call an ambulance."

One of the guards reached into his pocket but then paused. After a beat, he started shrieking too. His eyes were fixed on the cat. He pointed at it and yelled.

"Chill, it's a cat! It's just a cat!"

"No, no, a duppy puss that," said Alicia.

Mars looked at them, alarmed. "A *what*?"

"Duppy," Heaven repeated under her breath. She clenched her hair. "That whooping," she said more loudly, "it's the Whooping Boy."

Heaven was right. This was the Whooping Boy's call, its warning of its impending arrival. Alicia had heard it in the bushes outside. That was what the stories said—twigs would crackle under its feet as it danced and killed its victims by blowing hot air on them.

There was another scream, and another. One by one, people started to yell like they were yelling for their lives. The people unaffected spoke all at once, talking over each other.

"Security has lost their shit, we should call the cops."

"About what? A cat?"

"Kill it! Kill it!"

"It's an animal, you fucking psycho; you can't kill it!"

The cat, still facing Alicia, Mars, and Heaven, turned its head all the way around to hiss at the other guests behind it. People jumped back. Some returned to the room, slamming the door shut; others started running.

"Nope!" Alicia continued down the hall. "We need that comb now or everything is just going to get worse." She looked at him. "Where is it?"

He'd seemed to have retreated into himself, pressed against the wall, and Alicia had to repeat the question, louder.

"Last room," he finally said.

Mars and Heaven followed her as she ran down the hallway into a dimly lit lounge with a black celestial ceiling. A backlit wall panel of golden brown slices of agate bathed the room in a flaxen glow that seemed appropriate for the luxury it contained; everything was ostrich skin and mohair and bronze. The comb wouldn't be too difficult to find—there were only a few shelves of action figures and collector's items and CDs. They started searching the shelves above the sectional sofa, trying to ignore the screaming and the *Whoop! Whoop! Whoop!*

At the end of the shelf next to the agate wall, Alicia found a picture frame gilded with golden leaves. *The* frame. The goal. Encased within it, the comb. The source of everything that had happened to her in the past twenty-four hours. For a moment, she couldn't move. Now that the comb was within reach, the triumph was almost unbearable; it gave way to a wave of emotion she could barely contain.

Its beauty threatened to make her cry. A short, long-toothed comb like an afro pick, with an ornate handle shaped into curves and swirls. It was exactly like River Mumma: Ancient and ageless. Exquisite. Extraordinary. It had a regality to it—a power, a gravity—and it drew Alicia in. She could understand the desire to take the comb, to keep it, to own it, but she could also tell immediately that the comb could never belong to any human.

Oddly, Alicia hadn't thought much about the comb itself throughout the day, hadn't imagined what it would be like when she saw it, when she found it. She'd been focused solely on getting to where she needed to go. River Mumma was certainly no longer conceptual to her, but somehow the comb had remained almost theoretical in her mind.

The longer she looked at the comb—stolen and misplaced, displaced, lost to its rightful keeper, put behind glass to be observed—the more her emotions swelled, intensifying with each second until they erupted into a crescendo of Alicia smashing the frame on the ground.

She picked up the comb—it was heavier than it looked and with more than just weight, but also history. Memories flashed before her eyes. She could see River Mumma throughout the centuries, each time her appearance different, her tail sometimes green, sometimes blue, sometimes pink. She sat on different rocks in rivers that were white or blue or yellow or green, some with small heaps of food and drink and jewels on their banks, some with piles of garbage, the comb, unchanged each time, in her hand.

She wiped away some tears. "Can I have the bag?" she asked finally.

Heaven handed her the shoulder bag, and she put the comb inside.

"Real quick, I think I know how to get the comb back to her," said Alicia. "But she likes offerings and we need to show her respect, so I don't think anything in this bag is coming back."

Alicia could see it in their expressions—they'd already spent the money they would have got trading in their pieces of jewellery. Mars had already deposited the money in his brother's savings account, Heaven had textbooks for the next term, they'd allowed their fantasies to turn into future realities. And now they were in the process of letting it all go. But they did let it go. They nodded to Alicia, indicating that they were both OK with the plan.

"Thanks," she said. "Really. Let's cut."

"What about——?"

"I don't think he'll mind now, after seeing a cat turn its entire head all the way the fuck around."

They left the lounge, but it was too late. Everyone still in the hallway seemed unable to move, transfixed in fear, staring at the monstrous Rolling Calf. Alicia noticed it had a blinding white hide this time, not the inky black of this morning, the fur a contrast with its fiery nostrils. Next to it was a young boy with unnatural pointed features like a warped Pinocchio, long hair past its shoulders, and devilish red eyes—the Whooping Boy. It was sitting atop another duppy, a horse with three legs—two in the back and one in the front that, like its snout, were entirely skeletal. Blank white eyes, with chunks of flesh missing from its flank, exposing muscle and bone, drool clinging to its undead mouth.

"The Three-Foot Horse," Alicia whispered.

She had been eight when Winston told her of this duppy, of its toxic breath and its speed, its disregard for the moonlight, unlike other duppies, who feared it. He'd laughed when she dove under the covers in terror.

Heaven whimpered and Mars's breathing shook. It all happened so fast. The Whooping Boy puckered its lips like it was about to whistle and instead blew out hot air, white like steam, that blasted one of the security guards in the face, scorching his cheek. The guard fell to the floor with a thud, writhing in pain as the side of his face swelled and bubbled, blistering as if his skin was being boiled.

Alicia's screams mingled with his strangled shrieks of pain, and before she knew it, she was being pulled down the hall.

XXIV

Everyone scrambled in different directions. Alicia heard security guards yelling into their walkie-talkies: "Assistance! Assistance! We need assistance!" She was surprised to see that the owner of the house was the one who'd grabbed her by the wrist and pulled her forward. They ran, Mars and Heaven in tow, into another lounge, decorated with posters, including the cover art of one of his own albums. They pushed through double black doors and descended into a large room with a pool that was all black granite and purple backlighting.

He stopped running and fished his phone out of his pocket.

"Why are you stopping? These doors aren't going to protect you," said Alicia. "They don't even lock, fam! Not that it'd matter."

"Alicia, remember the salt in the bag," said Heaven.

She sat on the sofa at the side of the pool and started tugging at the stubborn zipper.

"They're paging me to make sure I'm OK," he said. "We need to call the cops or something!"

Heaven rolled her eyes. "They're not going to help!" She watched Alicia struggle with the zipper and sat down next to her. She held the bag, trying to make the zipper straight so the slider could glide down smoothly. "What are they going to do, shoot at a spirit?" she continued. "Be serious!"

Mars was pivoting on the spot. "Let's go!"

"Fuck!" The man hung up the phone and started running again, and so did Alicia and Heaven, Alicia still trying to unzip the bag as she hurtled forward.

As soon as they started moving again, the Rolling Calf appeared, its impossibly large body the height of the room. It breathed out fire. The pool ignited, turning into a lake of flame that jumped and danced in unpredictability.

The blaze spread, scorching a half-circle around the Rolling Calf. The duppy seemed galvanized by the flames. Alicia blinked helplessly as reflections of the fire flickered in the ceiling, in the floors, in the columns of black granite, like a house of mirrors.

"Salt!" Heaven screamed. "Alicia! Use the salt now!"

"I'm *trying*!"

The flames were getting closer, shape-shifting into hands wreathed in fire as in Alicia's vision of the cotton tree, eagerly crawling toward them.

The bag burst open when they reached the doors on the other side of the room. Alicia watched the Rolling Calf charge toward her as she fumbled with the box of salt. The duppy reared its head, ready for another blast, but she found the opening and poured some salt on the floor before backing out of the room.

They didn't rest. They kept running in single file, Alicia at the end of the line, pouring a trail of salt behind them as they went.

He led them out of the pool room to another staircase. "Is my house going to burn down?"

"I don't know about duppy fire," Alicia said as they climbed. "Heaven?"

"I'm not, I don't—"

"Maybe not," Mars said. "At the park, the fire didn't seem to ruin the grass, and I don't hear a fire alarm, so . . ."

"But it's gone, right?"

"No, it's not even trapped; we didn't salt the other door," said Heaven as they continued to sprint up the stairs. "We just bought enough time to get away."

"Plus the salt's finished," said Alicia, tossing the box behind her. She stopped climbing the stairs.

"Alicia?"

"*Leish!*"

"What are you doing?" Heaven ran back down a couple of steps. "We have to go!"

"We're just running aimlessly!"

"Not aimlessly," said Mars. "He's probably leading us to a panic room or something." He looked up and shouted, "You have a panic room, right?"

"You dun know I have a panic room!"

"A panic room doesn't save us from duppies, so it is completely useless in this situation. We need to go somewhere else anyway," Alicia shouted up at him. "Where's the nearest river?"

He blinked at her and Alicia threw up her hands. "Nearest creek? Stream? Spring? Anything!"

"The West Don River is probably five minutes away by car," he said finally.

Alicia nodded. "Guess you're driving us. Where's the garage?"

"I have people here! I can't just leave!"

"You want to protect them? Help *us*! The sooner the comb is returned, the sooner this will go away. All this is happening because that bull, the Rolling Calf, doesn't want River Mumma to get this comb!"

He kissed his teeth and charged down the stairs to lead them another way. The mansion was a maze. They twisted and turned through hallways like burrows that took them to various rooms, like a lounge with a psychedelic drawing of a mushroom and a long blue couch that snaked around a coffee table with a shisha pipe on it, and another, not quite a library but with bookshelves and maps and paintings. The rooms led to even more hallways, like a warren, and Alicia wondered if it would ever end, if they would ever see outside; a bizarre image of them running toward the centre of the earth flashed before her eyes. The house echoed with noise—distant screaming and yipping, barking, the sound of running footsteps. One of the guests ran right past them, down a hall perpendicular to theirs, the duppy cat chasing after her, hissing and growling. He moved like he was about to follow her, but Alicia yelled at him: "Bro, focus up!"

They continued on. Every once in a while they could hear static, like someone had turned on their walkie-talkie, but instead of voices speaking through it, there were just more screams; sometimes the screams were people calling for him, asking where he was.

"We're almost there."

As soon as he spoke, they all skidded to a halt, staring in horror at the other end of the corridor. The Whooping Boy on the Three-Foot Horse. Snaked around the horse's snout was its own tattered and bloodied tail, which looped into reins held by the Whooping Boy.

The Whooping Boy yanked on the reins, letting out an inhuman yip of malice, and the Three-Foot Horse reared on its hind legs, kicking out its cadaverous front one; its neigh was the scream of a thousand horses, which made everyone jump.

"Other way!" Heaven yelled. "Other way!"

They turned and ran back the way they had come, the horse just behind them, the quick clacking of its three hooves—*cooti-cup, cooti-cup*—on the marble floor. The gnashing of its teeth and the clicking of its skeletal snout sounded too loud, too close.

"Don't let it get closer; the heat will make you sick!"

Alicia instructed their guide to throw down everything he could to stall the duppies and make them count the items. "Anything in your pockets! Anything on your walls!"

He took off his thin gold chain and threw it behind them, unclasped a watch, pulled off a diamond ring, letting them fall to the floor.

"We would help," said Alicia, as he started taking out his earrings, "but we already got rid of everything we could earlier today."

Mars laughed without humour. "Even everything we couldn't!"

Alicia chanced a glance behind her. The duppies were stalled by the items, but the Three-Foot Horse still opened its mouth to try to blast them with its breath. It only ended up burning holes in the walls, warping and melting the marble.

He wrenched open a door and took them outside. It was nearly pitch black, save for the moon. The snowfall was picking up, and they were met with a cacophony of howls and barks; it was as if every dog in the neighbourhood was on high alert and communicating its fear.

"That can't be good," said Mars.

They ran along the expansive patio, and the effort combined with the cold air shredded Alicia's lungs, making her cough.

"Where is all your security?"

"Probably inside. Shit!"

Finally, they made it to the garage. He took a small remote out of his pocket and clicked it. As soon as the garage door began to slide open, he rushed forward, and then yelled in pain. A shadow had leapt from the door onto him.

"What fresh hell is *this*?" Alicia whispered—until she saw the bushy striped tail and the small black paws that looked like tiny hands.

"It's just a raccoon," she said. "They've been more aggressive lately!"

"Get it off! Get it off!"

He was twisting frantically, grabbing at the animal, which was skittish and scrambling on his head, clawing and scratching his face.

Heaven tried to pull it off without getting bitten or scratched herself.

Mars ran into the massive garage and stopped in front of a shelf with keys dangling from multiple hooks. He chose a sleek black one, and one of the ten luxury cars lit up in response—the chrome black Mercedes in the middle. He ran over, unlocked the door, and smashed down on the horn.

The raccoon recoiled and scurried away, leaving the man groaning loudly in pain. He, Alicia, and Heaven joined Mars in the garage, which looked more like an airplane hangar. The light revealed just how gruesome the attack had been: deep, bloody gashes all over his face and arms.

"Yuh need to get checked out for rabies, like, real quick," said Mars.

"How are we getting to the river now?" said Alicia.

"Take the car. Just turn on Lawrence and go all the way down," he said between anguished sighs. "The river is behind the school parking lot."

Heaven started to protest. "But we don't know how to—"

"Thanks," said Alicia, cutting her off. "So you probably don't have salt because rich people never have anything in their kitchen. Do you have a whip?"

He stopped wincing and grimaced at her.

"Not even for sex?" she pressed.

"I—? Move off. This is your business how?"

"There are a few ways to get rid of a Rolling Calf, and one of them is flogging it with a whip; it just seemed like it's the easiest for you to do."

"But if you leave, they'll leave with you," he said. "It's you they want—you just said that."

"Think of it as a precaution. A lot of shit happened today that none of us thought would ever happen, nuh true?"

Suddenly, fire plumed at the other end of the garage, engulfing a car in flames.

"The *Royce*?"

They looked around for the Rolling Calf, but it was nowhere to be found. Instead, the Three-Foot Horse appeared with the Whooping Boy sitting atop it, cackling, kicking its feet up.

Whoop! Whoop! Whoop!

"Alicia," Heaven said, "give me the bag and then just get into the car."

She blinked. "What—?"

"Don't think." Heaven snatched the bag off Alicia's shoulder. "I've got you. Get the comb to her."

Heaven sprinted out of the garage and down the driveway, holding the bag up for the duppies to see that she was now the one in possession of the comb. The Three-Foot Horse galloped after her, blowing out hot air, shrivelling the trees around the property to ash, igniting the plants, narrowly missing Heaven, who ducked and ran at the same time.

"Do you have a death wish?" Alicia screamed. "Heaven!"

Heaven bellowed something that Alicia couldn't discern until she'd yelled it a few more times. "The moon is covered!"

Alicia understood. "Mars, back in the car! Now!"

Mars sat back in the driver's seat as she jumped into the passenger's side.

"The Three-Foot Horse can run in moonlight, but it disappears in the dark, can't get you in shadows, shade, stuff like that," said Alicia, watching Heaven run into the street. "Heaven lured it into the dark. We have to catch up to her."

Mars pushed a button, turning on the ignition. "You know I only have my G1, right? I don't know what any of this—" He gestured at the array of buttons and screens in front of him.

"Just don't crash into anything."

Mars slammed down on the gas, and the car shot forward.

"Too much gas!"

He eased the accelerator just in time, keeping the car from crashing into the burning hedges. Neither the Three-Foot Horse nor the Whooping Boy was in sight when they made it to the empty street. Dogs continued to bark incessantly. Alicia imagined that the neighbours were peering out from their windows, calling the police or each other to gossip and theorize about the smoke billowing from the rapper's house.

Heaven was standing beneath an oak tree that still had its leaves. Mars slowed and Alicia rolled down her window. When Heaven bent down to speak with her, Alicia hit her across the head.

"Ow!" She touched the impacted part. "Ah wah duh yuh?"

"That was fucking reckless!" Alicia exhaled deeply. "Thank you."

"I'm going to stay and help. You've got Mars. Here." Heaven handed her the bag.

Alicia put the bag on her lap, feeling the surprising weight of the small comb.

"Walk good, eh?" said Heaven.

Alicia nodded and Mars drove off. Heaven got smaller and smaller in the side-view mirror, the night a protective blanket over her.

XXV

Sirens wailed and lights flashed, at first a piercing red and then red, blue, and white. Alicia told Mars to stay calm as he stopped driving so the fire trucks and the police cars and the ambulance could speed past them in the opposite direction. After a beat, Mars continued to drive.

"They're going to pull us over," he said.

"No, they're not."

"Was I even driving in a straight line?"

"They're going to the mansion. That's why there are fire trucks. That's why there's an ambulance."

"Nah, fam, I'm saying, they don't all have to go there, right? One could turn around and flag us down. I wasn't going the speed limit either. I'm not even going the speed limit now."

"We can't slow down, the duppies might catch up! Honestly, I think we're good."

"Can you just check?"

Alicia looked in the side-view mirror, and when she couldn't get a proper read, she twisted around in her seat so she could look out the rear windshield.

"Be careful! I don't want to be sued for damages and shit because you scratched up his interior. How much do you think this car costs? There is a literal fridge in the back seat, Leish. The most money I've ever seen in my life is in your bag, and he spends that on a *watch*! No, suh!"

"I'm literally just sitting, Mars; it's cool. No one is turning around," she said, watching the tail lights of the different vehicles.

He sighed. "This day isn't real, I swear. This morning I was on the TTC, and now I'm driving a fucking $700,000 car."

"So," said Alicia, smiling at him, "you're welcome."

Mars grinned but then turned serious. "You know one of the duppies is going to come for us."

"I know," said Alicia. "I also know that we don't have anything. We don't have salt, we don't have a knife, we don't have a whip or a leaf of life like Oni had in her jar—"

Mars made a "cut it" motion with his hand. "Don't worry about that. I was reading up when you were in your likkle coma ting. I'll do what I have to do. I'll make crosses out of branches," he said. "If the Rolling Calf comes for us, I'll find us a spot directly in moonlight. I'll strip down to my fucking underwear and make that thing count my clothes, OK?"

Alicia laughed at that imagery but was mostly grateful for Mars's sincerity.

"You have my sword; you're good, fam."

He touched Alicia's shoulder, giving it an affectionate squeeze, which in turn made Alicia put her hand on his, but then she pointed ahead of her.

"Shit, Mars! You're going to miss the turn!"

Mars swerved sharply on Lawrence Avenue East and the car started sliding, the rear skidding outward, drifting sideways. There were no other vehicles near them, just the snow-covered guardrails and the leafless trees behind them. The car didn't seem to be slowing down, and the road was downhill. There were no longer any guardrails and a blue-accented brown-brick building that looked to be a school was coming up on the left. The tail end of the car spun even farther outward.

"Steer!" said Alicia.

"I *am*!"

The car decelerated at what first appeared to be a dead end. It stopped in front of a broken chain-link fence that failed at keeping drivers out of an unremarkable wooded area. The green steel trusses of the Bayview Bridge loomed above in the near distance, but the road curved left. Mars followed the turn, and they found themselves in a parking lot beside the school they'd passed.

"This can't be what he was talking about, right? I don't see anything but Dumpsters."

Alicia nodded her head toward the windshield. "You can keep going. Up ahead. You see over there?"

Mars continued down a path crowded by clusters of trees and barely wide enough for a car, then drove into another parking lot with streetlamps, a few red-and-white York University signposts.

"There's nobody here," said Alicia.

"Exams," said Mars by way of explanation. "I think it's mad funny that we actually ended up at Glendon."

Alicia tugged open the bag and then took out the Tiffany bag. "This is technically campus, which is school, so this has to be what he meant," she said, putting on the necklace River Mumma had bought.

"What are you doing?" said Mars.

"Getting ready for River Mumma."

Alicia picked up the next of River Mumma's purchases and

clasped the rose gold bracelet onto her wrist. It felt heavy and cold, unlike Grandma Mabel's bracelet.

"OK, where should I park?"

Alicia looked out the window and frowned. Only a few of the lamps were working, creating a small pool of light in the centre of the parking lot and casting the rest in shadow. Nothing felt right until she saw a pop of red in the distance. Somehow, she knew it was a pedestrian bridge; the red railings were mostly obscured by the ashen trees that surrounded the lot, but the bridge called to her like a beacon. She pointed to it.

"You hear that?" said Mars as they neared the bridge. He opened his window. "That trickling?"

Alicia did. "The river must be close."

It was a little difficult to see through the dark and the cluster of tree branches, but when Alicia stretched forward enough, lifting herself off the seat, she could make out a stream running alongside the parking lot. That was her way to River Mumma. Relief surged through her—they were in the right place. But that gave way to uncertainty—sundown had already passed, she was technically late and didn't know how River Mumma would react, if she would even still be around, if her plan would even work, if she really was *too* late. But she still had to do this.

Mars drove into a parking spot, and Alicia gasped when a white shape materialized in front of them.

The Rolling Calf. It had found them. It stood in front of the car, blocking the way to the river below, snorting so that little puffs of flame came out of its nostrils. Its neck was curved toward them and its shoulders were hunched. It was ready.

Alicia banged on the glove compartment. "Where's the moon when we need it?"

Mars pressed his lips together, visibly searching for a solution in his mind. "Is there rum in the fridge?" he said finally.

She furrowed her brow but then shifted so that she was kneeling on her seat and could reach over to the fridge in the back. She pulled out a half-empty bottle of Bacardi 151.

"Yeah, there's rum."

"Heaven said that her aunt used rum to trap it—oh true, she had a lighter, though. It's the fire that does the trapping. Rum distracts it, but maybe that's enough time for you to do what you need to do," said Mars.

"Do you know how long rum distracts it? It can follow me, it can follow you. No, we need to trap it."

"Her aunt had a lighter," said Mars.

Alicia shook the bottle. "It says flammable. The label is literally a warning sign."

"But we still need fire."

Alicia nodded her head toward the Rolling Calf. "It sees me and breathes fire, we have fire."

"OK, but she said she drew a cross—"

"Mars! We're just going to have to improvise that!"

He sighed, then took the rum from Alicia. "OK, I'll go out first. Once I pour it out, run."

Alicia nodded. "And leave right after it's done."

Mars unscrewed the bottle before he opened the door, and then he ran out. The Rolling Calf moved its head, looking away from Alicia to Mars, distracted by the scent of rum. Alicia watched Mars run in different directions, first down and then across, pouring the rum as he went. The Rolling Calf moved away from the path to the river. It started licking the liquor off the ground in the parking lot, slurping and gurgling.

Alicia scrambled out of the car and ran toward the Rolling Calf, stopping directly in front it, holding out the comb. The Rolling Calf sensed it immediately and stopped licking the rum. Alicia held her breath as it reared its head, mouth wide, belly rumbling with the gathering of fire. Right before it exhaled, she sprang to the side, colliding with Mars, so its fire didn't catch her and only ignited the rum, which blazed into the shape of a massive fiery cross on the asphalt. The Rolling Calf roared in frustration, unable to leave the spot it was rooted to, unable to chase Alicia to the river.

Alicia held on to Mars. "Find moonlight!"

He nodded. "Be careful, Leish."

They went in separate directions. Alicia ran down the small hill that sloped toward the river, snow trickling into her boots. Once she reached the bank, she stopped. As she looked at the brownish green water, a calm took over, bringing with it a clarity. Nothing drew her to this spot, no cards, no external magnetism, but she was exactly where she was supposed to be. She wasn't plagued with doubt, just poised with surety. Alicia turned around to look at the Rolling Calf, stuck in a trap of its own making, and waited until she was sure it saw her; this time she refused to look down or look away, and when she was sure it saw the comb she held in her hand, she walked forward.

XXVI

W hat she thought would be a step was actually a plunge into icy water that shocked her system. Instead of wading waist-deep through the river, she was engulfed in its depths. It was deeper than she'd expected, but she didn't struggle, even in its freezing temperature. She wasn't drowning. She wasn't swimming either. She was floating. Submerged but suspended, as if her body was the same density as the water and it was lifting and sinking her at the same time. In harmony.

Soon, dense groupings of kelp, tall like shoots of bamboo, surrounded her in towering leafy columns like trees in a forest, and she knew that she wasn't in the Don River anymore. She was able to breathe, which meant she probably wasn't earthbound either. This was a different kind of place. The water, now a milky warm that soothed her aches and sores, shimmered a luxurious gold. Alicia looked below, expecting pebbles and stones, only to see that the riverbed was covered entirely in sapphires and rubies, emeralds and silver coins, gold goblets, strings of pearls, millions and millions of gems and jewels.

Ahead, in the middle of the forest, a large tree sprouted from the treasure-laden floor. Even though she could see it in its entirety, the tree had to be several thousand feet tall, with heart-shaped leaves and flowers—some yellow, some orange, some crimson—that looked like hibiscus. From the centre of its trunk, a single stream flowed out and up, splintering off into hundreds of rivers, like aquatic branches, each divergence a different hue of blue and green and brown and white, and Alicia suddenly knew. There was only one way something this extraordinary could exist. This tree, this river . . . it was the source, the fountainhead, the beginning of all rivers on the island.

This was River Mumma's home.

Alicia's vision adjusted, allowing her to take in more of her surroundings. She saw, littered throughout the water, the wreckage of a large ship, and the debris of dozens of cars, their remains overrun by coral—the manmade claimed by nature. White wisps floated around. Their presence made Alicia inexplicably sad. No sun or moonlight could reach so deep down (if the sun and the moon even existed where she was), and yet it was both light and dark in this watery abyss.

A wisp appeared in front of Alicia and transformed into a white-eyed face, pale and bloated, its expression contorted into a permanent scream, and in a blink, it was gone.

Souls them. Of the people mi drag down here.

The voice, velvety and mesmerizing and dangerous, took over Alicia's head first, and then River Mumma materialized before her. She was familiar to Alicia, yet radiant and unapproachable. Her hair was now an afro, a large nimbus decorated with seashells; her tail was blue rather than the green of last night; and her face had the same youthful roundness of this afternoon, but with eyes that revealed ancient wisdom.

Is there more than one of you?

Alicia had never thought to ask the question before, but now that she was on the verge of returning the comb, she wanted to know if she was giving it to a shape-shifter or a different being altogether; she'd only assumed she had been talking to one being throughout the day.

I am many, and many are me.

We're back to the vagueness. Fun.

She hadn't meant to say it—she'd thought it, but it was all the same to a deity.

River Mumma gestured to her right, and a table appeared beside her. *The* table. The one she guarded. The one the stories said many gave their lives to try to claim as their own. Alicia could see why—its presence made her heart hungry. It was somehow more than a table, it was a promise; Alicia could see everything she'd never have to worry about if she got hold of that kind of wealth. Nuisances like loans and meals and rent and . . . life. It would all just be taken care of.

Quickly, all the spirits gathered together and shot toward the ornate gold table, swarming it like a school of fish. They were no longer wisps, but bodies with faces like the one Alicia had just seen, all of their arms outstretched. Their cries of longing transformed the watery realm from beautiful to eerie, and different screams rang out from the different wrecks, echoes of the collisions that had brought them here.

River Mumma motioned with her hand, and the golden table disappeared. The spirits transformed back into wisps and the echoed screams stopped. Alicia couldn't decide whether she'd got an answer, but she also realized that her question was irrelevant. One River Mumma or dozens, the result had to be the same—giving back what was hers.

Nothing happened when Alicia handed River Mumma the comb. Nothing visual or tactile, anyway. No golden light radiated from the pick to commemorate the return to its rightful owner. River Mumma didn't even crack a smile; she just gently ran her fingers along the teeth and the handle before the comb disappeared.

Nothing happened and yet something did happen. At that moment, Alicia was exactly where she was supposed to be. Giving River Mumma back the comb didn't make her feel like she'd met a requirement or succeeded in a task, but the urgency that had propelled her all day stilled. A calm took over, bringing with it a clarity, a certainty in herself, an inner recognition of her own ability to get through the day, almost like peace.

So you're not going to take this away? She gestured around her. *And you'll go back to the rivers? You got out, you had your fun, you made your point. You're good now, right?*

River Mumma shrugged. *Sunset done gone. Yuh nuh keep to the deadline.*

Right, but that legit doesn't matter, does it? Abandoning the world over an arbitrary timeline is too fickle. Even for you.

Alicia saw River Mumma's jaw clench, and she softened her tone to show her respect.

I just mean that I'm here. Even when it seemed like it couldn't be done, even when I could've given up, I came. I gave you back what's yours because this was meant to be with you, and you are meant to be with us. We need it. We need to remember. We can't remember if you're gone. But I am sorry about missing the deadline. That's why I came with this.

Alicia extended her arms, and River Mumma observed the jewellery draped on her wrist, draped around her neck. The earrings in her palm.

It's an offering. From me and my friends. And, like, true, they were technically yours first, but they became ours and they became valuable to us, but no word of a lie, we're happy giving them back. I hope that counts for something.

The accessories suddenly vanished from Alicia's body and she took that to mean River Mumma had accepted the gift, which was her way of saying she would return to the rivers.

For your prize.

The space beside her, where the golden table had been just seconds before, glinted, and even though she couldn't see the table, Alicia knew it was there.

Want it?

A part of her did. A part of her was willing to be one more among the many who'd reached and strained for a table that was always beyond their grasp, in the slim chance that she would actually be able to possess it. She considered it, then said,

Can I have a different prize?

River Mumma smiled knowingly.

Ah wah yuh seek, pickney?

A gasp of air.

Alicia emerged from a creek that was home to a few fallen trees. She waded toward land before anyone could see her, and when her movements weren't bogged down by her clothes, she realized that they weren't actually wet this time. An extra perk from River Mumma; the first two were waiting for her on the snowy bank. She climbed out of the greenish brown water and sat at the bottom of a small hill next to her prizes: her unbroken cellphone and a plastic bag. The screen lit up when she touched her phone, revealing multiple texts and missed calls.

Immediately, Alicia video-called Heaven. She picked up right away, but the screen read "video unavailable" instead of displaying Heaven's face.

"Hello?" said Alicia.

There was nothing but garbled, broken noises until she heard, "Bro, it says Alicia's calling, shut up!"

"Oh, word?"

Alicia exhaled. Tears of relief sprung to her eyes, not to be stopped—Heaven and Mars were safe, and she felt lighter because of it, even whole.

It was a few more seconds before the video started working, and when Heaven saw Alicia, she screamed. "It is her!" She turned the phone sideways so Alicia could see Mars.

"Aye!" said Mars, drawing out the vowels. "What a fucking night, eh?"

"Understatement."

"How'd you get your phone, though?"

"River Mumma kind of granted it to me." Alicia could barely see them. "How did you get yours?"

"Security gave it back to me when everything was over; they just wanted me gone."

"Where are you?"

"Glendon Forest!" said Heaven.

"You disappeared into the river, and then a few seconds later, the duppies vanished, just gone," said Mars. "I wasn't really panicking because I didn't think you'd drowned. The way you just sort of dropped in, it was too . . . it looked . . . it just, it didn't look natural. But like, still, I had no idea where you were."

Heaven started speaking. "It'd been a minute since I'd heard from either of you and then I realized you didn't have your phones, so I went looking for you. Mars was easy to spot—he was still by the entrance of the forest—and we decided to just follow the river and see if you turned up."

"And the Three-Footed Horse? The Whooping Boy?" said Alicia.

"On the real, me and everybody at the house kind of trashed it, throwing rice everywhere we could so the duppies would have to stop and count the grains if they went through that hallway. Then I remembered burning incense can drive a duppy out of your house, and he had some, so everyone lit sticks and we all ran around until we were sure they were gone. Hence why they just wanted me out of the house."

"Rhatid. What about the cops, the fire trucks?"

Heaven shook her head dismissively. "They said someone threw a cigarette butt in the tree and that's why it caught fire."

"And they took mans to the hospital for a rabies shot, but who cares!" said Mars. "What happened with you?"

"Right? Like, where'd you go?" said Heaven, taking back the phone. "Did you give River Mumma the comb?"

"Yeah, she has it. Everything's good. Everything's criss, you know. It's over."

Those words felt strange for Alicia to say, even though they were, in fact, true. River Mumma had the comb, she wasn't leaving the world, and the duppies wouldn't chase them anymore, but the closure she'd expected evaded her; she didn't feel a sense of finality. Instead, it was almost like her body was vibrating with anticipation, though she couldn't say for what.

"So where are you now, then?" said Heaven.

"I'm—I don't really know, actually. It's like a park? Hold on."

She stood up and flipped the camera around so they could see what she could. She didn't know if it would help. Her surroundings were all trees and snow, some houses and small apartment buildings atop the hill behind her, and a brown official-looking building across the stream.

"Oh, you're in the Cedarvale Ravine," said Mars. "I walk it sometimes to get to Eglinton. You're not too far from St. Clair West, then. It's five minutes away."

"Bless, you can just catch the train to Lawrence West," said Heaven. "Take the 59 and you'll be home."

"I'm not really feeling home right now, to be honest. I guess she knew that, and that's why she made sure I came out here," said Alicia. "That, and I'm hungry because I'm starved, still. And your favourite spot is around here, Mars."

"Want to link up?" said Mars. "Because no lie, mi hungry, and we can just chill."

"And you can tell us everything you haven't told us, because I'm not even getting the highlights, sis," said Heaven.

Alicia nodded. "Bet."

"Cool. It's going to take us a minute to get there, though."

"No worries. Take your time."

"Keep your phone close," said Heaven.

They hung up. Alicia stood still for a moment, taking air into her lungs. Even though she hadn't drowned, it felt good to breathe. The simple act of inhaling and exhaling was a new sensation now, entirely different from even this morning—not a passive necessity but an active link to the world around her. It made her oddly restless.

She bent down and picked up the plastic bag, opening it. All the items her mother had asked her to pick up were inside, as well as a few additions made by River Mumma. She reached in and took out Grandma Mabel's bracelet.

"Thank you," she said out loud, putting it on her wrist.

It was going to make the next call a bit easier to get through. She dialled as she walked down the path to the main road and put the phone to her ear. As soon as she did, she flinched, nearly dropping it, when her mother picked up and started yelling, her accent unbridled.

"Miss Twenty-Six, ah wah time work over? But wait, mi call your work and yuh nuh even show up! Yuh muss'a *mad*! All day, mi ah call, mi ah call, cyaah even get one text back! Nine months mi carry yuh inna mi belly, and mi cyaah even get one text back from mi daughter! *Bright*."

Alicia grinned. It was actually rather comforting listening to her mother's rant—an expected and mundane reaction in a day characterized by unpredictability.

"Ah wah happen?" she said. "Yuh nuh listen to me?"

"Yeah, I—"

"'Yeah'? What is 'yeah'? Ah wah tone is this? They say it's a good thing fi have pickney, yuh know, but Lawdamassy, out all day, out all night! Mi just pray for Christmas mi get a daughter with a heart—"

Alicia walked the rest of the way holding her phone like she had it on speaker, and then she started texting Heaven while her mother continued her outburst.

Mom's acting like it's not 7PM on a Friday.

LOL. Where'd you tell her you've been all day?

Gonna need your help with that one.

True. True. I've got some ideas.

It was only when Alicia reached the restaurant ten minutes later that she had a chance to speak.

"Anything yuh haffi say to mi?"

She cleared her throat. "I picked up everything you wanted from the store," she said. "Even got some Irish moss."

A pause. Alicia knew what that meant. Silence indicated that her mother's frustration was ebbing and she didn't want to admit it. It was a typical reaction, one Alicia had encountered many times, but even so, it was different from the times before—she could hear the voices and chants, the songs of earlier today in her mother's silence.

"I also want to say that I got most of your texts. They were helpful," she said. "They, um"—she considered her words—"they prepared me for a few things that happened today."

Alicia waited for Ms. Gale to have the last word before hanging up, and then she walked into the vividly coloured restaurant with its green walls and brown chairs and tables. She headed straight for the counter, its display case bright with different pops and juices.

A young woman in a black shirt and white apron came to the front and asked for her order.

"Hi, yeah, so can I get a side of plantain and—"

"Sorry," she said. "We don't have that right now."

Alicia blinked. "OK," she said. "Ox—"

The cashier shook her head. "Not right now."

Alicia licked her lips and then pressed them together. "You know when it'll be ready?"

"Soon," the woman said, tilting her head.

"I'll just wait." She had nothing but time. "Can I get a bottle of Ting for now and you let me know when it's ready?"

The cashier nodded, walked over to the fridge, taking out a green bottle. Alicia paid for the drink and sat at a table beneath a line of Island flags hoisted above a large, joyous painting. She twisted open the bottle, looking at the different alerts listed on her phone.

The door chimed open and two women walked into the restaurant, stopping their conversation to place two orders of jerk chicken and rice with the cashier. Alicia listened to them return to their debate, entertained by how passionately they made their cases no matter how outlandish they sounded.

One of them rolled her eyes, exasperated. "Even if I went along with you, there are no bumbaraas dragons, aliens—none of that in the GTA!"

"Three fires in one day. Explain that! The news said one was at the man's house right out in his yard—"

"Said it was a cigarette—"

"It's not natural."

"I don't know why no one's first thought is arsonist."

The voices faded and Alicia let another journey engulf her. Her body didn't tense and she didn't panic; she calmly held on to the sides of the table as a way to keep herself oriented. This time, she didn't go far—she went to Heaven. She and Mars were still in Glendon Forest and the river raged beside them, splashing onto the bank, waves rushing and jumping, almost like the water was sentient. Heaven edged closer to the river, enthralled. Just when Alicia thought she was going to fall in, she stopped walking and looked into the water. River Mumma looked back from beneath the surface, shifted yet again to a different appearance, her bubble braids floating around her. She lifted her hands as if she were reaching toward Heaven, and then suddenly next to Heaven's feet were the pieces of jewellery Alicia had offered to River Mumma.

The vision released her, and Alicia took a sharp intake of breath when she found herself back in the restaurant. She looked around, but no one seemed to have noticed what had happened. Quickly she called Heaven but didn't even get a chance to say anything when she picked up.

"I saw her! And she gave the jewellery back to us! For sure, I thought it was gone, but I should've known, you know; they do say she rewards people, and because we completed the task, I guess she thought we were worthy!"

Mars was hollering in the background. "*This* is how you end a fucking quest!"

Those words again. Heaven had said them with a kind of victory, like they conquered the day, the jewellery their well-earned reward, but the surprise when Alicia saw the necklace and bracelet, the earrings—the happiness she felt for Heaven and Mars—was no match for the feeling she could now name. Alicia understood the anticipation that was keeping her wired: it was chaos but it stemmed from a stillness inside her from the river, a source of calm that gave her chaos definition—she didn't feel unshaped, she felt fluid. Expansive. Primed with possibility. Alicia looked at the video again, and smiled. She felt like she was beginning.

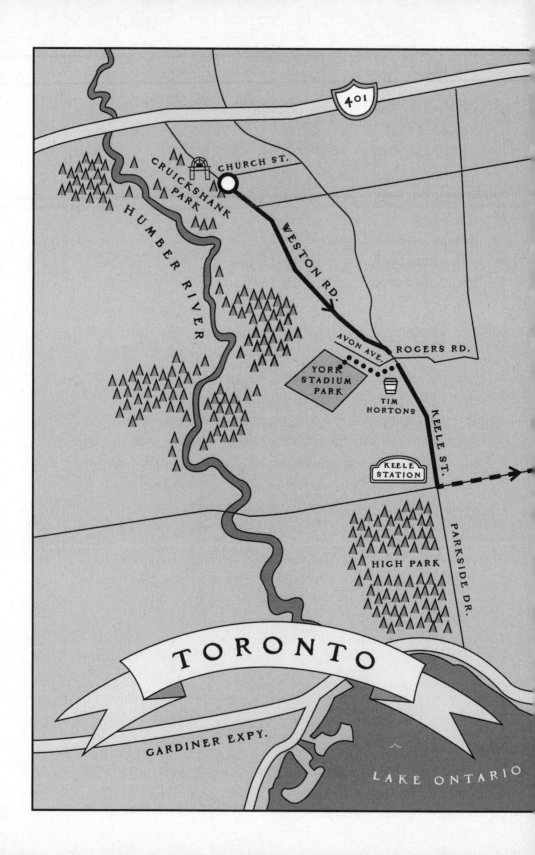

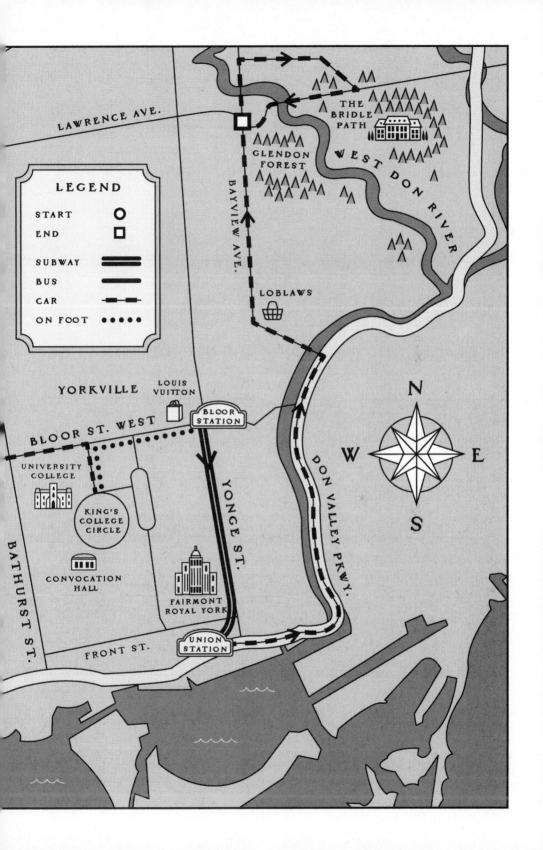

LEGEND

START ○
END □

SUBWAY ━━━
BUS ━━━
CAR ━ ■ ━ ■ ━
ON FOOT • • • • •

LAWRENCE AVE.

THE BRIDLE PATH

GLENDON FOREST

WEST DON RIVER

BAYVIEW AVE.

LOBLAWS

YORKVILLE

LOUIS VUITTON

BLOOR STATION

BLOOR ST. WEST

UNIVERSITY COLLEGE

KING'S COLLEGE CIRCLE

CONVOCATION HALL

YONGE ST.

DON VALLEY PKWY.

N
W E
S

FAIRMONT ROYAL YORK

BATHURST ST.

FRONT ST.

UNION STATION

ACKNOWLEDGMENTS

River Mumma is the book I never knew I always wanted to write, and I would like to thank all the people who helped it come to fruition.

First, I would like to say thank you, always, to my mother, Rogene, who showed me endless support, who helped me record routes throughout the city, who encouraged walks through Glendon Forest and Cruickshank Park, who took pictures of various buildings and settings so I could have reference points when deeply entrenched in writing or edits. You helped root this novel in Toronto.

Thank you to my editor, Deborah Sun De La Cruz, who trusted my instincts as a writer but whose masterful eye and keen perception elevated this novel to be the best possible version of itself.

Thank you to my agent, Amy Tompkins, for always having faith in my projects and my writing, for understanding my process, and for always having my back.

Thank you to my friends Ashley Hasfal, Denise Da Costa, and Aaron Slater, for all your suggestions, for listening to my ramblings, and for helping me remove blocks that stifled creativity. You kept my work honest.

To the Canada Arts Council, thank you for providing funding to give me the time and means to work on this novel.

I would like to thank my grandmother Evelyn, for her retellings, stories, and teachings, which have stayed with me and found a place in my work, and I would like to thank the various texts I consulted to widen my knowledge and strengthen my imagination, providing context and depth to this story:

Arvilla Payne-Jackson and Mervyn C. Alleyne, *Jamaican Folk Medicine: A Source of Healing* (Kingston, Jamaica: University of the West Indies Press, 2004).

Edward Seaga, "The Folk Roots of Jamaican Cultural Identity," *Caribbean Quarterly* 51, no. 2 (2005).

Myriam Moïse and Fred Réno, eds., *Border Transgression and Reconfiguration of Caribbean Spaces* (London: Palgrave Macmillan, 2020).

Sasha Turner Bryson, "The Art of Power: Poison and Obeah Accusations and the Struggle for Dominance and Survival in Jamaica's Slave Society," *Caribbean Studies* 41, no. 2 (2013).

Steeve O. Buckridge, *The Language of Dress: Resistance and Accommodation in Jamaica* (Kingston, Jamaica: University of the West Indies Press, 2004).

Sasha Turner, *Contested Bodies: Pregnancy, Childrearing, and Slavery in Jamaica* (Philadelphia: University of Pennsylvania Press, 2017).

Emanuela Guano, "Revival Zion: An Afro-Christian Religion in Jamaica," *Anthropos* 89, no. 4/6.

Olive Lewin, *Rock It Come Over: The Folk Music of Jamaica* (Kingston, Jamaica: University of the West Indies Press, 2000).

Kathleen E.A. Monteith and Glen Richards, eds., *Jamaica in Slavery and Freedom: History, Heritage and Culture* (Kingston, Jamaica: University of the West Indies Press, 2002).

Max Stackbein-Bussey, "Magic and Divination in Jamaica's Freedom Struggle, 1728–1824" (master's thesis, Arizona State University, 2021).

Brian L. Moore and Michele A. Johnson, *Neither Led nor Driven: Contesting British Imperialism in Jamaica, 1865–1920* (Kingston, Jamaica: University of the West Indies Press, 2004).

Rapid Eye Movement. "From The Grass Roots of Jamaica (1969)." Published on June 27, 2020. YouTube video, 0:4:10.

Ewan, Sheena. "Cultural Sensitivity Review." Review of *River Mumma*, by Zalika Reid-Benta. November 4, 2021.

© Rogene Reid

ZALIKA REID-BENTA is a Toronto-based writer whose debut story collection, *Frying Plantain,* won the Danuta Gleed Literary Award and the Rakuten Kobo Emerging Writer Prize for Literary Fiction. *Frying Plantain* was longlisted for the Scotiabank Giller Prize, and it was shortlisted for the Toronto Book Award, the White Pine Award, and the Trillium Book Award. Zalika served as the 2021–22 Writer in Residence at Western University and was the chair of the 2021 Scotiabank Giller Prize. She received an MFA in fiction from Columbia University, was a John Gardner Fiction Fellow at the Bread Loaf Writers' Conference, and is an alumna of the Banff Centre Writing Studio.

zalikarb   Literati167